DIVIDED
LOYALTIES

DIVIDED LOYALTIES

A novel by Stephanie Waxman

Copyright ©2010 Stephanie Waxman

Library of Congress Control Number: 2010902571
ISBN: 0-9709092-3-3
    978-0-9709092-3-7

Cover concept by Stephanie Waxman
Book and cover design by Beth Escott Newcomer/Escott Associates

In memory of my parents
For my children and grandchildren

NEW YORK
1936

Who built the seven gates of Thebes?
In the books are listed the names of kings.
Did the kings heave up the building blocks?

Question of a Literary Worker
Bertolt Brecht

I

THE SEPTEMBER DAY WAS HOT and muggy. Men slumped on stoops, smoking. Women sat at open windows, fanning themselves. People sagged in bread lines. Even the children skipping rope seemed barely able to lift their feet off the pavement. Jill's underarms were damp and she could feel her spit curls drooping against her cheeks. A man was selling roasted potatoes off a pushcart and the aroma made Jill's mouth water. All she'd had for breakfast was a cup of coffee, but if she spent her only nickel on a potato instead of a bus ride, she'd have to hoof it all the way uptown in this sweltering heat.

A thin woman with hollow eyes and a couple of raggedy kids at her feet held out an empty cup. "Lady, please?" She was no older than Jill, yet here she was with two kids and so poor she had to beg. Jill reached into her pocketbook for her nickel just as the bus rolled up. The doors gasped open and she climbed aboard.

The bus was stuffy and crowded, but in the back she found an empty seat with a crumpled copy of yesterday's paper. She didn't care that Governor Landon was running against Roosevelt and she didn't give a hoot that someone somewhere was trying to organize steelworkers into a union. She quickly flipped to the theater section and devoured the article about Helen Hayes, who was appearing in *Victoria Regina* at the Broadhurst Theater. What she wouldn't give to see Helen Hayes!

A heavyset woman smelling of sausages plopped down next to her, her fleshy thighs pressing against Jill. Jill noticed how she was wheezing with the effort of having made it up the steps and down the aisle. She noticed how delicately she opened her pocketbook, how tattered the Bible was that she took from it. She even noticed which verse the woman began to read (Job 12:15) and wondered what kind of burdens she was carrying. It was Jill's job to notice things about people.

She folded the newspaper and thought about the audition. Nurses, nurses. She searched her meager experience to find something that would help her land the part of Nurse McGinty on the new radio soap opera. Then she remembered the weary face of the nurse who had appeared in that bleak corridor to tell them about her mother. What was her name? She had asked if they wanted a cup of coffee. Jill wanted that coffee so badly, any way of delaying the news, which she had already read on Nurse O'Hara's face. O'Hara! That was it. Nurse O'Hara would be her model for Nurse McGinty. They were both Irish. That was a good sign.

The elevator in Loew's State Building was mercifully cool. In the ladies' room she tucked in her blouse and tried to remember not to lift her arms so the wet spots wouldn't show. She noticed her slip peeping out below the hem of her borrowed skirt and rolled it over at the waist. She straightened her seams, applied fresh lipstick, and then surveyed the whole picture. She was not pretty by conventional standards—her nose was too narrow, her lips too full. But her eyes were large and her hair was so black it made her skin look translucent. Her mother always said her hair was her best feature.

She prayed it would be a blind audition so that the producer and director would only *hear* her. That way, it would be her voice that counted. If they saw that she was only twenty-one, she'd never get a shot at Nurse McGinty.

Three men were in the engineer's booth staring at her through the plate glass.

Oh, brother, she thought. Okay, she told herself, act older.

"Good morning, Miss...?"

"Fullbright," she said, leaning into the microphone with her most mature voice, looking directly at the man who addressed her. He was a large man and spoke in a too-loud voice. She supposed he was the director.

"Miss Fullbright, you'll be reading the speech on page five. Nurse McGinty is telling a man that his wife just died on the operating table." He sat down and jotted something in a notebook. One of the other men, no doubt the engineer, was fiddling with dials. The one in wire-rimmed glasses—the producer?— was paging through the script. They all wore gray suits. She wondered which one had the power to hire her.

She took a minute to look over the speech. Her stomach growled and she wondered if the mike picked it up.

She tried to concentrate on her mother's nurse—the starched white collar and three-cornered hat, the clipboard under her arm. Jill could practically taste the hospital food she ate. She thought of the compassion on Nurse O'Hara's tired face. Then she took a breath and began.

When she was done, she was directed to a hallway where several other Nurse McGintys sat on folding metal chairs. Not one looked younger than thirty. Jill sighed and sank onto a chair. She chipped away at her nail polish, thinking of all the other ways she could've read the scene. "That is not positive thinking," she could hear her mother say. Millicent Fullbright was a big believer in the power of positive thinking. So, out of respect for her mother, Jill reviewed the success she'd had since she stepped off that Greyhound bus wide-eyed and eager less than a year ago.

Her father had been opposed to her going to New York. When Millicent died, Jill postponed her plans, enrolling instead in the Lamont School of Music and Drama. Even though the classes were good and she was improving her craft, she missed her mother terribly. Her own grief was doubled when she was around her father who used the bottle to deal with his sorrow. She ached to get on with her life. One day, she walked out of Elocution and made straight for the Denver bus terminal, where she purchased a one-way ticket to her destiny. Though it was hard for him to let her go, Russell finally gave her his blessing along with a hundred dollars, which Jill sewed into the lining of her only coat.

She had good luck finding a room in a boarding house called the City Federation Hotel for Women, practically on the Hudson, for ten dollars a week, which included meals that tasted like sawdust. She managed to land a few parts—a gangster's moll in *Junior G-Men*, the Virgin Mary on the *Ave Maria Hour*. She played a maid in two episodes of *Your Unseen Friend*, and one day she even stood next to Orson Welles in the elevator.

But being a radio actress wasn't exactly a steady job. Three nights a week she worked as an usherette at the Paramount Theater in a navy-blue uniform that smelled like the girls who wore it the rest of the week. Saturdays, she modeled for an art class, earning a dollar an hour. She could get two dollars if she'd take off her clothes, but she'd sooner sell apples on the street.

Her real dream was to be on Broadway. She tried out for a walk-on in the crowd scene in *The Eternal Road* but didn't make it. Her spirits really sank that day. Turned down for just a walk-on. She definitely would've been cast in an O'Neill play if she had only agreed to the indecent terms set forth by its producer, a squat man with a nasal voice who tried to put his tongue in her ear. As she tore out of his shabby office, she heard him yell, "You'll never get cast with that attitude, Miss Fullbright!" Jill rushed back to the boarding house to tell Gloria, another aspiring actress. Gloria shrugged and said, "What's the big deal? You should've let him fool around, at least enough to get the part."

So here she was, sitting in a room with older, more experienced actresses, clinging to her virtue and looking forward to a lunch of Saltines smeared with catsup at the counter of some coffee shop.

The director came out. All the actresses glanced up like a nest full of hungry birds. "Jill Fullbright?"

She looked at him, hope seeping out of every pore.

"Congratulations."

Jill held back the urge to throw her arms around him. She followed him into a cluttered office, where he spoke quickly as he searched through piles of papers. "Nurse McGinty will be featured in thirteen episodes at twenty-five dollars an episode."

She could quit her other jobs! Her empty stomach did a somersault.

"She'll contract TB and be treated by Dr. Malone. She and Dr. Malone will fall in love and Nurse McGinty will die. The nurse who replaces her will also fall in love with Dr. Malone, but he won't be in love with her and she'll make him feel guilty about Nurse McGinty's death." Without waiting to hear her response, he handed her the script and thrust some papers at her to sign. "Rehearsal is tomorrow at ten," he said, meeting her eyes for the first time and offering a smile.

Too excited to wait for the elevator, she ran down all eleven flights. When she reached street level, breathless and giddy, she remembered how hungry she was and dashed into the Walgreens drugstore across the way. Drawing a breath, she recognized the man with the wire-rimmed glasses from the engineer's booth hunched over a cup of coffee at the counter. She was not a forward girl where it concerned men, but she wasn't shy either. She went right up to him, smiling, and stuck out her hand. "Nurse McGinty."

He gave her a blank look. Then a slow dawning smoothed his face into a warm smile. He shook her hand, removed his hat from the stool next to him and said, "Please, join me. May I buy you a cup of coffee? A sandwich? You must be hungry. I'm sorry we kept you all waiting so long. That's the trouble with this business. There's very little regard for the actor's time."

It was his treat so she ordered roast beef, mashed potatoes, creamed corn, and chocolate pudding. He was a talkative fellow and gave Jill an earful about the inner workings of the show. His name was Martin Levy, and he was the writer.

"Nabisco wants each episode to center on the doctors and nurses, but I'm fighting for other hospital workers to be major characters, too. The wages of the people who empty bedpans and mop the floors are appalling. I mean, how's a man supposed to support a family on twelve dollars a week?"

He wasn't much to look at, not very tall, a pale complexion.

He seemed to be in his late twenties, but his hair was already thinning. There was a faint musty smell about him, as if he didn't get enough fresh air. Still, there was something that drew her in, a quiet kind of intensity in his green eyes.

She flew up the stairs of the City Federation Hotel. Her roommate, Louise, was sitting cross-legged on her bed, staring into a compact, drawing on eyebrows.

"I got it!" Jill cried.

"Darlin'..." Louise said with an accent that conjured up mint juleps. Whenever Jill was around her she found herself speaking in that same drawl, and she knew that if she ever had to portray someone from the South, she'd have no trouble.

She ran across the hall and knocked hard. "Thirteen episodes!" she shouted. "Bring a glass!"

"Hooray! I'll be right over," Gloria yelled back.

Jill returned to her room and reached into a drawer. She found the bottle of sherry among a jumble of slips, girdles, and brassieres.

Rudy Vallee, Louise's canary, was chirping away as usual in the corner, but for once his noise didn't bother Jill. Rudy Vallee was a nervous little bird, no bigger than a child's fist, and despite how pretty he was with his pale-yellow coat of feathers ending in a white tail, his jittery motion, bobbing head, and constant chirping drove Jill crazy. But today she poked her finger in his cage and said, "Sing for me, Rudy Vallee! Sing a song for Nurse McGinty!"

2

JILL TURNED OUT TO BE ONE heck of a good nurse. She began to think that she could actually bandage a wound if she had to. She and Martin spent more and more time together, discussing the twists and turns of the soap opera. One afternoon he asked her out on a date. When she accepted, he went beet red. For all his loquaciousness, Martin was a shy man.

She borrowed Gloria's pink seersucker dress, which was a bit frayed at the hem but better than her tired blue dress or gray suit, which Martin had seen a hundred times. As she dabbed perfume behind her ears, she thought about how boring her other dates were—sitting on Henry Arnold's stoop or walking around Tompkins Square Park with Harris Jones. Sitting or walking. Most fellas didn't have two dimes to rub together. But Martin was making something of himself. And his conversation was always lively.

He took her to a Sunday afternoon lecture in the Great Hall of the Cooper Union in Greenwich Village. The place was packed to overflowing, so she and Martin stood in the back. A tall man with a pasty face spoke into the microphone. By the way he said his vowels, Jill knew he was from Brooklyn. He spoke passionately about the plight of the working class and claimed that those in the audience were part of a generation that could transform the country. "All political and social structures are determined by the economic conditions of people," he sang out, describing Marx's vision of a classless society and how the Great Depression had caused a "spontaneous movement" of working people who were determined to turn the country around.

These ideas were new to Jill. She had heard her father rant against FDR's New Deal and worry over being able to hold onto the hardware store. But politics had never interested her. Her focus had always been her acting career.

Afterwards, they walked over to the Horn and Hardart Automat on Broadway and 13th. Even though it was Sunday, the streets were crowded; folks trying to escape the oppressive heat indoors settled for the muggy heat on the sidewalks. Jill and Martin passed beggar after beggar. Martin gave away so many pennies that Jill worried he might not have enough to buy them dinner. A rush of shame washed over her. She thought of whole families she'd seen sleeping on newspaper in the subways. Old men shoveling snow for a dime. She remembered the woman in rags begging for her kids. The words of the lecturer made her think of things in a new way.

The Automat was practically empty. As they opened the little glass doors and pulled out chicken potpies, Martin said, "See, Jill, in capitalism, there's private control of production, which means that only a few people run things. In Russia, Stalin has done away with private ownership." When they got settled at a table he continued, "Imagine if, instead of a few rich men owning everything and the average Joe owning just the shirt on his back, the workers owned the means of production, too? Then the wealth wouldn't collect at the top."

Jill took a bite of her chicken pie and thought about what she owned: her paltry collection of clothes, a radio, and her mother's pearl necklace. What else did she own? Her talent? She had worn down the heels of her only pumps peddling it each day and had finally sold it. "Well, they do own their ability to work," she said.

"But what if a fella can't work?" Martin said, getting fired up. "That's where Marx's vision is so beautiful, so humane and so totally logical. Marx said, 'From each according to his ability, to each according to his need.' That's what the Bolshevik Revolution was all about. And now, in Russia one man can't just use another man and toss him away like an old shoe if the guy can't work anymore."

Jill liked the way Martin's green eyes sparkled when he spoke, the way he waved his hands in the air when he made his points. She was eager to learn what he had to teach her about the world, the bigger world that she'd never given a moment's thought to. She suddenly imagined ironing his shirt, then felt embarrassed, as if he could read her mind.

"You're a worker, Jill. What if you and Nabisco shared the profits equally? Just imagine."

That was a dizzying thought, one her brain could barely absorb. It was beginning to dawn on her how many people worked compared to how few ran things.

"It's the Communist Party that'll galvanize the proletariat!" Martin declared, reaching across the table for her hand.

His hand was warm and soft. She didn't know what the proletariat was, but she felt convinced it should be galvanized.

Then she heard her father's words: "Communists are godless murderers."

But this communist certainly didn't have evil in his heart. He was the most sincere, most passionate person she'd ever met.

He spent his time worrying about what was good for mankind. He wore his zeal like a warm coat.

Her father had once been a joyous man. Jill remembered him dancing with her mother in the pavilion at Elitches Gardens. Then came the Depression and he became worried and gloomy. When her mother died so suddenly, Russell's grief bordered on despair.

But Martin was the picture of optimism. He believed so fervently that people could actually change the way things worked, who owned what, and so forth.

"So," Martin said, a twinkle in his eye, "you agree?"

"Sure I do," she said, smiling.

They walked arm in arm to West 22nd Street and then over to the river where a slight breeze brought a measure of relief. They stood in the soft light of the early evening, looking out over the greasy shimmering water toward New Jersey. Then they noticed some commotion on the wharf. Drawing nearer, they saw a crowd yelling and waving fists. A German passenger ship sat in the harbor. From the top of its mast flew a flag with a swastika. A boy had shimmied to the top of the pole and was trying to cut it down while the captain barked at him in German. The crowd taunted the captain and shouted encouragement to the boy, who finally cut the flag loose and flung it into the murky water. The crowd went crazy.

Martin exclaimed, "Now, that's encouraging! Usually folks would rather watch a ball game than engage in political protest."

Yesterday, Jill wouldn't have noticed and wouldn't have cared. But now, standing beside Martin, her arm linked in his, she felt the same surge of optimism. Something had been stirred in her that day, and when Martin asked for a kiss, she gave it to him eagerly.

3

MARTIN WAS HAVING TROUBLE concentrating on the article he was writing for New Masses. His roommate, Al, was snoring on the couch, but that's not what interfered with his concentration. He found himself re-playing the kiss over and over—the way Jill's mouth had yielded, the feel of her soft skin against his cheek, her delicate scent. He got up and crossed to the icebox and pulled out a bottle of root beer. He took a few gulps and looked around at the dark, dank basement apartment. The place was crammed with books on political theory, world history, and Marxism. Hundreds of books by learned people about important subjects, but not one of them explained the mystery of the human heart.

Martin had never courted anyone before. When he was a kid he had his first kiss with Julie Klein, an older cousin, in the alley behind the synagogue after his bar mitzvah. In college he'd gone to parties and taken a few girls to the movies. But once he got involved in the Communist Party, he had no time or interest in anything else. The party provided him with an analysis of world affairs and a clear understanding of the forces inciting a working class revolution. Arguing the finer points of dialectical materialism engaged and challenged him. This and the simple camaraderie of other Party members had been enough for him.

Now he was being pulled in a different direction. He knew it was up to the man to drive things, but he found himself taking his cues from Jill. She was spontaneous, a free spirit, whereas he felt constrained, boxed in. Granted, it was a box of his own choosing, but it still confined him. When he talked to Jill about political matters, the way she looked at him—her hazel eyes wide and hungry for knowledge—he was touched in a place that both intimidated and thrilled him.

He lit a cigarette and glanced at the page he had written without seeing the words. He knew that if he could persuade her to join the Party, he would be on surer ground. He'd just have to get up the nerve to ask.

JILL STRUGGLED WITH THE books Martin had given her. But reading treatises by Lenin was not like reading plays by Ibsen. Some sentences took her half a dozen tries before she got the gist. She had always been a quick study when it came to learning lines and grasping the essence of a character. Now she was challenged to apply her skills to the world of political analysis. Little by little, she began to understand the aims of the Communist Party. She agreed that when Lenin said a new type of party was needed to overturn the capitalist class, it had to be something other than the Democrats or Republicans.

Still, Jill was not really the "joiner" type. In high school she had joined the choir, but she couldn't stand being dressed in the same blue gown, singing the same notes as the others in her section. She wanted to be the soloist. Even though her voice wasn't quite at that level, she still felt she belonged in front. That's what drove her into the drama club, where she won the lead in every play.

But being with Martin, both at work and outside of work, had filled her with a new kind of enthusiasm. She wanted to be part of a movement to improve the world. She probably would have joined anything if it had meant spending more time with him. And in spite of the misapprehensions she knew her father would have, when Martin asked her, she said yes, pledging herself to the Communist Party with him as her sponsor.

She clutched his hand as they entered the building on 103rd. The lobby was narrow and smelled like onions. The wail of an infant came from behind one of the doors. Stepping around a baby buggy and two girls playing jacks, they climbed five flights and stood in front of apartment 5B catching their breath. Jill stole a glance at Martin. She was nervous.

A plump man with a thick moustache opened the door. He slapped Martin on the back and smiled at Jill. "I'm Ray," he announced, "and you must be the new recruit. Welcome aboard."

Makeshift bookshelves ran the length of one wall. A shabby couch sagged against another. A card table held a pot of coffee, a jumble of mismatched cups, and a small bust of Lenin. An ornate chandelier, left behind from grander days, dangled from a stained ceiling and cast a dull light. The whole place emitted the vague aroma of cat urine.

Martin pointed to a flag of the Soviet Union pinned across the window. "The hammer is for the industrial workers and the sickle is for the agricultural workers. Communism is all about working people." He flashed a smile and squeezed her hand. She didn't want him to let go of it. A tall, loose-jointed boy with orange hair extended a bony hand to Jill. "Hi. I'm Al, Martin's roommate." His expression told her that he knew all about her.

Carol, a stocky girl who wore two yellow braids pinned to her head, came over and introduced herself. When Martin presented her to Libby, a pale and slender girl with a freckled face, Jill exclaimed, "Libby Roth!" She turned to Martin. "Libby and I have been on auditions together." Libby said, "I'm so glad you're joining."

Ray called the meeting to order, read the agenda, and then Libby read the minutes from the last meeting. Al gave the financial statement, which included a welcome to the new member. Then he asked Jill, "What sustainer can you pledge?"

Jill shot Martin a glance. Martin explained, "Dues are a dollar a month, and in addition we each pledge a voluntary amount."

Jill reached into her pocketbook and grabbed three dollars. Was that too much or too little? She was desperate for everyone to think she was generous.

"Two dollar sustainer," Al announced, without giving away his opinion. Libby made a note in a black ledger. Ray gave a report from the Central Committee about the upcoming elections. Then he turned to Jill. "It hasn't been decided yet what Party action should be, whether we should run candidates or not."

Martin said, "Of course we should. We should run someone in the local *and* the national election."

"The national election?" Ray said, clearly taken aback. "You mean run someone against Roosevelt?"

"That's not a progressive move," said Al.

"I agree," said Libby. "Think of all the concessions he's made to the working man."

"Concessions?" cried Martin. "Roosevelt's not a friend to the worker. He's in bed with big business, that's obvious."

Jill thought of her father, who also hated Roosevelt. Was it possible that he could become a communist if Martin explained it all to him?

Carol spoke up. "But Martin, there's no doubt that the New Deal is progressive. The WPA alone provides hundreds of jobs." Carol was around Jill's age, but from her confidence and the knowledgeable way she spoke, she seemed like someone over thirty. She leaned forward in her chair and delivered her opinion in smooth, even tones, slowly and thoughtfully. Then she turned to Jill and said, "Do you think it's in the interests of working people to back Roosevelt, Jill?"

Jill didn't want to say she thought the President was good because that would be going against Martin. So she just shrugged and prayed that Carol would ask someone else. But Carol was still looking at her. "Or do you—"

A cat jumped onto Jill's lap as the front door burst open and a large man with curly black hair and piercing blue eyes exploded into the room. "Comrades!"

Ray looked up. "You're late, Elliot," he said, annoyed. "We're discussing whether or not to run candidates."

Elliot boomed, "Jews are fleeing Berlin and you're talking about elections?"

"Sit down, Elliot," Ray said. "The international situation is on the agenda. Be patient."

But Elliot was not the type to be patient or go by an agenda. He didn't speak, he thundered. Everyone listened whether they wanted to or not. It seemed the sheer force of his personality could move an inanimate object. He declared, "Aren't you forgetting Dimitrov's call for a United Front Against Fascism?"

Martin surprised Jill when he said, "Elliot's right. Our primary job is to oppose fascism. The answer to every decision should be based on whether or not it would help the fight against fascism."

Jill's mind was a jumble of new ideas. She was trying to

memorize the various points of view so that later, when she and Martin were alone, her questions would sound intelligent.

Finally the meeting ended. Someone brought out a jug of red wine. Bing Crosby's voice filled the room. Elliot and Martin, instead of discussing the Party line on fascism, were arguing about religion.

"God and communism cannot coexist!" Martin insisted. "Communism is when people have control over their lives. Religion asks people to give up control to God."

Her father's words "godless communism" rang in Jill's ears.

"Crap!" shouted Elliot, downing a glass of wine. "A belief in God enables people to overthrow the government, or any other damn thing they set their mind to. Most people need Him for courage."

"Him? Him?" Martin cried. "That just goes to show your lack of imagination, Elliot. Why does God have to be a Him?"

"Ah-ha!" Elliot exploded. "So God is a female!"

Elliot turned to Jill with a mischievous grin; before she knew it, he was holding her, spinning her around to the music. She tried to pull away, but he held her firmly by the waist. His hands were giant paws and she could feel their hunger through the fabric of her dress. Elliot buried his face in her hair, inhaled her perfume, and said loud enough for all to hear, "I'd pray to a female god any day..."

Why didn't Martin do something? She caught his eye as they twirled by. He just shrugged and smiled tolerantly.

MARTIN AND JILL WALKED down Columbus Avenue. Jill didn't take his arm; she seemed withdrawn. Martin looked at her sideways, trying to read her expression.

She turned to him. "Does Elliot always use shock to make his points?"

"That's Elliot. He tends to be theatrical."

She was quiet again. Then, "And do you really believe there's no God?"

"I believe God is just another idea that man has created," he said simply.

"But God's the Creator," she said, incredulous.

"That's the big question, isn't it? Did God create man because He was lonely, or did man create God because *he* was lonely?" Then for emphasis he added, "I mean, nobody even thinks about God unless they want something."

Jill became thoughtful again; he wondered if he'd crossed a line. But having her grasp his point of view was critical; his ideas about religion were central to his entire philosophy of life. He tried another point of entry, hoping to win her to his side with simple logic. "What if *we* made the changes and didn't wait around hoping and praying?"

"Yes," she said slowly, "I see your point. It's good to take charge of our own destiny. Still, God is the source of my inspiration. And I'm not about to drop Him out of my life, no matter what communists say."

He felt stung.

They walked in silence. It had cooled down; a cobalt sky appeared between the tall buildings. They had arrived at Central Park. He wondered if she even wanted to linger there or if she'd rather have him walk her to the bus stop. He spotted a bench and sat down. He was relieved when she sat, too.

"Weren't you raised with religion, Martin?"

"Sure I was," he said quickly, trying to gain ground. "Mama keeps kosher. Pop goes up there in the synagogue and reads the Torah."

"The what?"

Then it hit him: he was her first Jew! He looked at her closely. Her face was open and questioning. She really did want to understand. "The Torah is the Bible—from the moment of Creation to the moment they're poised to go into the Holy Land. Pop doesn't believe all of it, but come Friday night, he's fastening on his best collar."

She considered this new bit of information. Then she offered, "My mother was Protestant and my dad was Catholic, but neither of them was religious. I went to Presbyterian Sunday school."

He relaxed; they were back in a regular conversation. He took a tentative step in the direction of his deep beliefs. "I've gone completely away from all that religious stuff."

"You don't even celebrate the holidays?" she asked sincerely.

"I celebrate plenty of holidays," he said lightly, hoping to get a laugh. "How about the day the Supreme Court overturned the convictions of the Scottsboro Boys? And May Day. I celebrate May Day."

"So you're not Jewish anymore?" She was serious.

"Oh, I'll always be a Jew."

The look on her face suggested that she couldn't handle one more contradictory thought. Still, he pressed on. "Being Jewish is about more than just the religion. There are lots of principles that I respect. Jewish ideas about education, for example. Mama used to say, 'In America the streets aren't paved with gold; the gold is in the schools.' She grew up in the old country—Lithuania, a regular hotbed for revolutionary ideas. She worked in a bakery in Vilna. Guess what her job was? To sneak pamphlets into the bread!"

Jill laughed. They sat quietly for a while. It seemed as if they were on the same side again. He wondered if he could put his arm around her, but she was waiting for him to finish his story.

"Pop lived in Vilna, too. Life was no picnic if you were a Jew. When the Czar started conscripting young men into the army, Pop escaped in a cart buried under a bale of hay. Once they got to America, Mama found a job in a bakery and Pop peddled ice. At night, they studied English and socialism. When I was about nine, they took me up Fifth Avenue so I could see all the beautiful buildings. I kept wondering why there weren't any dumps there like in our neighborhood. Mama said, 'That's the capitalistic system.' Right then and there I decided I hated capitalism."

He wondered if Jill's own mother even knew the word capitalism; he imagined that the center of her world had been pinochle and casseroles. He thought of asking Jill about her mother, but what he really wanted was to hold her, to kiss her mouth, to feel her slender body close to his.

But she seemed far away, and suddenly quite fragile. He wished he'd never entered this messy labyrinth of ideas. He was an idiot for bringing up religion at all, for challenging something that was obviously important and very personal to her. Let her have her damned God, who cares? He turned to her, ready to retract his challenges, anxious to assure her that what she believed didn't bother him one bit. But before he could utter a word, Jill threw her arms around him and kissed him. Then, embarrassed, she pulled away. He was stunned and burst out laughing. She laughed, too. Then, emboldened by her spontaneity, he pulled her close.

4

JILL LOOKED FORWARD TO the weekly Party meetings. She arrived armed with questions about Russia, about theories of class struggle, about dialectical materialism. She loved it when Martin put his arm around her in front of the others. She liked being seen as his girl.

Elliot didn't dance with her anymore or embarrass her by sniffing her perfume. That had been for Martin's sake. When Jill found out that Elliot was a theater director, his arrogant behavior made sense. And though becoming friendly with a director could be useful to her, Jill stayed out of his way. He disturbed her.

Thanks to the volume of fan mail about the romance between Nurse McGinty and Doctor Malone, Nurse McGinty did not die of tuberculosis. Martin came up with the idea of a mis-diagnosis, a bit far-fetched since she'd been coughing up blood for weeks. But Nabisco knew better than to kill off a good thing. They'd hit the jackpot with the McGinty-Malone story line; the soap was a hit. Martin and Jill would be employed well past the thirteen weeks they'd contracted for.

To celebrate, Martin bought tickets to the Second Avenue Yiddish Theater, and it was then that Jill met his parents.

That afternoon, she took special care with her makeup, wore her mother's pearl necklace, and had Gloria fuss with her hair. Martin and Jill made their way through the crowded lobby where people were chattering in Yiddish and nibbling on knishes and strudel from the Second Avenue Deli. When he spotted his folks, Martin put his arm around Jill and guided her toward them. His father had a full beard and smelled of after-shave. His mother's eyes sparkled the same way Martin's did. They both had thick accents that Jill would have had to study a long time to perfect. They shook hands smiling as Martin made introductions, but when he announced her last name—Fullbright—they became agitated and spoke rapidly to Martin in Yiddish. Martin's face turned red and his voice was shrill when he answered them. Jill had never heard him raise his voice unless it was about political matters during Party meetings. She couldn't imagine why his parents were so upset or what they had said to cause Martin such consternation. She was frustrated that they had all cut her out of the conversation.

"Come on," he said sharply, taking her elbow and pushing her ahead of them into the theater. Inside it was noisy and airless. Martin sat between Jill and his mother, as if to shield Jill from his mother's bad manners. His mother and father were carrying on an animated conversation. Martin kept his eyes fixed on the program. Jill leaned in close and asked, "What did they say?"

He took a breath and turned to her. "They're upset because you're not Jewish. This is one area where their progressive thinking falls short."

Jill's heart sank. His parents were against her without even knowing her. It was as if she were being turned away without even getting to audition.

THE FIRST TIME JILL VISITED the basement apartment where Martin and Al lived she stood in the doorway dismayed. The place was small and cramped and smelled of mildew. She spotted a cockroach and jumped. Al laughed. "You can play with the cockroaches but you may not take them home!"

Jill stepped gingerly into the room and looked around for a place to sit. "I don't get it. You both have good jobs. You can afford a better place."

Al and Martin exchanged looks. Martin said, "We prefer to give our money to the Party."

She had nothing to say to that. It was yet another instance that showed she had a lot to learn about "subordinating personal desires to the greater good."

In the subsequent weeks, the three of them spent hours sitting around the little wooden table in the basement drinking coffee and discussing Party objectives and how they could use their art to further the cause of the workers' struggle. Martin was writing a play with proletarian heroes. Al was working on a collection of short stories about garment workers. And Jill was thinking about her acting in a new way. Up until then, she'd always just used her best instinct. She'd go into the studio, rehearse for an hour, and then go on the air. Now that she was a communist, she thought about what she was saying in a different way. She tried to delve deeper into Nurse McGinty, a well-paid worker with a higher education. Maybe Nurse McGinty looked down on uneducated people. How would that affect the way she talked or issued orders? But then Jill remembered the compassion of Nurse

O'Hara. She was so tender when she told them about her mother. Jill wanted her characterization to be in line with their progressive ideas, but she also wanted it to be true to the spirit of Nurse McGinty. So she ended up not changing her at all.

Sometimes Jill cooked for Martin and Al. She had learned the basics from her mother and cooked for her father after Millicent died; though the way Russell passed up Jill's meals suggested she wasn't very good at it. But Martin and Al weren't choosy. They appreciated her efforts, even if the menu was limited. Jill also offered a feminine touch: she hung lace over the Venetian blinds; she bought red carnations and put them in a jelly jar. Martin didn't approve of such frivolity, but she did it anyway. The place needed cheering.

Party work took all their spare time: they met with their unit each week and sold *The Daily Worker* door to door. They tried to recruit minorities. It was their unit that came up with the slogan *"Black and white, unite and fight!"* They marched in solidarity with electrical workers who were trying to get a union going. They led a delegation to the Welfare Board demanding relief for the unemployed. Once a week Jill and Libby assembled mimeographed pamphlets that outlined the aims of the Party, listed concrete actions it was organizing, quoted Stalin. As Jill stapled the pages together, she remembered how Martin's mother had secreted anti-czarist propaganda into baked goods. Jill felt a kinship with her now that she was also part of a long tradition of resistance. But Martin's mother would never know this as long as the woman continued to reject her.

Martin took Jill to see the Group Theatre's production of *Waiting for Lefty*. At the end of the play, the entire audience stood and shouted, "Strike! Strike! Strike!" along with the actors. When they left the theater Martin thrust his fist into the air in the communist salute. "What was that line, Jill? An uppercut. The good old uppercut to the chin!" She joined him in the salute, quoting from the final scene, "Workers of the world...our bones and blood!" They marched down the street arm in arm chanting, "Bones and blood! Bones and blood!"

At least once a week, Martin was one of several speakers— sometimes as many as eight a night—standing on a crate on the corner of 86th between Lexington and Third Avenue, each man selling his cure for Depression troubles. There were always crowds. Some of the folks who gathered to listen were out of work and just liked seeing a show for free. Others stood in earnest, desperate for something to believe in.

Martin preached as if it were a revival meeting. "Fellow workers, what does it mean that German Jews have been stripped of their citizenship rights? Why should we here on 86th Street give a damn? Because, my friends, if Hitler has his way, it will be happening here, too, right here in New York City!"

A sour-faced man yelled back, "What the hell! The Jews own too much anyhow!"

Jill blurted, "Anti-Semite!"

But Martin addressed the man with respect. "Sir, what we here in America treasure most, what makes our country unique and strong, is what Hitler fears most—a melting pot."

A woman holding a small yapping dog spoke up sharp and challenging, "But realistically, how could all that happen in America?"

"Ma'am, fascism is systematic. In Germany it began with a series of anti-Semitic campaigns. First, an official boycott of Jewish firms, then liquidation of Jewish businesses. And, today, German Jews are officially deprived of all rights of citizenship!

How could it happen in America? Sinclair Lewis just wrote a book called *It Can't Happen Here*. It's a shocking answer to your question."

Jill watched Martin—his tie loose, his hat askew, his shirt rumpled as always. He held the audience in the palm of his hand. He had fire in his soul. She thought that if he ever got tired of writing, he'd make a good actor. He kept the audience waiting until just the right moment to deliver the heart of his message. "The civil liberties of the common man are being trampled under the iron heel of fascism!" He certainly wasn't a handsome man, but to Jill he looked very impressive—smart and bold and flushed with commitment. Pumping every word full of passion and purpose, he finished by bellowing, "Fascism is evil! And the Communist Party is willing to fight it tooth and nail!" By then the crowd was shouting encouragement and applauding. That was Jill's cue to pass out the pamphlets.

Martin stepped down. He took off his glasses, mopped his brow with a handkerchief, and then beamed at Jill as if together they had just wiped fascism off the face of the earth.

"How do you do it?" Jill asked, not hiding her awe. "No script. Not even notes."

He took her in his arms. "You inspire me, that's how!" He kissed her passionately and gazed into her eyes. "God, you're lovely! Those eyes, that perfect profile. If I were an artist, I'd paint portraits of you all day long."

"Oh, Martin..." she said, pleased and embarrassed.

"Maybe I'll learn to draw one of these days. After we stomp out fascism!" He laughed as he stuffed the remaining pamphlets into the crate.

AL WAS VISITING HIS MOTHER IN Brooklyn and Jill was making dinner. She stood at the sink peeling potatoes, one of Martin's old shirts wrapped around her waist for an apron. Martin was sitting at the table studying Marx's book on dialectical materialism. A window behind him provided a view of the ankles and feet of passersby on the sidewalk. The occasional scratching of Martin's pen in a notebook was the only sound. Jill realized that this was the first time they'd been alone in the apartment. If her father knew, he'd have a heart attack. But really there was nothing for him to worry about; Martin was a gentleman. He knew she was a respectable girl, happy to neck with him in the park but saving the rest for when she got married. Nowadays, especially among some of their comrades, that was considered old-fashioned. Carol and Ray weren't even married but lived as husband and wife.

Jill loved this feeling, as if they were married and this was their home. Of course, their home wouldn't be in a basement, and they wouldn't be eating off of chipped plates. She was about to put the potatoes into boiling water when there was pounding at the door. Martin opened it and Elliot swept into the room as if they were expecting him.

"Evenin', comrades!" he roared in his theatrical way, tossing his hat onto the couch. He always entered a room as if nothing of importance was going on until he appeared.

Martin took his coat. "Just in time for dinner."

Jill tried to catch his eye. She didn't want to share their evening, especially with Elliot.

"It's spirits I'm after, not food."

Jill delayed putting in the potatoes, hoping he'd go quickly. Martin brought out the only bottle of wine. He poured three glasses, handed one to Jill but jumped into a political talk with Elliot before she could signal her displeasure. "I don't know, Elliot," Martin said. "United Front sounds swell but who will lead it? Roosevelt?"

Elliot laughed his hearty laugh. "Look, if the Social Democrats hadn't been so scared of the communists, Hitler might not be a household word today. We have to pull everyone together to keep fascism from gaining ground."

Martin lit a cigarette, took a long pull and said in a thoughtful voice, "So, how does the real left keep from getting swallowed up by the reformist section of the capitalist class, which is bigger and stronger now than we are?"

Elliot was there to stay. Jill put in the potatoes, picked up a knife, and began to slice carrots. Their words drifted in and out of her head: New Deal. Proletariat. Bourgeoisie. Bolshevik. They went on and on as only Elliot and Martin could do, finding slivers of disagreement in every idea. Then the conversation shifted. Elliot started grousing about work. He rocked back on the legs of his chair. "Radio is too damned confining. I've got to find a stage play to direct."

This got Martin excited. "I'm almost finished with *Factory Whistle*. I'd love to see what you'd do with it. Let's rent a hall and just put it on. Jill could play Beatrice. Right, Jill? Libby could play her sister. Just in our unit alone we could pull a cast together. It'd be great to put it on before the election."

Elliot seemed to consider the proposal, but Jill knew that a thrown-together production was not what he had in mind. Something shuddered in her chest. She knew he was about to say something that would crush Martin's enthusiasm.

"Nah, that's penny ante. I want Broadway." He reached for

the wine. "Now, when you're a famous writer…"

Martin's tone was cool. "That's hardly in my plans. I write for the Party, not my own glory."

Elliot said quickly, "Well, of course, I know that. That's all any of us really want. Still, the more power you have, the more influential you are. That just stands to reason."

Jill put down a place setting in front of Elliot, hoping to change the direction of the conversation. But Elliot pushed away from the table. "No thanks, Jill." Then, with a wink, added, "I've got a pretty little dish waiting for me uptown."

He put on his hat. As he went out, he said, "I'd like to read the finished draft."

Martin nodded. But Jill knew he'd never give Elliot his play, and she also knew Elliot would never ask again.

5

By the late fall, the meetings were filled with discussion about what was happening in Spain. Franco was using military force to bring down the Popular Front government. Hitler and Mussolini were sending forces in to help him. When the International Brigades began arriving in Spain to support the Loyalists against Franco, the conversation at Carol and Ray's became heated.

"Let's be clear," said Elliot forcefully. "No matter what's going on in Spain, the number one priority for us here is Party building."

"What good is Party building while Hitler's on the loose?" Martin asked.

"The Party is the only force willing to stand up to Hitler!"

"I agree," said Carol. "The Party is our best shot at forcing his hand."

"Moscow is calling for volunteers to go to Spain," Martin countered. "That's where we all should be today—in Spain fighting fascism, not sitting around arguing dialectics like a bunch of petty-bourgeois intellectuals!"

"Come on, Martin," said Ray, "that's hardly fair."

"Yeah," said Al. "It's no small thing to pick up a gun and run off to Spain."

Martin continued vehemently, "What else can we do? There's a democratically elected government in Spain. With German and Italian forces helping Franco, it's doomed to failure. The democracies are sitting on their asses with policies of non-intervention. How can we just sit by and watch? It's a chance to take a stand against fascism!"

"Aw, get off your soap box," Elliot muttered.

Martin countered, "Elliot, you're the one who always says that our primary job is to oppose fascism."

For once Elliot said nothing. Then, with no particular flourish, Martin said, "Well, I'm joining. I've already submitted my name."

Jill glanced up, not sure she'd heard right. The room suddenly fell silent. Jill's stomach clenched. She wanted to run to him, throw her arms around his neck and tell him no, no, you can't do such a dangerous thing! But she bit her lip and watched her comrades consider the gauntlet Martin had hurled at their feet. It was clear that his plan was completely foolhardy. Surely someone would convince him of that.

Finally, Al exclaimed, "I agree. It's the right thing to do. Count me in!"

Ray looked at him, a new light in his eyes. "I suppose we really could make a difference."

The conversation was like a runaway train headed toward disaster, and everyone was jumping on board! My God, she thought, he's really going. He'll be thousands of miles away, in a foreign place where he'll face terrible danger. The idea of being separated from him was unbearable. She jumped up. "Me, too!" she cried. "Women should go, too."

Martin shot her a glance, a mixture of wonder and pride. Then Elliot announced unapologetically, "It's foolish to think we should all go to Spain. We need to build support for the Loyalists here."

"That's true," Martin conceded.

There was more discussion, this time about the need to put pressure on Roosevelt to send arms to the Loyalists, how important it was to keep the Party strong, how more of them could go at a later date if necessary. The initial flurry of excitement died down and in the end it was decided that Martin alone would go.

Jill's heart folded over on itself. She struggled to keep her expression neutral during the talk about logistics. The U.S. State Department had prohibited all travel to Spain; anyone who volunteered put his citizenship at risk. Therefore, secrecy was essential. Arrangements had to be made for transport. Border towns were closed, so how Martin would get into Spain would have to be worked out. How much money would he need? Where could he convert dollars to pesetas? Would he be able to receive mail directly, or would it have to be diverted for security reasons?

Jill barely paid attention. She couldn't wait to be alone with him. Finally, after they dropped Al off at the subway, she and Martin headed for Central Park. She was determined to present a coherent argument that would convince him not to go. But before she could organize her thoughts, he turned to her and said, "I was so proud of you, that you wanted to volunteer."

"Umm," she said in a quiet voice. Then panic ripped through her and she blurted out, "But why do you have to go? It's not *your* war!"

"Any war that fights fascism is my war."

"But, Martin, what if you get killed?"

"I might die. But it's worth it if we can stop fascism."

"How can you say that? We're talking about your life! Are

you actually willing to lose it like that?"

He said nothing. They found a bench and sat down. Tears were getting in the way of Jill's thoughts. "Martin, it's not that I don't respect your convictions—"

"It's easy to have convictions but unless I act on them, what's the point?"

The afternoon was chilly and already dark. Jill wished she were in his dreary basement making dinner instead of sitting here talking about him dying.

Martin said, "If Spain turns fascist, then Belgium and France won't be able to hold out. Then England, then China, then—"

"I thought communists believed war was bad. Look at all the wasted lives in the Great War."

"We do believe war is bad. The so-called Great War was nothing more than an imperialist blood bath. My brother was cannon fodder in that war."

"Your brother? I didn't even know you had a brother."

"He won the Congressional Medal of Honor, rescued twenty people under gun fire. I was only a little kid, but I still remember him." He turned away from her. "Daniel...used to give me rides on his back..."

She touched his arm. "But then, why would you...?"

"The Great War was supposed to make the world safe for democracy. If we win this war, we really would make the world safe for democracy." When he looked at her his eyes were wet. "Don't you see? I have a chance to make up for my brother's loss."

A man passed with his dog. The simple act of taking a dog for a walk filled Jill with longing. Why couldn't she and Martin have a regular life?

"Come on, honey," he said. "Instead of imagining the

worst, think of Democrats, socialists, and communists fighting together and winning peace in Western Europe."

He had never called her honey before and her heart lurched. At the same time, she felt hopeless. With her limited knowledge of world affairs, there was no way Jill could persuade him not to go.

He lifted her chin and looked into her eyes. "But I'd feel better going if I knew I had a wife to come home to."

It took her a moment to catch his meaning. He spoke without formality, without an engagement ring, just in his own way, right from his heart.

"Oh, Martin," she said, beaming through teary eyes.

He took her in his arms and kissed her. When he walked her to the bus, his arm draped around her shoulder, the Christmas lights strung up along Broadway seemed to be dancing just for them.

6

December 8, 1936

Dear Dad,

I'm sorry it's been so long since I've written. The show has kept me busy, and I've also met someone who I've been spending a lot of time with. In fact, I'm getting married! His name is Martin Levy. He writes scripts for my show and that's how we met. He also writes for a magazine called "New Masses." He's a graduate of New York University and a Phi Beta Kappa, too. We're getting married January 10. Don't buy us a wedding present. Buy a railroad ticket instead! (Can't you get Sid to run the store?) I'd love to see you and I think the change would do you good.

Martin's beliefs are different from yours, but I still think you two will like each other. He's very educated and interested in intellectual things. (Also, he doesn't trust Roosevelt either.)

Love, Jill

December 13, 1936

Dear Jill,

Do you realize that "New Masses" is a Communist

publication? And I'm sure that Levy is a Jewish name. Please listen to me, Jill. You're very young and impressionable. I insist that you break off this liaison immediately. Whatever you do, do not give this man any money and under no circumstances sign your name to anything. You are very naive and young. The International Jewish Bolshevik Conspiracy is a serious threat to Democracy and Freedom. I'm afraid that you've been duped by this young man. Here is fifteen dollars so you can go with your roommate to Atlantic City and have a good time and forget about this fellow.

Think of your poor mother. I beg you, don't do something that would break her heart.

Love, Your Father

Jill wanted to use the fifteen dollars to buy Martin a suit for the wedding, but he convinced her the money should go into the Party coffers. She thought it ironic that her father's money was helping to spread communism. It upset her that her own father didn't trust her. Did he think that if the devil himself showed up with a marriage proposal, she might accept it? Jill knew his fears would vanish if he could just meet Martin.

Martin's parents refused to attend the wedding, too. His mother's words were, "Marrying a *shiksa* with no rabbi? That's not a wedding!"

Martin told Jill, "The hell with what everyone thinks. We don't need their blessing. We have the entire international labor movement on our side!"

The subsequent weeks were filled with activity. Martin was busy making travel arrangements, gathering essential items for the months overseas, and working another writer into the radio show. Jill was figuring out the details of the wedding—the blood test, the marriage license, the appointment at City Hall. Louise took her shopping for her wedding dress. They poked along 14th Street, looking in windows. Jill's mother had been a whiz with a needle and thread, able to make any dress without a pattern, so naturally Jill had always imagined being married in one of her creations, something in white satin with a detachable organdy train.

They stood outside a window looking at bridal gowns. Louise pointed to a lacy one with tiny pearl buttons at the neck. Jill loved the way it nipped in at the waist. She admired the detail work on the sleeves. "Martin would think it's too lavish."

"It's your wedding day. Wouldn't Martin want—?"

"To use money on a one-time expenditure is against our political beliefs," she explained. She pulled her collar up against the wind and turned away from the window, not wanting to tempt herself.

In the end, she settled on a lilac suit from Klein's. It didn't have satin, lace, or pearl buttons but according to Louise, it flattered her figure and made her hazel eyes go blue.

A few days before the wedding, on her way home from the studio, it turned bitter cold and suddenly hail pelted down. Jill escaped into a church and stood in the nave shaking off her hat, aware of the sudden quiet. She hadn't been to church in years and her recent conversion to communism had pushed aside any interest in things religious.

A few other parishioners were inside, some seated, some kneeling, some lighting candles. The walls were lined with statues of the saints. Above the altar, Jesus hung from the cross. She sat in a pew in the back. Amber light filtered through one of the panes of stained glass and fell across the room in a narrow slant, including in its sweep a woman kneeling at the altar lighting a candle. From the way her head hung and her shoulders rounded, Jill thought she must be in mourning. With a stab of recognition, she knew without a doubt that the woman was grieving for her husband! The woman's pain sliced through Jill like a knife. How could Jill ever endure Martin's death? She dropped to her knees and pressed her palms together. Please, God. You already took my mother, isn't that enough? Don't let him die, too.

When Jill came outside, she was dazzled by bright light. There was no evidence of the recent hailstorm. She stood on the steps and closed her eyes, feeling the warmth of the winter sun. A calm settled over her. She felt it was God's blessing and, deep down, knew that things would turn out all right.

She wanted to run all the way to Martin and tell him about her religious epiphany. But she knew he'd scoff. He would remind her that the only time we pray is to ask for something. She decided to keep God's benediction tucked inside.

7

JANUARY 10 BEGAN COOL AND clear but gradually turned dark
with billowy gray clouds. Martin slumped against the window
of the bus, hat over his eyes, hoping to catch a few winks. He
had barely slept the night before, anxious about the last minute
details of arranging for transport and lodging when he arrived
in France, and troubled by the uncertain fate that awaited him
once he landed on Spanish soil. Mostly though he was worried
about tonight, his wedding night. He had gone with a few girls
in college, had necked and held hands and felt under a few
sweaters. But he was still a virgin.

Al, not much more experienced, had explained things the
night before with the help of a bottle of corn liquor and a couple
of cheap cigars, his way of giving Martin a proper send-off into
matrimony. When they'd gone through the bottle and were both
sprawled in a drunken stupor on the couch, Martin asked,
"How will I know what to do?"

Al champed on his cigar and slurred his words. "You won't.
But Martin Junior will."

With those feeble words of advice and a hangover, Martin
had awakened with the ancient Hebrew words on his lips,
"Please, God, may I arise like a lion!" And here he was at 3

o'clock in the afternoon, barely able to hold his head up, let alone arise like some wild jungle beast.

BY THE TIME LOUISE, GLORIA, and Jill left the City Federation Hotel it was drizzling. Carol, Ray, Libby, Elliot, Al, and Martin were already in the judge's chambers.

The ceremony was brief. They promised devotion and love everlasting. When the judge said, "...'til death do you part," Jill felt the magnitude of not only Martin's commitment to fight in Spain, but also her own pledge to stand by him in his choice. "I do," came from deep in her soul. They were pronounced husband and wife and kissed each other and hugged their friends. Elliot wanted more than a hug, and pressed his mouth onto Jill's, but she kept her lips clamped shut. He let go of her saying, "She's all yours," and pushed her toward Martin, who caught her with joy on his face.

Jill tossed Louise her bouquet and everybody threw Rudy Vallee's birdseed at the newlyweds as they ran out into a downpour. They turned and waved good-bye before climbing into a cab and beginning their married life.

Martin took Jill for a drink in the lounge of the Astor. The Tommy Dorsey orchestra played up-tempo rhythms. Martin didn't know how to dance so they just sat close, sipping champagne and watching couples sway cheek to cheek as Edythe Wright sang, "Head Over Heels In Love." Martin was pitched forward, intent on catching every lyric.

We could make believe I love you
Only make believe that you love me
Others find peace of mind in pretending
Couldn't you, couldn't I, couldn't we...?

He whispered to Jill, "This song feeds the working man's fantasies of escape."

She smiled and squeezed his hand. It touched her that Martin's political ideals permeated his every thought.

They walked to the Empire Hotel in the slow falling rain. In the restaurant they were given a corner table with real cloth napkins. They ordered roast chicken, but neither of them did more than pick at the food. Jill kept thinking, tomorrow at this time I won't be a virgin.

Martin signed them into the hotel registry: "Mr. and Mrs. Martin Levy," and then they took a shaky little elevator to the sixth floor.

Jill's stomach was on its own elevator. She had only a vague idea of how marriage was supposed to be consummated. She felt herself swing between excitement and terror at the prospect of finding out. Her friends had been of little help. Carol's only suggestion was that Jill should have a few drinks beforehand to "loosen up." Louise was still a virgin and therefore had no advice to offer. Gloria's escapades led her to give Jill only the briefest instruction, "If he'll let you get on top, you'll have a great ride!"

Jill missed her mother, though Millicent Fullbright was certainly not one to explain such things. The day her daughter started menstruating, she was totally flustered. Jill, fear on her face, had run into the kitchen, thrusting out her bloody bloomers. Millicent, blushing, had avoided her daughter's eyes and walked brusquely into the bathroom. "It can't be stopped," she said over her shoulder as Jill stood behind her like a confused puppy. Millicent opened a drawer and dug out some cotton cloths folded in neat squares. "You can use these from now on." Jill was horrified. She thought she was going to bleed every day. No, Jill's mother would not have been the best person to ask about sexual intercourse.

The elevator jerked to a stop, and they found their room at the end of the hall. Martin turned the key in the lock, flicked a switch, and the room was flooded with light. Crowding the small space was a chest of drawers, an easy chair, and the bed. The window was shut against the rain and the air was heavy and still. The radiator hissed. They hung up their raincoats.

Jill wondered if she should take off everything all at once. She wanted Martin to tell her what to do.

Martin put his glasses on the dresser and sat on the bed, looking at her with love and longing. She came over and sat down next to him. The bed caved in the middle and they laughed. He put his arm around her delicately and whispered, "My wife."

He turned off the light. By the dim glow of the street lamps they undressed with their backs to each other. Jill unpacked her small valise and put on her nightgown, then quickly slid between the stiff, cool sheets, pulling the covers up.

Martin stood by the bed wearing only his pajama bottoms and asked shyly, "May I look at you?"

She murmured yes and he drew back the covers and peeled off her nightgown. He stared in the semi-darkness at her naked body, then slipped into bed beside her. When he pulled her toward him the feeling of his hairy chest against her breasts startled her. They completed the act before Jill had time to consider Gloria's advice.

Afterwards, he asked anxiously, "Did it hurt very much?"

"Just a little," she said. "There might be blood."

He turned on the bedside lamp and they both looked. But

her thighs were pale and white. Jill ruffled his hair. "Look at us, just look at us!"

He gazed at her. "I'm the luckiest man alive." He pulled her toward him and they snuggled under the covers and listened to the rain.

"How many children do you want?" she asked.

"Two of each," he said.

Then Jill began to weep softly.

"Don't cry, sweetheart. I'll be back in no time."

"It's not that," she said. "I'm just so happy."

He kissed her brow. "I know, I know…"

He drifted off to sleep. Jill propped herself on an elbow and studied him in the dim light—his pale skin, his soft lips. When he exhaled he snored softly. She put her face close to his and inhaled his breath. She could imagine growing old with him. She smoothed his thin hair off his brow and noticed her wedding ring, a cheap thing that Martin had picked up on 14th Street. Jill didn't mind that the gem was worthless; she felt like the wealthiest woman in the world.

She rolled onto her back and looked out the window. Neon from a bar across the street blinked through the rain. Gloria and Louise were probably sitting around doing each other's nails, chewing the fat. Jill was a million miles from their world now.

8

THEY GOT UP THE FOLLOWING morning and stopped by the basement apartment to pick up Martin's duffel bag. Al smiled discreetly, as if nothing had changed. "Everyone's meeting at the subway," he said off-handedly, telling Jill and Martin what they already knew.

Carol, Ray, Libby, and Elliot were waiting for them. As they climbed onto the train, Elliot made eyes at Martin, "Well?" Martin ignored him. But Elliot persisted. "Come on, how was it?" Jill pretended not to hear.

"Get your mind out of the gutter, Elliot," Martin said.

Elliot protested. "We're entitled to a report, don't you think? Isn't it on the agenda, Ray?"

But Ray wasn't paying attention. He'd found a copy of *Life Magazine* on the seat. "Hey, get a load of this," he said. "It seems that a Mr. Robert Cuse found a loophole in the U.S. Neutrality Act and forced the State Department to grant him an export permit so he could send planes and munitions to Spain!"

"No kidding?" said Martin, grabbing the magazine. He quickly read the rest of the article. "But wouldn't you know Congress rushed new legislation to plug the loophole. Naturally, the shipment never made it out of the harbor."

Elliot looked at Martin. "Well, comrade, that's certainly a sign that you made the right decision."

Suddenly it struck Jill that the reason Elliot didn't make the same decision was that if he got killed fighting in Spain, he'd never become a famous director. She quickly brushed the thought away. Elliot was over-bearing and arrogant, but everyone knew that he was a devoted communist.

They stood shivering on the dock. Steely gray clouds promised more rain. Martin said his good-byes. When it was Jill's turn, she tried to hold back tears but it was no use. She cried freely.

"Be brave," he said, wiping away her tears. She nodded and bit her lip. He hoisted his duffel bag onto his shoulder and made his way up the plank of the *SS President Roosevelt*. Jill kept watching Martin's strong back until the crowd swallowed him up. She turned to her friends for comfort, but they were not paying attention to the ship or to her heartache; they were in a huddle, and on Ray's cue broke into the "Internationale."

Arise ye prisoners of starvation!
Arise ye wretched of the earth!
For Justice thunders condemnation;
A better world's in birth.
'Tis the final conflict,
Let each stand in his place.
The International Party
Shall be the human race.

Ray squeezed Jill's hand, "Chin up, old gal." She smiled at him gratefully.

Elliot said, "Let's go to Rossoff's. I'm starving."

It was difficult for Jill to resume her old life. Her heart wasn't in it. She had become so deeply connected to Martin, and then suddenly, he was gone. From the moment his ship headed out, she felt bereft. She took some comfort in going to work every day and making Nurse McGinty come to life in spite of the fact that a new writer had been put on the show. She adopted a better attitude toward Rudy Vallee and decided his chirping was a song of determination. Still, she couldn't stop worrying about Martin. Each day that she didn't receive word from him, her concern increased. She became more and more convinced that his smart thinking wouldn't be enough to protect him. Even though he was brave and impassioned, he was too intellectual to be a real soldier.

Finally at the end of February, a letter reached her.

February 19, 1937

Darling,

I am sitting under an olive tree half-listening to the Commissar of the Lincolns (the name of my battalion). He's reminding us that we're not fighting under the orders of the Comintern, we're part of the Spanish Republican Army now! He's a small wiry Negro. It occurs to me that this rag-tag "people's" army of ours is completely integrated, from commanding officer to the rank and file!

The ship was a bit of a bore. The petty-bourgeoisie sipped their drinks, watched rotten movies, promenaded on the deck, laughed and talked about superficial things, and ate big meals. Those of us on "a mission" couldn't wait until we docked.

We took a train to a small border town (I can't disclose its name) and crossed the Pyrenees during a night so black I had to hold onto the shirttail of the guy in front of me, a skinny kid from New Haven named Eddie. We raced against sunrise to get across without being seen. By dawn, my hands were so cold I couldn't open them.

When we finally touched Spanish soil, one of the Polish fellas began singing the "Internationale." I was so moved that I welled up. Jill, this is the global dream of communism I've always envisioned: comrades joining together from all over the world to get the job done. Many have already experienced fascism in their own countries and their stories are grim. Listening to them reaffirms my belief that I made the right decision. Fascists are on the move. As a Jew and a progressive, I'd be among the first to fall under their ax if they ever came to our shores. So, rather than "wait and see," I'm taking a stand.

I feel your support from across the ocean. How I miss you and long to get a letter. Please write to me: c/o Mme. Gillette, 1 Haute Place, Paris.

I hope you will continue to develop yourself politically during this time, even though I won't be there to nag you and tell you what to read. (Read Engels' The Origin of the Family, Private Property, and the State. *Elliot will help you with it.)*

Everywhere we go we are met with the Popular Front Salute. The good old uppercut to the chin! It's thrilling to have encouragement from strangers. I sign off now with my own fist raised. Give my regards to all our comrades. Long live the Soviet Union!

I dream of holding you in my arms again soon and end this letter by saying, muchos besos para ti. *(Many kisses for you!)*

Love and Salud, Martin

The reality of war and the dangers that Martin faced filled Jill with so much apprehension that she got sick. She dragged herself to Dr. Herbert's and laid on the examination table debating whether or not to tell him the source of her concern. The smell of disinfectant increased her nausea. Dr. Herbert came back into the room, his rotund body navigating clumsily through the small space. He sat down heavily on a little stool, put on his bifocals, and opened her chart. Jill said tentatively, "I think it's from worry. I've had a lot on my mind lately. Or maybe it's the flu...my roommate just got over it."

"It's not the flu and it's not nerves," he said, peering at her over the rim of his glasses. "You're going to have a baby."

She sat up. "How can that be?"

"Come now," he said, "you're a married woman; this is what happens."

"But we were only married for one night before my husband had to go out of town."

"One night is all it takes."

She walked out of his office in a daze and picked her way gingerly over icy packs of dirty snow, taking special care not to fall. She was due at Carol and Ray's and headed toward the bus stop. The crowds jostled her; the blare and belches of the passing cars gave her a headache. It began to snow lightly and she shivered inside her tweed coat. The bus stop bench was too wet to sit on, and she wanted badly to sit. She suddenly knew that the last place she could sit tonight would be on Carol and Ray's sagging couch. She simply wouldn't be able to concentrate on a discussion of Party policy.

She turned in the direction of the Loew's building and sat at the counter in the coffee shop across the street where she first met Martin. She stirred sugar into her tea, going over her conversation with Dr. Herbert. There was no way to get word to Martin immediately. She tried to picture what he was doing, where he was sleeping. She imagined a dirty place with flies and stale bread. She could see him running through the dusty Spanish streets, his strong legs hurrying special messages to some commander. She imagined his soothing voice and quiet confidence and felt near tears. When would he come back? What if it wasn't in a few months? What if it was longer, much longer? Worse yet, what if he didn't come back at all? She would be left alone with a child!

"Hey, Beautiful."

She glanced up and saw Elliot sliding onto the stool next to her.

"Elliot? Aren't you going to the meeting?"

"I've got a rehearsal downtown." He signaled the waitress for coffee and lit a cigarette. "What's your excuse?"

"I—I'm not—I've got too much on my mind."

He studied her. "Is it Martin? Is everything okay?"

She meant to say, I'm expecting news. But it came out, "I'm expecting."

Elliot's head jerked up so quickly that the ash of his cigarette fell into his cup. He said with a grin, "Well, let's hope if it's a girl she gets your looks, and if it's a boy he doesn't get Martin's!"

She smiled and took a sip of tea. Then she blurted out, "Oh, Elliot, I don't know what to do! This wasn't our plan. What if something happens to him, or what if...?" She looked at him, her eyes imploring. "It's too soon."

"You're just in shock. That's why they give you nine months to get used to the idea." He took a drag on his cigarette. "Look, you'll make a wonderful mother. Martin will be happy as a clam. You'll move out to Jersey and join the PTA or something."

This made her laugh. "It's so hard to believe it's already happening, right now, inside me." She touched her belly and he looked at her hands resting there. She quickly became self-conscious and changed the subject. "When are you going to start a family, Elliot?"

"First I have to do what Martin did, don't I? Find a gorgeous wife."

She smiled. "But, Elliot, do you really want a wife and family?"

He looked out the window at some kids playing stickball, slipping and sliding on the ice. "What I really want is to direct motion pictures."

"I can imagine you doing that," she said honestly.

He looked at her, getting enthusiastic. "I want to be able to control where it is that the audience looks, what it is that they hear. On the stage it's always the whole picture. In movies, you can have close-ups and long shots, cut the dialogue to fit the mood, do whole scenes with no dialogue at all. Or a series of scenes. Montage sequences."

He snuffed out his cigarette. "Some day I'm going out to California."

"What about the Party?"

"What's one thing got to do with the other? I'll always work for the Party. Put it on the big screen, reach more people. Like Eisenstein."

They took the bus downtown, and he walked her to the door of the boarding house. She reached out her hand for him to shake but he ignored it, pulling her toward him in an embrace. The smell of him and the strength of his hold, though brief, put her off balance. She figured it was just the "maleness" of him. Now that she was pregnant, she was probably overly sensitive to hormone differences.

By the time she tiptoed into her room, careful not to wake Rudy Vallee or Louise, her thoughts were completely on the baby. She undressed and, wearing only a slip under her robe, went down the hall to the bathroom. She took off the robe and studied her profile in the mirror, trying to discern a bulge. But her stomach was flat as a pancake.

She thought of her career, of making it on Broadway. She would have to put her dreams on hold. God had other plans for her. He had chosen now for the miracle of life. She was going to be a mother.

She cursed herself for so carelessly tossing her precious secret to Elliot. Martin should have been the first to know. And he wouldn't know for weeks. How could she ever explain to him that she told Elliot first, without making him feel cheated?

She slipped between the covers with a flashlight and a piece of stationery. She decided to simply eliminate the whole part about telling Elliot and began by simply saying, "Darling! We're going to have a baby!"

9

SHE FLOATED THROUGH THE following morning on a cloud, beginning to marvel at the changes taking place in her body. On a crowded bus a man gave her his seat. Their eyes met for an instant and Jill was certain that he had divined her secret.

At the post office, something stopped her from mailing the letter to Martin. She had omitted the fact that she had told Elliot and that bothered her. Married people should have no secrets.

When she got back to her room, she took a fresh sheet of paper and rewrote the letter. This time she told Martin about bumping into Elliot and how Elliot had joked about them moving to New Jersey. She was satisfied that she had told the truth in a way that wouldn't upset Martin. She put the new letter in the envelope. Just as she sealed it, Louise came running into the room. "From your husband!" she said, tossing Jill a letter. Jill tore it open.

March 2, 1937

Mi Compañera,

I saw up close what Comrade Lenin meant when he said, "Bullets are the final argument." Remember Eddie? That kid from New Haven? He got shot. It happened right in front of me. I tore off my shirt and tried to stop the bleeding, but it just gushed through the cloth. I held him and told him that he was brave, but I don't think he heard me. He kept crying for his mama. And then he started moaning something awful. A few minutes later, he was dead. Only seventeen years old, poor kid. At least we have the comfort of knowing that he died for a working class cause.

Sweetheart, these are the cold realities of war. But please know that I am okay. I'm getting used to the steady diet of mule meat and garbanzo beans and the cold weather and seeing up close what it means to stand up for one's principles. I'm feeling strong and hopeful. We must stay positive and focused on our goal. Destruction to the fascist mad-dogs!

We're moving to a new town and I have to help with the transfer. We've been given a new address where we can receive mail: c/o Socorro Rojo Internacional, Place Altozanos, 20 G.P., Albacete, Spain.

I close by saying, NO PASARÁN! (The watchword to Franco's forces: You may not cross into Loyalist territory!)

I hope to get a letter from you soon.

Your loving husband, Martin

The picture of the soldier stayed with Jill all day, and each time she saw a mailbox, she passed it by. It was very important that her letters not give Martin anything to feel bad about, so even though she didn't believe in lying, she thought that in this instance, it would be better to leave out the whole part about Elliot. She was thinking through the details of that decision as she undressed for bed that night when suddenly, a terrible cramp doubled her over. She limped down the hall to the bathroom.

"What's wrong?" Gloria asked, her mouth full of toothpaste. Jill couldn't speak for the pain. She and Gloria both saw blood trickling down her legs, spreading onto her girdle like crimson ink onto a blotter. Jill had the sharp sensation of being split in two. She began to shake uncontrollably. Gloria yelled, "Somebody call a doctor!" Several girls came running and huddled in the doorway watching her bleed. She let out a long, mournful howl as she clutched her belly, trying to keep the life inside her from sliding out onto the white tile.

By the time Dr. Herbert arrived, she was already in bed, though she couldn't have said how she got there or who had cleaned up the blood. The doctor reassured the girls that it was just a heavy menstrual period. Jill was grateful because she didn't want anyone to know. He gave her a shot to make her sleep. Louise handed her a hot water bottle and thoughtfully took Rudy Vallee into Gloria's room.

Jill closed her eyes, hoping the medication would take effect immediately. She started to doze then realized with a start that her letter never got mailed! At first she was relieved. She had spared Martin the pain of this terrible loss. But then came the thought that by not mailing the letter she had somehow caused the baby to miscarry. It was all mixed up with the fact that she had told Elliot and not told Martin. She had participated in some kind of subterfuge. Losing the baby was her punishment.

10

THE NEXT THING SHE KNEW, she was awake. It felt like afternoon; the room had no windows so it was hard to tell. But Jill could sense the emptiness of the place. She lay in bed, suddenly yearning to hear the chirps Rudy Vallee made. Her head was fogged from the drugs. The world, which had always felt so solid under her feet, was suddenly like quicksand. She couldn't get a toehold.

She tried to imagine what she would write to Martin. Poor Martin, so far away, seeing friends die, eating mule meat and garbanzo beans. How could she add to his misery?

She rolled over and closed her eyes. A picture of her mother floated into her head, sitting in the front seat of the family Studebaker in her dull plaid dress, adjusting the netting on her blue hat. She was a stout woman with a square face. Her hands were always rough and red, as if she'd just washed the dishes in scalding water. The fact is she did wash a lot of dishes with little help from Jill. Jill was an actress, devoted to her scene studies and vocal warm-ups. Millicent indulged her daughter because she believed she had talent.

They were late for Jill's high school graduation and Jill was moping in the back seat. "If you hadn't forgotten to iron my gown—"

"I had other things on my mind," her mother said distractedly, pulling white gloves onto her rough hands.

"What could possibly be as important as my graduation?" Jill said.

"Believe it or not, there is something," her father mumbled.

"Russell, please."

"Well, Millie, why shouldn't she know?"

"Know what?" Jill demanded.

They had arrived at the school. Russell parked the car then turned to look at her. "The doctor said your mother shouldn't work so hard."

"What doctor?"

"Never mind," her mother said.

"Why does everyone treat me like a child?" She slammed out of the car and flew into the gymnasium.

After the ceremony, as Jill and her friends were hugging each other, sobbing, promising to stay in touch forever, a loud cry came from the far end of the gym. A man's voice echoed through the hall: "Help! Somebody!" The whole audience, like one large curious animal, turned toward the crisis.

Jill spotted her father's pale face. She pushed toward the front and there was her mother, collapsed on the shiny wooden floor, her blue hat crushed beneath her head, her jaw slack. The last words her mother had heard her say were filled with resentment and anger.

What if the last words Martin heard from her were about their baby, the lost promise of new life? If he had to give his young life for his beliefs, then he should go out of this world believing his wife was just as he left her—waiting for him to come home, waiting to start a family.

Jill padded down the empty hall to the phone and dialed Elliot's number. "You haven't told anyone, have you?" she asked in a thin voice.

"Told who what, Jill?"

"About me…about expecting…" There was a silence while she held her breath, waiting for him to answer.

"No–o, I don't think so, why?"

"You don't think so? Can't you be more certain, Elliot, for God's sake?"

"What's this all about?"

Her head began to pound. She took a deep breath. "Meet me at the White Horse Tavern."

When she arrived, Elliot was already in a booth nursing a Manhattan, his tie loosened, his shirt open at the collar.

As she slid in opposite him, she said quickly, "I'll have whatever you're drinking." He signaled the waitress then waited for her to speak. She'd been crying; her face was a mess. She reached for his pack of cigarettes and took one out, but her hand shook when she tried to light it. He took it from her and lit it with his own cigarette. When he handed it back she finally met his eyes.

As an actress, controlling her emotions was something Jill had been trained to do. Why was it suddenly so hard, with Elliot's clear blue eyes holding on hers, waiting, wondering. She inhaled the cigarette but the smoke made her gag. She began to cough, then she burst into tears. "I lost the baby!"

In an instant he was beside her, his arm around her shoulder, pulling her close. She cried into her hands. Finally, she managed to say, "Martin never knew."

He said softly, "Oh…Martin never knew."

"And I thought it'd be best if he never did."

"You have my word," he said simply, kissing her forehead. "You have my word."

11

January 11, 1938

Mi Compañera,

It's hard to believe it's been a whole year since you and the gang waved me off on the SS President Roosevelt. We didn't dream that the fight against Franco would still be going on, did we? And, even though it's been so many months, I'll never get used to the actual experience of war—sleeping under a thin cover of straw, never bathing properly, watching a nineteen year-old lad lead our platoon, trying not to shit in his pants. It's quite a picture, isn't it, Jill? Me, a bookworm from the Lower East Side, carrying a rifle on my back and a can of ammunition in my hand. I had never even held a gun, and now I'm facing Hitler's Condor Legion and Mussolini's fighter planes.

But it's not all struggle; we still manage to get some time for recreation. Guess who came to sing for us? Paul Robeson! It was raining and cold, but when he sang "Ol' Man River" in his warm, rich bass voice, it was as if we were all warm and dry sitting together at Carnegie Hall. The boys went crazy cheering.

Sweetheart, thank you for the mittens and tobacco.

Next time could you send some chocolate? It would probably be melted by the time it got here, but it would still make me very popular with the fellas.

What I want most is letters with that delicate lavender scent you wear. I yearn to be with you, to hold you in my arms. I dream about making a child together. Do you ever dream of that?

Your loving husband, Martin

JILL REREAD THE LAST LINE AND swallowed hard. She folded the letter and tucked it into the back of her makeup kit on top of the other letters. She studied herself in the mirror and wondered if there would ever be a way for him to tell, just by looking at her. Then she forced her mind away from such fruitless speculation and simply savored the comfort of knowing that Martin was safe.

She smoothed back her hair into a bun. That, together with the heavy pancake makeup, made her look at least twenty-eight, "Martha's" age. She glanced at the wall clock. She still had time before her entrance in Scene Two, so she got out her box of stationery and uncapped her pen. Then she sighed, picked up Martin's letter and fished in her pocketbook for change. An older woman wearing a maid's uniform came in and sat on one of the stools facing the large mirror. "Ida was late interrupting me and I had to ad lib until she finally said her line."

"Oh, Alice!" Jill said, "Tonight of all nights, with Miss Hellman in the audience!"

"Imagine adding new words in front of the playwright. I'm completely mortified."

Jill gave her a sympathetic look, then threw on her robe and walked into the corridor. She could hear the voices on stage raised in argument. A stagehand nodded to her as he propped a rolled up carpet against a flat. She rounded a corner and dropped two nickels into the wall phone.

"Yes, hello?"

The sound of her mother-in-law's voice never failed to make Jill's stomach flutter. She cursed herself for not waiting until after the show to make the call.

"Hello, it's Jill."

"You got a letter?"

"Yes."

"*Guttsadonk*. Please. Read."

It was always the same: clipped sentences, long pauses. Each woman straining to be polite. Martin refused to write to his parents directly until they formally—and warmly—accepted Jill as family. And, because it was humiliating for his mother to get all the news about Martin from Jill, the already tense relationship with her mother-in-law was doubly aggravated.

Leaving out the personal parts, Jill read the letter aloud. At the end she heard a heavy sigh. "I'll call when I get another one," she said with as much friendliness as she could muster.

"Yes, good-bye," was the reply.

Jill went back into the dressing room, passing Alice who was waiting in the wings for her cue. Jill considered how best to respond to Martin's question.

January 28, 1938

My Dearest Martin,

To answer your question, Darling, of course I think of starting a family. But I do not waste too much time dreaming, because the dreams often turn into worry about the future. Remember what you once said about filling the worker's mind with fantasies? I do better when I concentrate on my work.

She thought about what to say next. It was essential that all her letters were cheerful and newsy; her task was to distract him from the cruelties of war. It would do no good to complain about her loneliness, about the boring predictability of Party work, about her yearning to have a regular married life.

Each time I go on stage with "Martha" I feel as though I know her better. It's strange, at first I wanted the role of Karen because she was so familiar. But Martha is more of a challenge. She doesn't know herself very well. (Which is the key to the whole play in a way.) Being in such a long run means I get to explore all aspects of the character. I thank my lucky stars each night when I'm taking my curtain call, looking out over the footlights into the darkened theater exploding with applause. I have to pinch myself: my Broadway dreams have finally come true. (The only thing that would make me happier is if you were in the audience!)

Elliot saw last night's show and was knocked out by my performance. I don't think he fully appreciated my talents from my radio work. He just returned from one of his trips to California. He has a few motion picture deals pending. He came back to direct "Abe Lincoln in Illinois" and is working Richard Gaines into the part since Raymond Massey had to drop out. It should probably be done in a smaller theater, but I think Elliot will do a fine job of creating intimacy in that barn, the Adelphi.

Sometimes I wonder if I'll ever work in radio again. Not that I didn't enjoy it, but I feel the stage is where I belong. Still, I am proud of my work in that last soap. I think I was able to influence the writers. By the time I left, Mrs. Harrington had some spunk! Why is it that female characters are always in the shadow of the men? They need to have their own shadows. (See how I was doing my Party work? Trying to get the writers to liberate their women characters!) Of course Lillian Hellman gives her characters plenty of spunk. It's wonderful saying lines written by a woman for a woman. (You are the exception to the rule that men can't write women's roles, my dearest!)

She put down her pen, poured herself some tea and glanced at the clock. The tea was tepid. She thought about the conversation with Martin's mother and, even though it meant she would lose the only contact she had with his family, she made a decision.

I read your letter to your mother today. It seems cruel to make her go through me to find out if you are okay. I think you should stop punishing them, Martin. They're getting old. I forgive them, so you should too.

There was a loud rap on the door and a muffled, "Five minutes, Miss Fullbright."

Everyone sends love to you as usual, especially—
Your devoted Jill

She spritzed some of her perfume onto the letter and stuck it in an envelope, then hung up her robe and stepped into Martha's dress.

12

MARTIN LEANED BACK AGAINST the bale of hay and pulled his coat tighter. The afternoon was bitter cold, a fierce wind pulling the chill off the snow-capped mountains. The smell of gunpowder hung in the air. He closed his eyes and held the letter to his nose, trying to catch the lavender scent. He couldn't hold onto the image of her face. But he remembered her laugh and her tender touch. He replayed for the hundredth time their one night of lovemaking. He felt himself getting aroused and quickly opened his eyes. The last of the sun was glinting off the broken glass and other debris strewn across the field. It resembled a demolition site for a new construction project. He had grown used to the sight of such devastation. Yesterday's bombing had been four hours nonstop. The buildings didn't have steel frames so they crumpled like eggshells. Nothing compared to the way people fell.

Beyond the field he could see where men were digging fresh graves. Among the dead was one of the young commanders, Jorge, a kid from Peru. He and Martin had just finished a game of Parcheesi. Jorge had gone off in search of his canteen when the first bomb hit.

Martin took out a stub of a pencil and a crumpled piece of

paper that he smoothed out on his pant leg. As he did before beginning every letter, he carefully considered how to formulate his experience so it wouldn't upset Jill. All the gruesome stories could wait until he was safely home.

February 14, 1938

My Darling Valentine,

Life here continues to be an experience in international solidarity. Yesterday I was playing Parcheesi with a Peruvian man while some Italian fellow sang a tune that a Swedish guy picked out on a Spanish guitar. I looked around and wondered if we weren't gathered at an International Party picnic. The rumor is that forty nationalities are here fighting Franco!

I am very pleased to know you are on the stage again and that it brings you such fulfillment. As for me, I've written another article for "New Masses" and two for the "Daily Worker." Did you read them? What do you think of my angle on Hitler's strategy? I find it good discipline to keep writing. (Though getting my hands on the only typewriter isn't easy.) I hope that, in spite of the demands of your play, you continue your studies. Party work will continue long after "The Children's Hour" has come and gone.

As for my parents, I suppose you're right. I will force myself to put my anger aside and write to them directly from now on. Please tell my mother where to send her letters.

Sweetheart, in your next letter, could you put in shoelaces, razor blades and chewing gum? Write back soon. I lap up all your delicious news like a hungry cat.

Your devoted Martin

THE SOUND OF COINS LANDING in the bucket startled Jill and she looked up to see a well-dressed man with a briefcase hurrying to catch a cab. She smiled. It heartened her that people from different walks of life understood the need to give money for medical supplies for Spain. She reached into the bucket and counted eleven one dollar bills lying amidst a jumble of quarters, nickels, and dimes. Last week Libby had collected almost seventy dollars. She sighed. She'd never get that much here in the park on such a freezing day. But Party directives said that collections went better in the park, so here she was with only Martin's letter to keep her warm. She took off her gloves and blew onto her hands; they were so numb she could barely hold the pen. She turned her attention back to her half-written letter.

But, Darling, some good came of twisting my ankle: I got to see three Broadway shows. I went with Gloria. We loved "The Women" (35 women and no men in the entire play!) and "Stage Door." Have you heard of "The Cradle Will Rock"? It's a musical about factory workers at the Mercury Theater that made me think of your play. Someday I want to see yours on the boards! Anyway, I'm fine now and believe me, three nights was long enough. I couldn't wait to get back. (By the way, rumor has it that Lillian Hellman is somewhere in Spain lending support for your efforts!)

I'm so glad you continue to write articles. Of course I read them all and think you're brilliant! Your analysis helped me understand how essential it is to kick the living daylights out of Franco. I try to find time to study the labor theory of value, but the ideas are so difficult to grasp. Even Al says they're hard. He's still working at "The New York Times" and just got bumped up. He's now assistant to the features editor!

Libby was fired from the Ethel Barrymore show. The producer wanted someone with a more mature voice. You know Libby, she's talented but she has a limited vocal range. She took it rather badly as it would have meant one hundred bucks and she could have used the money.

My father still hasn't answered my letters. I thought by now he'd accept things as they are. He's so stubborn and no doubt drinking himself into a stupor night after night. I worry about him and it does hurt to be cut out of his life so completely.

I will close this letter with good news. Yesterday, I saw an ambulance on the dock getting ready to be loaded onto a relief ship and here's what was painted on its side: "People of the Lower East Side in Appreciation of the Anti-Fascist Struggle of the People of Spain." So, my dearest, don't give up hope. Our government will be sending arms soon.

Your loving Jill

April 15, 1938

Well, my Darling,

"Soon" hasn't arrived yet. And you can't fight three highly trained armies with one ambulance. I know Roosevelt won't budge; he's worried about tangling with Hitler. Even the carnage at Guernica didn't convince him. If he knew how many American boys were dying, would that change his mind? Crushing the iron heel of fascism without world support exacts a heavy toll.

Martin put down the flashlight and massaged his leg. When he'd first caught the bullet the pain was sharp and made him yelp. Now it was just a dull ache. He lifted the tent flap again and peered into the night, but still there was no one. It was almost ten o'clock. Where were they? He closed the flap and moved the flashlight around the small space. Pedro was sprawled next to him in a deep sleep. Earl was in the corner smoking. He turned off the flashlight and closed his eyes. He pictured Jill on stage, going out for drinks with her fellow actresses, lying in bed reading his letters. He wanted to tell her that at Brunete, 600 of the 900 Americans who fought had died. He wanted to tell her how terrifying it was to be fighting with outdated weapons. To tell her that they were running out of munitions. That tanks weren't firing. He wanted to tell her that there was a very good chance that he'd lose his right leg since medical supplies had dwindled to almost nothing.

But he would do nothing of the sort. He turned on the flashlight again, but before he could write anything, he heard, "Come along, soldier." He opened the tent flap and saw Ronnie, a young English chap sitting atop a cart next to a peasant who held the reins. "At last," said Martin, crawling out of the tent. Ronnie pulled him onto the rickety cart, which began bouncing along the dirt path. They traveled for over an hour. The only light was the dim glow of a quarter moon. The air was icy and by the time they approached the village, Martin was shivering. The cart jerked to a stop. The driver spoke in rapid-fire Spanish. Martin understood that they were at a villa, which had been vacated by a wealthy landowner who'd been forced to flee. It was here that a "hospital" had been set up.

Ronnie grabbed a large box from the cart and led the way

into the kitchen, Martin limping behind. A young Spaniard drawing water from an indoor well greeted them with the customary salute. Candles caused shadows to flicker around the stucco walls. The room was frigid and, though there was a large brick fireplace, only gray ashes lay inside. A large delicately carved oak table sat in the middle of the room. On the counter were syringes, scalpels, bandages, and a stack of medical reference books. A thick layer of dust coated everything.

"This is the operating theater," Ronnie announced. "We use the upstairs as a ward." He was emptying the box of sheets and towels. We had bottles of alcohol, but they must have broken on the way here. That's why everything smells like antiseptic."

A large Negro woman wearing a tattered red coat over a nurse's uniform entered. "Is this the leg?" she said to Ronnie, barely taking in Martin. Ronnie nodded and asked her, "Did you ever manage to make coffee?"

"With no wood?" she said. And suddenly Martin yearned for a cup of coffee. Hot and steaming. He was chilled to the bone.

"Okay, soldier, pants off," she ordered. Martin slipped out of his pants and climbed onto the oak table as she indicated. Her face was drawn and ashy. It was unlikely she'd had a decent night's sleep in a while. "Right or left?" she asked.

"Right."

She examined his leg where the bullet had entered below his knee. "No chance of getting it out. Best we can do is try to keep it from getting infected."

She picked up a needle from the counter.

Martin said, "I always carry my spoon in my boot since the boys fight over eating utensils, so it's ironic that the bullet went in just above the spoon." He was babbling to keep from noticing that she was sharpening the needle on a stone. The sliver of hope that he'd clung to vanished.

She swabbed his leg with damp cotton, and Martin knew it wasn't damp from alcohol.

To get his mind off his grim odds, he changed the subject. "Where are you from, Nurse?"

"Oregon."

"You're a long way from home."

She sighed. "I'm where I need to be."

"How's that?"

Then for the first time she looked him in the eye. "As a nurse and as a communist, I knew I belonged in a place where women and children were being killed."

Her statement brought tears to his eyes, but before he had a chance to respond, the needle went in sharp and fast. When she withdrew it, he impulsively reached out and pulled her toward him, burying his face in her skirt, sinking into the softness of her belly.

"I know," she said quietly, touching the top of his head.

Then suddenly she moved away from him, crying, "Oh why the hell not!" and began rummaging through shelves, banging open cupboards. "Aqui!" she exclaimed when she found a stack of wooden plates. She cracked them against the side of the table and threw them into the fireplace. Ronnie looked stunned, then grasping her meaning, grabbed one of the medical journals, ripping out pages and hurling them in on top of the broken plates. The Spaniard laughed and tossed in a match. The paper caught and ignited the plates. Before long, a fire blazed. The Spaniard pumped water into a large kettle and the nurse opened a tin of coffee. Ronnie shouted, "Hallelujah!"

Martin leaned back on the table and closed his eyes. He felt the heat of the fire against his skin, and something inside him began to let go. No matter what the future held for him in this damnable war, he would always have this night: a cup of hot coffee and the deep camaraderie of three fellow communists.

13

My Dearest,

I bless the nurse from Oregon for saving your leg! What a dreadful experience. And, even though you don't put much stock in prayer, I do pray (daily) for your continued safety.

So, what's the exciting news around here? Not too much to report. Yesterday I got a letter from Louise. She and Walter are happy in Chicago even though they live near the elevated train and their apartment rattles several times a day. She misses Rudy Vallee, but Walter laid down the law about living with such an annoying bird. As you know, I used to feel the same way about Rudy, but now I welcome his racket. At least he's communicating which is more than Rosalie does! She's such a shy girl, minds her own business, never says a word. You'd think she was living alone instead of sharing a tiny room with me. (If only Gloria had moved in, but she likes having a room all to herself.) Anyway, I left a copy of "New Masses" on Rosalie's bed and hopefully she'll want to talk about it. I wish I had more time for Party work, but you know how time-consuming theater is. I did manage to raise sixty-two dollars for medical supplies to send to Spain. I also collected several bundles of clothing from the girls at the boarding house.

The battle to repeal the embargo is gaining support. Our unit helped organize a "Jamboree for Spain" with Fats Waller, Cab Calloway and W.C. Handy. They made great dance music and everyone had a ball. We raised three hundred and fifty dollars!

I know it must get discouraging sometimes, but Sweetheart, please don't give up hope.

Always, your loving wife, Jill

May 20, 1938

Dear Jill,

Thank you for the snapshots. I especially like the ones of you on the steps in front of the theater. You look gorgeous in that sundress and the hat with the wide brim. The photos make me miss you even more, if that's at all possible.

You say don't give up hope, but that's easier said than done. The morale has fallen sharply. Political work isn't being done. There has been an increase in the number of desertions. There's a general feeling of disin-tegration. It's hot as hell. Everyone's breaking out in boils. We haven't eaten vegetables in months. Last night I dreamt I ate a carrot. When Ernest Hemingway visited, he remarked, "I suppose everyone has lice." Quite observant! Ten minutes after the de-lousing truck leaves, the lice are back.

If only we had new weapons. A fascist victory now would be a terrible blow to the democratic forces of the world.

I imagine going to that bathhouse on Monroe Street and enjoying the hell out of the five minutes you get in hot water for two cents. Maybe I'd give them four cents and buy ten minutes! But there is no bathhouse here and certainly no hot water. I'm sorry if I sound discouraged.

I miss you, darling, more than words can say—
Martin

June 3, 1938

Dear Martin,

You sound very blue, and for good reason. I suppose you can only keep up your optimism for so long. It's horrible to imagine you with boils and no proper food and not even a bath.

I've been feeling down too since we finally came to the end of the run. I miss the routine of going to the theater, sitting in my dressing room, waiting for my cue. I miss the fellowship among the actresses. And then I think about how far away you are, and I feel even worse. I still believe in the struggle and wouldn't dream of you coming home before Franco is defeated. But I miss you so much and yearn to have you near me. I write to Roosevelt every morning, right after I do my vocal exercises, and urge him to sign a collective security agreement among all democratic countries. I just know victory will be ours soon. We must keep our hope alive.

Rosalie has moved to Cleveland and now Rudy Vallee and I are sharing the room with Julie, a chipper girl training to be a schoolteacher. Her good cheer has the opposite effect on me. Sometimes I wish she would just stop smiling and chattering and be quiet. Isn't that mean? One good thing is that she's behind the war effort 100% so when I get a letter from you she understands my relief.

We must cling to our belief that our side will prevail, and with this fervent hope I sign off, your—

Jill

June 23, 1938

Dearest Jill,

It's been decided—the Loyalist Government is sending us home. I can't remember ever feeling so defeated. They're shipping off all the international volunteers. There have been too many heavy losses. The hope is that, with all of us gone, maybe Franco will send the Italian and Germans away too. Then the final outcome could be determined by armies of Spaniards. Let's face it, it's a dim hope. (I read about Joe Lewis knocking the living daylights out of Max Schmeling. I'd like to see that as some kind of a good omen, but at this point it's a stretch.)

It should take about a month to make all the arrangements. This is brief, forgive me. Soon I will share everything in person.

Your loving husband, Martin

14

"HE'S COMING HOME!" JILL shrieked, waving the letter as she ran into Gloria's room.

"That's great, honey!" said Gloria from the dressing table where she was pinning up her hair.

"I can't believe it," Jill said, falling across the bed. "He's really coming home."

"You're sure lucky he made it. But honey, are you worried about..." She put down her comb and faced her. "I mean, how do you know you'll still love him? Aren't you worried what it will be like after so long?"

"He's my heart's desire, Gloria. It's as simple as that. My one, my only, in sickness and in health. Some day you'll understand."

As Jill pictured her reunion with Martin, one painful memory kept pushing into her thoughts. Should she tell him? Even though Martin was coming home in one piece, it seemed unfair to begin their married life on such a sad note. Perhaps some other time, after they were settled, she'd share that painful part of their history.

In truth, it wasn't really part of their history at all—it was only part of hers. In a strange way, hers and Elliot's, the only one (besides Dr. Herbert) who knew about it. If it hadn't been for Elliot, she wouldn't have been able to pull herself out of the deep melancholy that followed the miscarriage. They would go to the White Horse Tavern after their unit meetings. She would sip a glass of sherry and cry softly, and Elliot would drink Manhattans and comfort her.

Jill was counting the days until Martin's return but then, in late July, she received a telegram saying he was stuck in Paris without a passport and it would take several weeks to sort things out. Meanwhile, Elliot had decided to relocate to California permanently. A few weeks before he was scheduled to leave, she sat with him in a booth talking about what a time of change it was, with him about to go and Martin about to return.

"Do you think I should find a place before he comes home, Elliot? Or is that the kind of thing Martin would want to have a say in? On the other hand, maybe he won't be in the mood to start hunting for an apartment after all he's been through."

She sipped her drink. Suddenly Elliot pounded the table making his swivel stick jump. "Jill!" he said, his eyes bright. "You should take my place!"

"Gee, I don't know, Elliot."

"The rent is only eighteen bucks, which you can't beat. I've already given the landlady notice. You should at least take a look."

They left the White Horse Tavern and headed uptown. Elliot's building faced an elementary school and Jill thought about how nice it would be to hear the sounds of children playing during the day. The lobby smelled like fresh paint. Elliot moved a bicycle out of the way and a cat pounced out from the darkness. "Get out of here, Spooky," Elliot said, then to Jill, "he lives in 3C, but he prefers the lobby." They climbed the stairs, and while Elliot fumbled for his keys, Jill looked around expecting to glimpse a disapproving eye. It was late, and she was entering a man's apartment.

He flicked on the lights. The front room was in a state of total disarray: half-packed boxes, stacks of books and pamphlets in disorganized heaps, posters rolled and piled on a faded brown couch. Elliot went into the kitchen to make coffee. "Or would you rather have a drink?" he called.

"No, I'm fine," she said, looking around. She'd been in his apartment a few times, but there had always been other people around, and she'd never really paid attention to the place itself. He came out of the kitchen as she was peeking into his bedroom.

"Afraid it's a mess. But you can still get the idea." He turned on the light. "It gets a nice bit of sun in the late afternoon. Mrs. Liebowitz is the landlady, a true revolutionary— she's been in the Party since the beginning."

She took in the room—the unmade bed, piles of clothes, suitcases, books. She went to the window and looked out at the jumble of buildings. Squares of black sky popped up between the skyscrapers, many of them only half-completed. Their glassless windows were like hollow eyes.

She sensed Elliot behind her. He touched her and she jumped. He spun her toward him and held her firmly. Then she felt his mouth on hers and a shot of electricity went straight through her.

She pushed away. "You shouldn't have done that, Elliot." She was trembling. "Martin is your friend...and my husband. What about all our other friends? If they knew...now you've spoiled—"

"You seemed to enjoy it."

"I didn't."

He looked at her a moment, then said, "I'm going to make a drink," and left the room.

Jill tried to calm her thumping heart and sort out the feel-ings that churned inside of her. She was scared to come out of the room. She couldn't bear to face him. Yet she certainly couldn't remain in his bedroom.

She crossed quickly to the front door. "Elliot," she stam-mered. She called louder. "Elliot, I'm going home." Her throat was like sandpaper; her words seemed to be entering the room from somewhere above her head.

He came out and stood in the doorway holding a tray of ice. "One kiss. Not the end of the world, is it?"

"But what about Martin?"

"I'm sure Martin's had a few kisses, too."

"You're wrong, Elliot. Martin isn't like you. He would never—"

"Look," he said irritably, "Do you want the place or not?"

"I couldn't, not now."

"Oh, for chrissakes." He returned to the kitchen. His voice sounded like her father's did whenever she'd done something ridiculous. He came out with two drinks and set them on the coffee table in front of the couch. "Won't Martin be happy to come home and find that his wife has stumbled onto a cheap apartment already furnished?"

"Furnished?"

"You think I'm going to cart all this crap across the country? Now, come on. Be reasonable. It makes sense, doesn't it?"

She looked around the room. She knew he was right. It did make sense.

He held up one of the glasses for her to take. "Comrades?"

She stepped forward and took it from him. "Yes, all right," she said, avoiding his eyes. "Comrades."

15

LATER, AS SHE WAS LYING IN her own narrow bed, listening to the soft sound of Julie's breathing from the other side of the room, she decided that she would erase that moment from her life. When she thought of this night, she would remember what a mess Elliot's place was, and she would remember looking out at the unfinished skyscrapers, and she would remember having a drink with him. But she would not remember the moment when he held her and made her tremble. She would destroy that memory and she would never tell anyone about it, because to tell someone would mean that it really happened. So finally, she closed her eyes with the reassuring knowledge that she had cut out the incident permanently. It was just like when her mother altered her blue seersucker dress: she opened the seam, snipped out the extra fabric, and then sewed the seam closed again. That extra piece got tossed into the garbage. And when Jill wore that dress afterwards, it fit perfectly.

The following Sunday, the unit meeting was canceled so that everyone could help Elliot do the final packing. Meanwhile, Jill gathered her things into her trunk and said farewell to the girls, giving Gloria an extra long hug. She looked around at the little room, which had been home during so many major changes in her life, and whispered good-bye.

She held Rudy Vallee's cage on her lap in the taxi. For an extra nickel, the cabby lugged her trunk up the stairs. She pushed open the door to her new living quarters. The gang was loudly debating the probable escalation of trouble in Europe as they drank beer and ate bologna sandwiches. Benny Goodman's orchestra was playing "These Foolish Things" on the radio. Rudy Vallee let out one of his chirps and everyone looked up. "Jill, come in!" said Ray.

Al made room for her to sit on the couch between him and Elliot. But Jill grabbed a sandwich and sat cross-legged on the floor, listening to the lively talk. Then the conversation switched to speculation about how Elliot's life would be in California.

"Ermine swimming pools," teased Libby, quoting *Stage Door*.

"Watch out or you'll get soft, Elliot!" Ray said, standing and putting on his hat. Al grabbed his hat too and Libby picked up her handbag. The party was breaking up. Everyone went downstairs and Ray hailed a cab. They all hugged Elliot good-bye.

Elliot grabbed Jill in a rough embrace and whispered, "You, I'll miss most of all." Then he released her with a laugh, and she caught her breath, grateful that he was vanishing from her life.

She went back upstairs and stood in the doorway surveying her new abode. The place needed a thorough dusting and she'd have to mop the floors. She emptied the ashtrays and gathered up the uneaten sandwiches and beer bottles, carrying them into the kitchen. She went into the bedroom. The afternoon light cut a wide swathe across the unmade bed. She would have to get sheets and blankets. Meanwhile, she spread out her coat and took a pillow from the couch. Then she began to fill Elliot's drawers with her things.

That night, as Jill drifted off to sleep, she thought of all the things she wanted to do to fix up what she had come to think of as the "honeymoon cottage." She fell into a deep sleep and had a muddled and disturbing dream about Elliot. She was startled awake by her own cry. She looked around, completely disoriented. It took her a moment to remember that she was in Elliot's bed, a realization that jarred her. She was shivering. She picked the coat up off the floor and put it on over her nightgown and went into the other room.

The floor was cold. She wanted to turn on a light but couldn't remember where the lamp was. She groped her way to the couch, pulled her knees up to her chest, and tried to remember Martin's face. But the dream was still inside her, disturbing her with its blurry images, its dark, erotic feeling.

She listened to the strange groans the walls made. A bit of moonlight seeped into the room. Jill searched around for her purse and found a book of matches, struck one and made her way into the kitchen. She struck another and found the light switch by the door. The kitchen was suddenly illuminated, calming her. She lit the stove and put on the kettle.

While she waited for the water to boil, she looked around. The stove would need a good scrubbing. She'd hang new curtains, too, though the window opened onto nothing more than a brick wall. She noticed slogans scribbled on the faded yellow wallpaper in Elliot's loopy backward scrawl: CLASS STRUGGLE and PEOPLE BEFORE PROFITS.

Sharing a shelf with a Sears Roebuck's catalogue and a jar of Nescafe was a tattered copy of *Ten Days That Shook the World*, back issues of *New Masses*, a collection of Haiku.

She reached for the Haiku book and something fell out. It was a calendar girl kneeling on a chaise lounge arching her back, her nipples poking through a gauzy chiffon bed jacket. On the bottom it said:

Elliot, I'll join your Party anytime...Daisy

The shriek of the kettle made her jump. She poured the water into a cup, added Nescafe, then sat down again and stared at Daisy.

16

MARTIN'S SHIP WAS DUE TO arrive August 16, 1938. He had
been gone over nineteen months. Jill tried on three different
outfits before settling on her lilac wedding suit even though it
was way too warm. Her hand shook as she applied her makeup.
Then she decided to wash it off; she figured tears would ruin it
anyway. She had bought a small bouquet of red carnations like
the ones she used to put in his basement and, pinning one to her
lapel, put the rest in a jar by the bedroom window.

The dock was jammed. She craned her neck, even stood on
her toes to single him out, but the stampede of people made it
impossible. She was startled when someone gripped her shoulders and turned her around. She didn't recognize him. He had
shriveled. His face was discolored and his shave uneven. He was
a much older man than the boy she had sent off to Spain.

He pressed her to him, crushing the carnation. Then he held
her at arm's length, tears staining his blotchy cheeks.
"Sweetheart!" he said, his voice thin and scratchy.

"You're back," Jill said, tears running down her cheeks, as
she knew they would.

She took off her gloves so they could hold hands in the cab.
His hand was rough and dry. She squeezed it and he squeezed

hers back as he stared out the window. She had so many questions, so much to tell him. But Martin's silence suggested that it'd be better to wait, to let him get used to the new sights and smells. There would be plenty of time. They had the rest of their lives. She gave his hand another squeeze.

Martin had been to Elliot's place many times so when they climbed the stairs, he stood awhile in the doorway trying to get used to the new look. He dropped his duffel bag and ran his fingers through his hair. "I can't believe I'm back," he said, "I just can't believe it's all over." His voice was gravelly, not at all the way Jill remembered it.

She wanted him to hold her, to scoop her up and carry her into the bedroom. To pull her back into his heart. But Martin was distracted, wandering around, looking out the window, gazing at a picture of Lenin as if he'd never seen it before. He was not used to being in a room with pictures and lamps. Jill noticed that he walked with a slight limp and she felt an ache in her heart for all he'd been through. He poked his finger into Rudy Vallee's cage. The bird flitted to the other side with a chirp.

"I'd love a cup of coffee," he said.

They sat with their coffee at Elliot's kitchen table. Martin reached into his pocket and took out something wrapped in newspaper. He handed it to her saying, "A Polish guy gave it to me." It was a small red handkerchief with the hammer and sickle on it. She smiled.

He spread out some worn photos on the table and scooted his chair closer to hers. "This is Joe, our chef, he was a real comedian, made everyone laugh. Died in Brunete. And here's Eddie, the kid from New Haven, didn't live past the first month. Here I am with a bunch of the guys from our battalion. And this picture was taken after one of the battles, part of the Aragon Offensive. We defeated the bastards, but it cost us eighty men. See, that's me standing in the back row." He took a swallow of coffee. "I wish you could've met some of these fellows, Jill."

"Me, too," she said, meaning it.

"And the Spanish people. So brave and determined. There were many celebrations before we left. Sad to call them celebrations since we were no closer to victory than when we arrived. But that's the Spanish spirit. Guitarists played malagenas. Haunting, ancient, beautiful music. They all wept to see us go. Did you read Ibarruri's farewell in *New Masses*?"

Jill shook her head, no.

"Her words are sheer poetry: 'Come back, when the olive tree of peace puts forth its leaves again, entwined with the laurels of the Spanish Republic's victory!' And I do want to go back. I want to show you the country."

He took another gulp then reached inside his duffel and pulled out several posters. He unrolled one and spread it on the table. It was a charcoal drawing done in large bold strokes depicting a soldier hitting a man with the butt of a rifle. The battered man wore a swastika armband. Another poster showed a close-up of a woman's foot in a rope-soled sandal crushing a concrete swastika. On the next one *CRIMINALES* was scrawled in red across the top. A woman was screaming. In her arms was a dead child, blood dripping from its lifeless body.

Jill burst into tears. He put his arm around her. "It's just a picture, darling. Imagine seeing the real thing." He rolled up the posters and put them away. "I guess I'm used to it."

They sat in silence.

The dark shadow of Jill's heart-breaking secret fell between them. She knew that now was her chance to say it. To tell him why his poster had made her cry.

"I need a shower," he said, pulling himself up wearily and going into the bathroom.

She wanted to run after him, hold him, pull him close and tell him. But she didn't. He was so raw, so new, so distracted. He'd seen enough carnage.

They were strangers. If only they could make love, Jill knew they could cross the awful divide. She went into the bedroom and got undressed and slipped between the covers.

A few minutes later he stood in the doorway. He was so thin his hips barely held up the towel around his waist. He got under the covers and pulled her toward him. "How I've dreamed of this moment," he said.

He climbed on top of her and kissed her ears, her nose. Jill whispered, "My precious Martin. Thank you, God, for returning him to me."

He rubbed against her and his kisses became frantic.

But he was limp. Finally he rolled onto his back and started to weep.

"It's all right," she said, touching his cheek.

"It's not all right," he said. "We lost so much."

Jill thought he meant the time they were apart. Then she had the panicky thought that Elliot must have told Martin that she lost the baby.

But he said, "Even in the face of defeat, the Spaniards said, 'We'd rather die fighting on our feet than live the rest of our lives on bended knees.' That's what they said. Even as they waved good-bye to the volunteers, who had been their greatest hope, they were more determined than ever to prevent fascism from winning in their country." Another sob choked him. "And we started out with such hope."

His voice trailed off. His eyes closed and Jill could feel him sinking like a small boat into a mammoth sea of remorse.

She had no words to comfort him. She looked out the window at the sooty sky, the unfinished skyscrapers. How could they ever reclaim their old happiness? She turned to him and touched his face. "I missed you so much."

With his eyes still closed, he murmured, "God, me, too."

17

THEY ACCEPTED AN INVITATION from Martin's mother for Friday night, the Jewish Sabbath. In Martin's old neighborhood they bought a cake and some flowers. From a corner delicatessen, he plucked six pickles from a barrel where they were soaking with dill weed and peppercorns. He explained to Jill that the pickles were a tradition that began when he was first old enough to run errands on Shabbus.

His mother answered the door and held onto Martin for a full five minutes before she finally let him go, wiped her eyes, and looked at Jill with a relieved smile. Jill smiled back. They had been through something together; a truce had been established. Now the object of their mutual devotion was home safe and sound.

The living room was small but cozy. There was an upright piano in the corner with pictures of family members, including a picture of Martin's older brother, Daniel. The windows were steamed up from cooking. The table was set with an embroidered tablecloth and gleaming silverware. Martin and Jill sat close to each other on the davenport opposite Martin's parents as Martin struggled to tell them all about his war experience. He began one story but before he could finish, it would remind him of another story. He started to describe the directives they were given, then was suddenly explaining the dwindling supplies, then the ongoing problem of the food. He was trying to paint a picture, but his thoughts were disorganized. He had never told the story before. Finally, he just said, "Unless you were there…"

There was a long silence. Then his mother stood, "What you need, boychek, is some real food. Come."

Jill followed her into the kitchen and picked up a tureen of barley soup. Martin's mother carried a silver tray that held a brisket surrounded by roasted potatoes, cooked carrots, and green beans. She covered her head with a lacy shawl and mumbled a prayer as she lit two white tapers. Other prayers were said over the wine and the freshly baked bread.

Martin shoveled in the food. For her mother-in-law's benefit, Jill said to him, "You must really love me to settle for my cooking after growing up with this."

THERE WAS NO HERO'S welcome for Martin or for the other Americans who came back defeated from that bloody war. No speeches, no parades, no official memorials. No one presented Martin with the Order of the Purple Heart for being wounded in action. He tried to pick up the threads of his life.

He was furious with Roosevelt for not supporting the Loyalists; incensed that the United States Communist Party was so closely affiliated with the Democrats. It was hard for him to throw himself back into Party work with a positive attitude. At their unit meetings, he paced around the room smoking one cigarette after another. Carol and Ray exchanged looks during one of his speeches.

"Handing over Czechoslovakia to Germany was a bribe! Believe me, the policy of appeasement was not adopted because

Chamberlain is naive. It's tacit collaboration with Hitler so Hitler will go after Russia. England and France don't care about the fascists. They want to destroy the labor movement in their own countries and internationally. Let's face it, they want to wipe out communism. Meanwhile, Hitler is getting stronger and stronger."

He was all wound up. There was so much he could never explain to his old comrades. What it was like to have a boy die in his arms.

At home, he was agitated all the time, distracted. He just couldn't relax. Jill tried to think up ways to get his mind off his sadness. They went to Café Society on Sheridan Square and heard Billie Holiday and Jack Gilford on the same program, a real first— a Negro and white person in front of a mixed audience. During the movie *Grapes of Wrath*, Martin actually let out a hoot of approval when Henry Fonda said, *"A fella ain't got a soul of his own, just a piece of a Big Soul, the Soul that belongs to everybody."*

They went to the World's Fair and sat in Futurama seats, which swung high above a model of an idealized United States. They flew across cities of the future from one coast to the other. Martin got a kick out of the fact that the designer had inadvertently omitted all churches. "The city of the future is godless," he mocked. "Now that's what I call progress!"

It was fortunate that Jill continued to get stage work, because it took awhile for Martin to even look for a job. He just wasn't able to concentrate enough to write. Finally, he put the word out that he was looking, and before long he was hired to write another radio soap.

They did their Party work. They read and studied. Martin contributed articles to *The Daily Worker*. Jill kept telling herself that soon Martin would be himself again. But months passed and it seemed that Martin, her anchor, had come unmoored.

Suddenly it was a new year. They passed out of winter and into spring and out of spring and into summer and then, the unthinkable happened, and the agitation that had danced around Martin since his return took him over completely.

It happened early on the morning of August 24, 1939. Martin, as was his habit, woke early to write. Jill had grown accustomed to his early rising and could sleep through the clacking of the typewriter. But on that hot summer day, she awoke to a different sound, a loud muffled noise. She propped herself on her elbows and tried to identify it. With a shock, she realized it was the sound of Martin sobbing.

She stood in the doorway and stared at him. He was standing in the middle of the living room, a newspaper in his hand, his shoulders shaking with convulsions. He noticed her and, without a word, handed her the paper. She read the headline: "SOVIET UNION SIGNS NON-AGGRESSION PACT WITH GERMANY."

"I don't understand," she said.

"Yes, you do! Damnit, don't play dumb, Jill!"

His words stung. He had never raised his voice, let alone insulted her. She stared at the paper, but everything blurred. He gripped her by the shoulders and shrieked, "Stalin is selling us out! Selling out the Party. Selling out the Movement. Selling out the boys who gave their lives in Spain! That's what's happening. Now do you understand, Jill? Now do you get it?!"

He began pacing. "What the hell was the Seventh World Congress all about for chrissakes? What was the point of Dimitrov's paper? Fighting the bastards, that's what. Fighting to the death against fascism. And suddenly, Stalin is to the right of

Roosevelt! Now that's a laugh, isn't it? So this is how the vanguard behaves in a crisis!"

"There's probably a reason for it. Why are you ranting like this?" Jill blurted out, frightened.

But he wasn't listening. Whatever dream Martin had held—whatever dream had held Martin together—was disintegrating.

He banged open the closet, grabbed his hat, and slammed the door so violently it sent Rudy Vallee's cage crashing to the floor. The cage door flew open and in an instant, the bird swooped through the open window into the sweltering heat of Manhattan.

Jill and Martin stared at the open window in stunned silence. Without another word, he put on his hat and left the apartment.

Jill rushed to the window and searched for the little bird. But all she saw were gray buildings.

MARTIN DIDN'T COME HOME ALL afternoon. The day grew hotter and hotter. Even with the windows open, the air was thick and still and sticky. Jill limped around with a damp washcloth on her neck. She jumped at every sound, hoping it was him, calm again, ready to take her in his arms and apologize for his angry outburst. She kept going to the window, scanning the skies for the little canary.

Their unit meeting was at seven. When Martin still hadn't returned home by 7:15, not knowing what else to do, Jill went alone. When she got to Carol and Ray's, he was already there, fuming as if he hadn't stopped all day. Jill stood in the doorway, but he didn't even acknowledge her.

"Does he expect us to line up behind the Party?" Martin shouted, waving his arms, spitting out his rage. "Is that really what he expects? Because he can forget that. I won't be part of a movement that shakes the hand of Hitler. I won't follow blindly.

Duty of the International Movement to support the Soviet Republic, no matter what? Solidarity, my ass! No, thank you. Not me. Not anyone I care to hang around."

Ray said, "Martin, come on, you're being irrational. Stalin is sincere in wanting peace."

Jill cried, "You've always loved Stalin."

He turned in her direction but looked right through her.

Carol added, "I think it's a ploy to delay things. Stalin's just buying time. Don't get so rattled, Martin."

But Martin was rattled. "Jesus. I'm pointing out that perhaps now is the time to seriously consider the leadership in Moscow. Maybe it's time to break with the Politburo."

"You can't be serious," Al said.

"I'm damned serious. We're thinking people. Should we jump just because Stalin snaps his fingers? If Moscow sneezes, does that mean we all have to come down with colds?"

Elliot was no longer around to tell him to get off his soapbox, but it was as if he were: suddenly Martin grew quiet. He sat down and lit a cigarette. "I've seen fascism up close. I've smelled it, I've tasted it."

He inhaled deeply and, looking at no one, said, "One day, I was in a field on the outskirts of Colmenar Viejo, a small village just north of Madrid. Women and children were threshing their grain." He sat quietly, remembering. "I was fascinated by the process, it seemed so primitive. They spread the grain out on the hardened earth. A mule hauled a rickety contraption around. It was basically just narrow wheels mounted on a shaft, and this was how they threshed their grain.

"I was standing there talking with one of the women, asking how old she thought this method was. She had a baby in her arms. She spoke no English and my Spanish wasn't great at the time, and we were laughing at our awkwardness and the baby was pulling at her breast for milk, when suddenly we heard a roar in the sky. Someone yelled, 'Fascistas!' As a soldier, I knew to immediately drop to the ground, but before I could grab her and pull her down with me, she ran toward the other women. They huddled together in the middle of the field screaming. I shouted to them to get down, but they didn't understand, and besides, they couldn't hear above the sound of the plane. It was the fascists' first visit to Colmenar Viejo and the women didn't know what was happening.

"A minute later, I saw one of the planes coming toward us spitting fire. The women and children started running in all directions. They were in the direct line of fire. The plane dove down to about thirty feet off the ground and in a split second I saw the expression on the face of the pilot. He was laughing.

"He didn't hit any of our men. I'm sure he didn't see us. But the women and children were a perfect target. The one I was talking to, with her baby's little hands still clinging to her dress, was lying in a pool of blood."

"Martin, please—" Jill begged.

"...her hands were calloused from pushing the threshing device."

He looked around the room at everyone. "The Russians were there. They know how much the Germans love peace."

No one said a word.

He was pulling away, like a train pulling out of the station, slowly at first, then gathering momentum and moving off into the distance.

CALIFORNIA
1950

We know what we are, but know not what we may be.

Hamlet
William Shakespeare

18

MOUNTAIN VIEW WAS A QUIET street, shaded by tall, drooping Chinese elms, which rose up all along the sidewalk. The houses were ranch-style, with ell-shaped driveways. Jill stepped out into the bright spring morning and felt the warmth of the sun through her chenille robe. Los Angeles never failed to delight her with its endless days of sunshine. She knew from speaking to her father that morning that Denver was buried under a foot of snow.

Her relationship with her father had taken years to patch up. After she married Martin against his wishes, Russell had refused all contact. She pleaded with him in letters, mailed pictures of her and Martin, sent Christmas cards. But he didn't respond. Finally, she stopped trying, telling herself he was as dead to her as she apparently was to him.

But when her daughter was born, she found herself wanting to hear his voice and she placed a long-distance call. When he said hello in his deep, raspy voice, she silently replaced the receiver in its cradle. She couldn't risk his rejection of her child. So the silence continued until she and Martin decided to move out to California. Jill realized that their train would have an hour layover in Denver, so she pushed aside her fear and sent Russell a telegram asking if he would like to meet his grandchild.

When the train pulled into Denver, Russell was standing on the platform. His hair had gone white and his pale skin hung in loose folds around his face. He had grown a droopy mustache, which tickled Jill's cheek as he brushed her face with a dry peck. The stink of liquor was gone.

They sat on wooden benches in the cold, cavernous depot where their voices echoed and bounced off the walls. They were awkward with their conversation, eager to reconcile the differences, which had been amplified by years and miles and anger. She handed him the baby. He held her easily, as if he held an infant every day. "She looks like you did," he said, pulling the soft pink blanket away so he could see her plump little hands. "What do you call her?"

"Millie," said Jill, and watched the name go straight to his heart.

"Millie," he repeated, barely audible, thinking of his own beloved wife. He looked at his daughter with grateful eyes. For the first time, he looked at his son-in-law, too, and offered him a tentative smile.

The following week as Jill and Martin were settling into their temporary quarters at the St. Elmo Hotel in Hollywood, a box arrived. It was a set of dishes. They were lime green, rimmed with yellow daisies. Jill thought it was the ugliest dinnerware she'd ever seen, but she was deeply touched. It was as tangible a peace offering as she could imagine, and she intended to serve her father pot roast on it at the earliest opportunity. That turned out to be a few years later, after Nathan had been born and they'd moved into the house on Mountain View. Russell visited, bringing a stuffed rabbit for Nathan and a storybook doll for Millie. He and Martin clashed whenever the conversation strayed into politics, so they had a tacit agreement to avoid that arena. Besides, Martin was at the studio most of the time, which left Russell alone with Jill and his grandchildren and this arrangement suited them all.

Jill checked her roses and plucked off a few dead leaves. Her roses were the pride of her garden and just beginning to come into their splendor. The bed, which edged the lawn near the front fence, held marigolds, petunias, and pansies. And now her bulbs were coming up—ranunculus and daffodils. She noticed that last week's heat wave had almost done in the sweet peas. Tomorrow she would buy some zinnias to replace them and some new impatiens and begonias for the north side of the house where the olive tree made it too shady to plant anything else.

The lawn was lush and well-manicured. Martin mowed it himself. He would never think of hiring a gardener or even a kid from the neighborhood. It wasn't to save money. It had to do with the principle of doing for yourself what you are capable of doing. Besides, it was the closest that Martin, such a city boy, would ever come to working the land. They'd had the sprinkler system installed last year even though it meant digging up the entire yard. They couldn't count on California rainfall to keep the grass green. In the summer, the sun scorched it the color of toast. At the end of summer, just as the days tipped into autumn, a dry, hot wind blew in from the desert across the wide expanse of the San Fernando Valley. Now, with the turn of a tap, the entire yard was watered.

Jill and Martin had been through a lot to claim this life. They had endured the difficult period of separation when Martin was in Spain and the trying times that followed when his optimism had turned to dust. Though Jill continued to work as a stage actress—and that had a steadying affect on them both—the mounting threat of Nazism had infected their everyday lives with fear and dread. Together with Martin's parents, they huddled around the radio listening to FDR's fireside chats, worrying about the fate of Martin's extended family in the Old Country. Once America had entered the war, things shifted again. Jill and Martin endured the blackouts, ration stamps, and air raids along with everyone else. Louise became one of many war widows when Walter was killed in action, and Jill realized—again—that she and Martin had been spared. For Martin, it was a different story; his injury kept him from fighting alongside the other American boys (Al and Ray had enlisted), and this frustration added to his growing sense of helplessness. When typewriter factories were converted to war production, the "42 Keys to Victory" campaign called for all privately owned typewriters to be turned over to the armed forces. Martin was torn. Jill insisted that he hold onto his Remington. So out of a sense of guilt more than anything else, he began writing again. *Flame of Hope* was his first attempt at fiction. He discovered that he enjoyed working on something over which he had total control, and most importantly, something that shifted his focus from his disenchantment with Stalin to something personal. The story poured out of him and was immediately snapped up by Simon & Schuster.

Without the demands of Party work, ongoing political analysis, and challenging Party directives, an opening was created. And even though the war brought its own worries, something new was kindled between Jill and Martin during this period. After his novel was accepted, Martin became more relaxed, showing a new lightheartedness, a sense of play. He took Jill skating in Central Park; to the Crazy Cat Club on Broadway; he even bought a series of dance lessons so they could learn to fox trot (though Martin never quite got the hang of it). They were having fun together. Then when Jill got pregnant, the anticipated joy of new life brought Martin fully back to life, too.

The baby changed Jill. Her acting ambitions suddenly seemed less important. Even though it meant putting her career on hold, she was ready for the change. She had been working since she'd first arrived in New York; now she was grateful to simply stay home with the baby.

With the end of the war and the return of American boys, the final remnants of Martin's depression disappeared. The mood in the country shifted as well. Truman signed the charter of the United Nations; the Employment Act committed the federal government to the goal of full employment; Congress increased the minimum wage from forty cents to seventy-five cents an hour; Social Security benefits were extended to an additional 10 million people; the Housing Act provided for slum clearance and construction of housing units for the poor. There was the Truman Doctrine and the Marshall Plan. It was a time of general prosperity, a time to enjoy life.

Now here they were in Southern California—Martin was working regularly as a scriptwriter and Jill was raising her family in this lovely house on this quiet, tree-lined street. She plucked a few oranges from a branch sagging under the weight of its bounty and dropped them into the pockets of her robe. Once again, she marveled that lemons and oranges and a strange little citrus called kumquat grew on her very own property.

She went into the kitchen and put the fruit on the counter. The tile was pale blue and matched the wallpaper, also blue with specks of yellow. It was a modern kitchen with a built-in electric range and a garbage disposal. She loved how bright and sunny it was, loved looking out onto the swing-set and olive tree in the backyard.

She filled a large pot with water and put it on to boil. She buzzed around the kitchen measuring vinegar, pouring cold water into cups, adding small color pellets. Then she squeezed the oranges, listening for sounds of the children. They would appear any moment, champing at the bit to get to Elliot's for the big Easter Egg Hunt. Elliot often threw parties in his luxurious home, though usually they were adult-only parties. But on Easter he invited the children. Carol and Ray would be there with their two children, who were the same ages as Nathan and Millie. Carol and Ray had been in Los Angeles only a year. The two families—in spite of the fact that Jill and Martin were no longer in the Party and Carol and Ray were Party functionaries—were close. Libby would be at the party, too. She had followed Elliot out to the coast to pursue an affair with him. The affair ended badly but rather than return to New York, Libby remained in California, finding work as an actress in the new medium, television. She still showed up at Elliot's parties. Al had returned to New York after the war to nurse his career as a journalist. He was happily married now and he and Martin wrote to each other frequently.

Elliot never married, always had a different starlet on his arm, and flirted with women unabashedly. Jill enjoyed his attentions but didn't take them seriously. She envied the women in his life not because they were his lovers, but because they were his stars. She still clung to the dream of returning to her career and longed to try her hand at screen acting. But Martin held firmly to the belief that a child's best interests were served by its mother and insisted that Jill stay home while the children were young. They had fought over it. She knew several actresses who left their children with baby-sitters and those kids seemed perfectly well-adjusted. In the end, they compromised: she would stay home until Nathan was in school a full day. But that was still two years away. And she would be two years older.

Not that Jill didn't enjoy being a mother. It's just that the wait was unbearable. "Patience is a virtue," her mother used to say, as young Jill stood by exasperated, waiting for her to hem a skirt or sew on a button while her friends waited outside. And now, Jill's career was waiting in the wings and she felt that same chafing feeling.

If it hadn't been for the Actors Laboratory Theater, she would have gone crazy. The Lab gave her a place where she could hone her acting skills, keep that part of herself alive. The Lab had been started by actors who, like Martin and herself, had fled New York for the promise of Hollywood. They brought with them the innovation of the Group Theatre and the enthusiasm of artistic revolutionaries. She'd taken classes from Jules Dassin and felt safe in his hands when he directed her in comedy, something she'd never done before. Hume Cronyn directed her in a scene from Cyrano, and used the word "stunning" to describe her work. Now she was studying with the wonderful character actor, Morris Carnovsky. She worshiped him, loved the ready smile on his cherubic face. His sweet manner didn't belie the strength he brought to King Lear or Macbeth. His approach to Shakespeare was unique. He'd have the actor sit and think the scene through, then get up and move and think it through again. Then, mumble the words. Finally he'd say, "Now do it!" By that time, the character leapt onto the stage. With Carnovsky, she was learning how to live in front of an audience—how to let people see what was inside: the good and the bad. She was understanding how to invest each part with true emotion, not just "acted" emotion.

She loved the easy camaraderie of her fellow students, sitting together at Schwab's after class. She loved, once a week, being an actress and not a mother.

Nathan tumbled into the kitchen completely naked except for socks and shoes with laces stringing behind. He was in tears. He'd just learned how to tie his own shoes, but his fingers were constantly forgetting which way to go. "I can't," he wailed, tugging on Jill's robe, his face red and blotchy.

"Come on, Nathan, try again."

He bent over his shiny new Buster Browns, his pudgy fingers working hard as his mother coached him, "Up and over and under the bridge, then make a loop. That's it, pull tight."

The bow was finally made. He grinned broadly and skipped out of the kitchen singing "Here Comes Peter Cottontail," his little penis bouncing in front of him. Jill smiled as she carefully spooned a dozen eggs into the boiling water and set the timer.

She poked her head into Millie's room. Millie was sitting at her vanity staring into the mirror with determined concentration, struggling with two barrettes. Jill came over and expertly clamped the barrettes into place. Millie wanted to wear her hair like her mother's: parted in the middle with cascades of dark waves on either side. She asked, "How come your hair never falls in your face without barrettes?" But before Jill could answer, Millie jumped up. "Mommy!" she said brightly, "Can we wear our mother-daughter dresses?"

After much prompting from Millie, Jill had had two identical outfits made, complete with jackets and straw hats trimmed to match. They were dotted white Swiss with full skirts, cinched at the waist with pink cummerbunds. Jill's mother would've been appalled at the sloppy way the seams had been finished, but at least the woman who sewed them had allowed a wide hem on Millie's so that it could be let out as Millie grew taller. The style was a little girlish for Jill, but she knew it flattered her figure and clearly it would make Millie happy, so she smiled. "Go get it. It probably needs ironing."

Jill went back to the kitchen, plugged in the iron and unlatched the narrow door that enclosed the ironing board, unfolding it from the wall. The timer went off. She turned on the faucet and put the hard-boiled eggs under the cold water. She smiled. None of the shells had cracked.

MARTIN WAS IN BED ENJOYING a smoke before the household forced him into activity. He wished he could spend the day at his office working on the script. It was hard to lend himself to the hearty camaraderie of Easter Sunday when he was so distracted. All his thoughts were focused on the characters he'd been midwifing.

He watched the smoke curl and catch the light streaming in through the blinds. Once again he realized he was happy, a thought that continued to bubble up and surprise him after he'd finally broken loose of his depression five years ago. After his novel was published, after Millie was born, his life was humming along and it seemed that things couldn't get any better. Then one Tuesday afternoon in February of 1942, his world took an unexpected turn, which brought an even greater sense of contentment.

By then, he and Jill were living in a railroad flat on the Lower East Side near Martin's folks. It had been snowing all day. Jill had the flu and was curled up on a kitchen chair shivering under three blankets, advising Martin how to give two-month old Millie a bath in the sink. The phone rang and Martin picked it up, his hand dripping wet. Weeks before, Elliot had given the galleys of Martin's novel to someone at Warner Brothers. On the phone was a Mr. Wilk offering him a contract at three hundred bucks a week. He pressed the phone against his shirt and told Jill. Her mouth dropped open, and she nodded her head as vigorously as her feverish state would allow. She wanted another child and dreamed of raising her children in sunshine and fresh air. So, as he stood with the dripping baby, staring out at the dismal New York winter, he accepted the offer.

When Martin announced his intention to move west, his mother dissolved into tears. She had become attached to the baby, making daily visits, loaded down with borscht, a loaf of challah, and often a hand-knit blanket or bonnet. Martin knew he would be depriving her of her only grandchild, and Jill and Millie would feel the loss as well. Nonetheless, he bought railroad tickets on the Chief and the little family headed toward the City of Angels. He'd been skeptical about lending his talents to the lower art form of motion pictures, but one look at the blue skies of downtown Los Angeles and a whiff of the orange blossoms in the warm air and he was sold. So what if writing for the movies was a commercial enterprise for a puerile audience in which you were guaranteed to lose your soul? Who cared if Hollywood was, as Bertolt Brecht called it, "the city of merchandisable dreams"? Or if it were true that, as Elliot had written to him, "In Hollywood, if you strip away the phony tinsel, you'll find real tinsel underneath."

Jill had a more cheery perspective: in the movies, not only could Martin tell stories that showed a sympathetic attitude toward working people and minorities, but he would also have an audience of thousands.

When presented with the contract, he was asked, "You

don't belong to any organizations that you shouldn't belong to, do you?" He didn't; that was no lie. He had dropped out of the Party without apology. But his political leanings never became an issue. The studios knew perfectly well that he and other writers were progressive. It was even rumored that Harry Cohn, head of Columbia Pictures, had said, "These guys are communists, who cares? They're talented."

After a few weeks at the St. Elmo Hotel, they had lived in a cramped one-bedroom apartment in Hollywood. By the end of the first year, he'd earned enough for the down payment on a house in Burbank, just a few blocks from the studios. He'd also bought Jill a real wedding ring, an exquisitely refined diamond in a setting of white gold. She'd been longing for a real ring all these years, and God knows she'd been patient. It gave him pleasure to finally be able to give her something of real value. Still, he promised himself he would never "go Hollywood," and had not bought a new model car or dug a swimming pool in the backyard.

He snuffed out his cigarette and congratulated himself on keeping his values intact without the discipline of the Communist Party to guide him. Naturally, he'd been approached by Party functionaries in California, but, separate from his sour feelings about Stalin, Martin was appalled at the direction the Party had taken in America. He thought the so-called "progressive capitalism" that Browder espoused was ridiculous. A peaceful transition from capitalism to socialism? As if the capitalists would one day just hand over the factories to the workers, folding as if it were a penny ante poker game. The Party, now called the Communist Political Association, had relaxed its discipline, taking in record numbers of recruits. They may as well have called themselves Democrats.

He had gradually come to believe that the struggle to raise the standard of ordinary people's living, to create a world without prejudice, were worthwhile pursuits in and of themselves. He didn't need to belong to the Party in order to defend those principles. In the end, he was content to call himself a progressive and focus his political energy on making the Screen Writers Guild a strong union.

Elliot had dropped out, too. It had grown increasingly difficult for him to adhere to the Party line. The final straw came, as it had for so many of their comrades, when Albert Maltz wrote an essay for *New Masses,* arguing that works of art should be judged by their creative contributions rather than by their implicit political positions. The Party was up in arms. Elliot was disgusted when Maltz recanted. The whole incident confirmed for him that things had deteriorated beyond repair. The Party's current leadership violated the whole intellectual life of Marxism; they had become an intellectual goon squad. It was time to move on. Besides, Elliot's star was rising. He had become one of Louis B. Mayer's boy wonders.

Martin's very first assignment had been to adapt a stage play about a steel factory, which he had found profound and deeply moving. He'd been teamed with a seasoned scriptwriter named Charlie Fisher. When Martin walked into Charlie's office for the first time, Charlie thrust out his nicotine-yellowed fingers for a vigorous handshake. They tossed around a few ideas, and then scheduled a meeting for a story conference with the producers. Beck, one of the producers, began the meeting by asking, "So, what do you think of the play?" Martin responded enthusiastically, "I think it's great." Charlie kicked him under the table and spoke directly to Beck, "Sure, the play's plenty good, but it's out of date. There's a war on now, and we want to make this factory a munitions plant and show that sabotage is going on."

When they got into the corridor, Charlie wheeled on him. "What the hell were you thinking? Never tell a producer that a story they've hired you to rewrite is great. No matter what you think, tell them it stinks! Otherwise, pal, you and I are out of a job."

Martin had never worked with another writer before, but he immediately took to Charlie. He was quick, smart and had an acerbic wit. He was a fast typist, too. It's strange how things had worked out. Martin would have never come to California if it hadn't been for the war. The war created a vacuum in Hollywood. Charlie was too old for the draft and Martin's gimpy leg had kept him from joining up. In a way it broke his heart that he couldn't be among the troops that had stomped fascism into oblivion. On the other hand, he'd seen enough blood, enough anguish in Spain. Martin learned a lot from working with Charlie. Writing for pictures was a very different process than writing novels, and it was certainly different from the sketches Martin had done for radio.

Eventually, Martin decided to write a script on his own. Elliot proved to be a big help. He hadn't served in the armed forces either; a slight heart murmur, the legacy of childhood rheumatic fever, had kept him out of the war and in Hollywood directing B movies. And though Elliot was no writer, he had an uncanny grasp of good storytelling. Martin came to him with an idea based on the "zoot suit riots." Elliot sat in his living room, a scotch rocks in one hand, a gold-tipped cigarette in the other, listening to Martin read from his notes. "It was June of 1943, a gang of white sailors stormed into the heart of the Mexican-American community in East Los Angeles. They broke into bars and theaters, assaulting anyone in their way. They beat any 'zoot suiters' they found and stripped them of their clothes—their zoot suits—and this was a big insult since these clothes were the fashion of the day for Mexican-American men. The police accompanied the caravans of soldiers and sailors, watched the beatings, and then jailed the victims! Truly unbelievable! The law just turned a blind eye. And given the context of what was going on at the time—remember the Japanese had been rounded up and put in relocation centers. So the racial prejudice—"

Elliot interrupted him, "But which character are we following? What does he want? What are the personal stakes? Let the characters drive the action, not polemics." He flicked his ashes into the fireplace and took a swig of scotch. "As Sam Goldwyn says, if you want to send a message, use Western Union."

Martin retorted, "The fact is, the riots did have political implications. I don't see anything wrong with using the medium to illuminate social contradictions."

"Neither do I. Storytelling is a powerful way to elucidate values. I'm not arguing against that. But we're in the film business to make films, not to change the world. Make it a love story or something."

Now *Zoot Suitor* was in production at Paramount with Robert Mitchum as a sailor who falls in love with a seamstress played by Greer Garson, who is engaged to the Mexican-American played by Tyrone Power. Before Martin had come over to Paramount, he'd asked Charlie if there was any difference between working for Warners and Paramount. "About the same," Charlie quipped. "In both places writers are treated like shit." At least at Paramount there were left-wing writers everywhere. Social themes were okay.

Life was good. He was healthy (though his leg continued to bother him from time to time). He had a contract at a major studio with his own office and a private secretary. His wife had a home she could be proud of. They had a circle of friends, many like themselves, transplants from New York. His children were growing up strong and healthy. Leaving New York was the best move he'd ever made.

Jill came into the room radiating accomplishment. "Well, the eggs are all dyed, and I left a plate of pancakes warming in the oven."

"Umm, pancakes," he said, putting on his glasses and swinging his legs onto the floor. Jill sat down on a satin-quilted bench and twisted off a lid from one of the many jars crowding her dressing table. Martin watched her smooth a pale peach liquid into her skin. She looked good. Her thick dark hair shone with luster and she'd managed to keep her figure in spite of two pregnancies. He was grateful that she'd let him have the morning to himself. He supposed he owed it the kids to give them this day. They were so excited about the egg-hunt. He got out of bed and kissed the top of his wife's head before leaving the room.

As Jill worked the makeup into the area around her eye, she detected a new crop of creases. On closer examination, she spotted a few silver strands at her temple and yanked them out. She was thirty-six. She wondered how old she would she look on screen. How could she wait for two whole years to find out?

19

By the time they had tucked the eggs into baskets, gotten everyone into their Easter best, packed swim suits and towels, had gone back because Nathan had forgotten Mr. Rabbit, and were finally in the station wagon headed toward Toluca Lake—it was well past noon and hot as a day in July.

Millie and Nathan ran ahead through the house and straight out to the backyard where the sun glinted off the water. The lake was narrow enough for a man to swim across without getting winded. Brick houses rimmed it and colorful little boats tied to weathered wooden docks dotted its shore.

Jill stepped onto the grass and looked at the long table laden with biscuits, ham, turkey, pickles, potato salad, coleslaw, deviled eggs, gingerbread, cookies, and Carol's famous German chocolate cake, which was melting on little paper napkins. Another table held an urn of coffee and bottles of booze. Beer and soda pop were in a tub of ice.

Elliot, his arm around the waist of the slender, sun-tanned lead from his last movie, was talking with Gene Kelly. Tanya Laney and Lloyd Bridges were in the middle of one of their vicious games of ping-pong. Other guests lounged on chaises watching the children splash by the edge of the lake or take turns with Elliot's bright red rowboat.

Suddenly Libby thrust a petition at Jill. "To raise money for the Hollywood Ten," she said, a cigarette dangling from her mouth. Libby had grown into a thin, chain-smoking woman who wore a squinty, worried look. She had remained in the Party and was greatly disappointed when Jill and Martin dropped out. Still, she knew Jill was a soft touch for issues like this one. The House Committee on Un-American Activities, or, as it had been dubbed by its opponents, HUAC—the House Un-American Activities Committee—was on a mission to purge the movie industry of so-called "subversives." The Hollywood Ten had been held in contempt of Congress for refusing to cooperate with the Committee and were now appealing their conviction.

Jill took Libby's pen and scribbled her name, then Libby dashed off toward Henry Fonda. Henry had been part of the Committee for the First Amendment, a group that opposed HUAC. Jill had joined, too, after hearing the impassioned words of John Huston. There must've been over three hundred people squeezed into the Coronet Theater the day Huston spoke. "In America we have the Constitutional right not to tell people whether we are members of the Communist Party or any other damn party! We have the right to think whatever we want to think. Isn't that what we all learned in high school civics?"

Jill would like to have been on that star-studded charter airplane that went to Washington—standing shoulder to shoulder with Henry Fonda, Lauren Bacall, Humphrey Bogart, Marsha Hunt, Vincent Hurlie, Frank Sinatra and all the rest, protesting HUAC's methods of investigation. She wanted to help spread the word that it was impossible to sneak subliminal messages into a movie and destroy someone's patriotism. She wanted to challenge the right of the Committee to ask questions that the Constitution and the Bill of Rights said were illegal.

But she remained home, glued to the radio. It was shocking to hear the disrespect the Congressmen showed to the Hollywood Ten—interrupting, raising their voices, bullying them. Of course, John Howard Lawson aggravated the situation with his aggressive ripostes to Chairman Parnell Thomas and had to be dragged from the witness stand. And Richard Nixon became completely flustered when Alvah Bessie took a condescending tone, pointing out that since General Eisenhower was currently refusing to say whether he was a Republican or a Democrat, Alvah Bessie refused to say whether or not he was a communist. It could've been worse. Up until the last moment, Lawson and Herbert Biberman had planned to approach the witness stand singing the national anthem.

The whole thing made Jill mad. So whenever the opportunity presented itself, she signed a petition or sent money. With liberal judges sitting on the Supreme Court, everyone felt certain that the case of the Hollywood Ten would be dismissed and the Committee would die a sudden death.

Phyllis Gladstone came over to Jill holding up Nathan's stuffed rabbit. She was a tall woman, raw-boned with mannish hands and yellow hair as coarse as wire. "I've been hired to baby-sit."

"You've made a friend for life," laughed Jill.

Jill had met Phyllis at the Lab, and the two became instant friends. They were among the few members of the Lab who weren't working as film actors, though Phyllis was trying to break into pictures. She had a naturally expansive personality and hadn't yet learned to rein it in for film.

But their friendship went beyond the fact that neither was

working in the movie business. Phyllis loved watching Jill on stage, the way she was able to completely shed her own skin and become a character. She was crazy about Jill's kids, adored Martin, and enjoyed being around a family, as she had no children or husband herself. As far as Jill was concerned, Phyllis was a strong actress, her own woman. She had a no-nonsense way of looking at the world and Jill trusted her. She also appreciated Phyllis's enthusiasm for her talent.

"Jill! Phyllis!" It was Charlotte, also from the Lab. Charlotte was a younger actress who worshiped Jill and Phyllis. She spoke in a high, squeaky voice, which Jill and Phyllis believed made it unlikely that Charlotte would ever make it as a film actress.

"You'll never guess!" cried Charlotte. "I've been signed by RKO!"

Jill stole a glance at Phyllis, but Phyllis was already grasping Charlotte's hand, exclaiming, "Oh, honey, that's wonderful!"

"Congratulations, Charlotte," Jill said, trying to quash her disbelief and envy. She stammered, "Excuse me, I have to…" and moved off in the direction of the bar, trying to get control of her feelings. She hated herself for being so small, for resenting Charlotte's good fortune. She reached for a glass then felt someone's hands around her waist. She could tell it was Elliot. No one else would be so familiar. "Elliot, hi."

"You look ravishing today. Is Martin still putting his foot down or are we ever going to see you at an audition?"

"Nathan is only five," she said defensively, wriggling free.

"Right, right. First and foremost, a mother. But, God, I hate to see all that talent go to waste."

He glanced at his watch. "Better get this show on the road, or we'll go over budget!" He took the whistle from around his neck and gave it an ear-piercing blow, the signal for the children to be rounded up and herded indoors by the women so that the men could hide the eggs.

As she corralled the children into the house, she wondered if everyone thought of her first and foremost as a mother. They closed the drapes so the kids couldn't peek out. Anne Shirley lined up everyone, even the little ones, so she could teach them the kick-ball-change step. Nathan kept tripping, and Jill could read his growing frustration. She suggested singing and led a round of "Here Comes Peter Cottontail" and then "Easter Parade."

The kids were getting impatient. Jill glanced at her watch. It had been long enough to hide the eggs. "I'm going to check," she announced.

After the dark of the indoors, the bright sun blinded her. Then she saw an alarming sight: the men standing in a huddle by the lake. Somebody's had an accident, she thought, quickening her step. As she approached, she heard the tenor of their conversation—somber, not panicked as if someone had died. She pushed her way into the circle. No one was getting mouth-to-mouth resuscitation. No one was injured. They were all just talking.

"The children are climbing the walls," she said.

No one looked at her.

Elliot was saying, "It'll all blow over. What are they going to do? Drop anyone who ever attended a meeting? That would be just about everybody in Hollywood."

"Well, they've made a hell of a start," Martin said. "Herbert, Samuel, Alvah…"

Now Jill was interested. They were talking about the Hollywood Ten.

Elliot continued, "Movies are big business. Do you really think Darryl Zanuck and Harry Cohn are going to knuckle under to a puny Congressional committee and fire their best talent?"

"After the Waldorf meeting, they vowed they'd fire all Reds," said Larry Parks, a tall, lean man with a mop of wavy hair.

"Nah," said Elliot. "I don't believe it. They don't all agree to anything. Each guy, whether it's Jack Warner or Louis B. Mayer, runs his fiefdom like a feudal lord."

Martin said, "Remember, Eric Johnson promised never to support anything as un-American as a blacklist. Those were his words, 'un-American.'"

Samuel Ornitz, a heavyset man in a rumpled pale brown suit, took off his glasses and, wiping them with his handkerchief, grimly weighed in, "Just proves, even the president of the Motion Picture Association doesn't have any power."

Vincent Hurlie ran his fingers through thinning hair. "Samuel's right," he said thoughtfully. "Since I was on that plane, my agent hasn't even been able to get me an audition. Unless I sign something saying the trip to Washington was masterminded by commies."

"Like Bogie did," said Alvah Bessie, a tall, angular man with stooped shoulders.

"There's a blacklist all right," Samuel insisted. "They're on a real witch-hunt. They won't stop until they've found a pinko under every stone."

Alvah waved a crumpled telegram. "Sending us to jail is an object lesson for the rest of you."

It suddenly hit Jill that the Supreme Court had refused to hear their appeal! That meant their convictions were being upheld. That meant that Alvah and Samuel, and all the rest of the Hollywood Ten were going to jail. She felt a shiver of fear.

Samuel heaved a heavy sigh. "Let's at least be as brave as the people we write about."

There was a pause while everyone considered the nobility of that challenge. Suddenly, Jill remembered the children and stepped forward, breaking the silence, "Isn't it time for the hunt?"

The double entendre was unintended, but the mood suddenly shifted. They looked at one another and shared a strained laugh.

20

IT WAS A YEAR LATER THAT Martin sat in his office on the Paramount lot looking out the window at two men wheeling a large piece of dappled sky onto a sound stage. The real sky was clouded over giving everything a silvery cast. The gray spring day matched his spirits. He forced his mind back onto his main character, a Nazi on trial for war crimes. He studied his notes again, looking for clues about which incidents from the world stage were germane to his story, but his mind kept drifting back to the events of his own day.

Like molten lava turning to volcanic rock, the atmosphere of fear had gradually solidified in the last year, ever since the Hollywood Ten had been sent to prison. The North Koreans, on the prompting of the Soviet Union, had unleashed an attack across the 38th parallel, and President Truman, without even bothering to ask Congress to declare war, had ordered U.S. forces to attack all along the Korean front. American boys were dying on foreign soil for a cause that had nothing to do with American security. But "security" was the watchword of the day. Or rather, insecurity. There were loyalty oaths, bomb shelters, and even concentration camps, so-called "holding areas" for subversives in case of a national crisis. The Rosenbergs were being held up as examples of the worst depravity to the sound of crowds cheering, "Let them sizzle!" Senator Joseph McCarthy had launched a series of attacks on alleged communist traitors who had infiltrated the federal government.

As part of the crackdown on communists, Party leaders were being sent to prison. Martin had learned that shocking fact late one night when, long after he and Jill had gone to bed, Carol and Ray showed up at the front door, their kids asleep in the back of their old Nash Rambler. "We're going to Mexico," said Ray, his voice barely above a whisper. "They're throwing communists in jail."

"What?" exclaimed Martin. "The Communist Party is a sorry excuse for a party, but it's not illegal."

"Being a Party functionary is."

Under the glare of the porch light, Carol looked pale, her eyes bloodshot. "Did you ever hear me plot to overthrow the government?" she asked. Before anyone could answer, she blurted, "And, if we leave the country, we'll be expelled from the Party for desertion. It's been the center of our entire lives for over sixteen years!" She burst into tears.

Jill put an arm around her. "Get the kids. You're staying here tonight."

Everyone agreed that the authorities wouldn't think to come looking for them there. In their panic, Ray and Carol had hardly packed a thing, so Martin and Ray snuck over to the apartment and, by flashlight, emptied bookshelves and closets into boxes. They stuffed everything into the Rambler. When they got back, they found Carol and Jill sitting in the kitchen drinking bourbon. Martin poured drinks for Ray and himself. They whispered late into the night. Ray felt they had no choice but to leave the country. If he and Carol went to jail, what would happen to their kids? They didn't want them paraded on national television like the Rosenberg kids had been—pitiful victims, children of traitors.

Martin looked out his office window again. It had begun to sprinkle. He took off his glasses and rubbed his eyes; his head throbbed. His leg was bothering him, too. He reached for a bottle of aspirin and threw several into his mouth, choking them back with stale coffee, then lit a cigarette and exhaled. It was 1951, and HUAC was back in town, ready to destroy the communist plot lurking behind every screenwriter's door. Things were heating up. Actually it wasn't heat at all; it was the chill of the Cold War.

The phone rang, and Martin reached for it gratefully. It was Jill reporting that Nathan and Millie's chicken pox was driving them all crazy and reminding him that he had promised to be home by six o'clock.

Martin welcomed the news. Something as normal as chicken pox.

JILL STOOD AT THE KITCHEN sink washing Nathan's hands. She had to constantly remind him to stop picking at the scabs. He kept forgetting, so she was forever scrubbing his hands with hexachlorophene. The radio was on, but she only dimly registered the voice of Senator Joseph McCarthy: "...*a conspiracy on a scale so immense designed to diminish the United States in world affairs, to weaken us militarily, to confuse our spirit—so that we will fall victim to the Soviet intrigue from within and...*"

"Ow!" squealed Nathan. "You're hurting me!"

"Mommm—y!" It was Millie wailing from the bathroom. Jill went and stood wearily in the doorway. Millie looked up from the bath, a pained expression on her spotted face. She soaked in a baking soda bath on and off throughout the day, but it did little to relieve the itching. There was nothing more Jill could do, but Millie called to her every few minutes to remind her that the bath wasn't helping.

It had been raining all week and the house was strewn with pick-up sticks, Erector set parts, the train set, doll clothes, miniature soldiers. The kids had hung sheets from every table, crawling in and out of "hide-outs" all day. Neither of them seemed to need naps.

Jill moved through the rooms in a fog, making beds, picking up paper dolls and tinker toys, rinsing dishes, listening to the incessant rain. She picked up a rag-doll in a sailor's suit and it triggered a memory—a remark Elliot had tossed off a few weeks ago that had lodged like a sliver beneath her skin. She thought it would work its way out on its own, but her heart had swelled in sympathy and held it deep inside.

Elliot had thrown a party at the Cocoanut Grove to celebrate his latest movie, *Sailor's Delight*. It was the first time Jill had ever been to the elegant nightclub that, since its opening thirty years earlier, had become the premier night spot for Hollywood's rich and famous. When she stepped inside, she was dazzled: its vast interior, detailed in a Moroccan motif, was dominated by real tropical palms with stuffed monkeys hanging from them. The blue ceiling was painted with twinkling stars. Couples spun around the dance floor to the music of Les Brown's orchestra. There was a colorful mix of chiffon gowns, expensive furs, and sparkling jewels. Over three hundred industry people were there to toast Elliot, including Louis B. Mayer himself. Lena Haskell, Elliot's latest star, a well-endowed girl with porcelain skin and flaming red hair, hung on his arm, a white mink trailing over her shoulder.

Jill and Martin were seated at a table close to the dance floor. A Negro with brilliantined hair circulated with caviar. Booze flowed freely. They dined on lobster bisque and chateaubriand. A photographer snapped their picture. Even though she was thrilled to be among such luminaries, Jill felt like an interloper. She was there not because she was part of the movie business, but because she and Martin were Elliot's old friends. She looked across the table at Martin who seemed bemused by the whole spectacle.

After dinner, on the way to the powder room, she spotted Elliot bending Robert Montgomery's ear. "The part is made for you," he was saying. "You not only get the girl, but you get to punch out Jimmy Cagney, too!"

Robert laughed, "Ah, jealous rage I hope."

As Jill passed them, Elliot pulled her back by her stole, not looking at her, still talking to Robert, "And if you're lucky, Jill will be playing the part of Phoebe."

Robert turned to her. "I didn't know you were being considered for Phoebe."

Jill laughed, pulling herself free. "Elliot's drunk."

Like a searchlight on Hollywood Boulevard, Elliot beamed his smile at her. "M-G-M wants a fresh face for the lead—someone older, more experienced. Rita is too young. So is Lauren." He bent over and took a whiff of the gardenia behind her ear and whispered, "Though I doubt Martin would ever allow it." Then he grabbed a clump of her hair and said, laughing, "Of course you'd have to go blond. Phoebe's a bit of a slut."

The way he said "slut" and the mischievous glint in his eye made Jill realize that he was teasing her. She laughed and retorted lamely, "Oh, yes, I'd have to dye my hair to be a slut..."

She went into the restroom and applied lipstick with a shaky hand. Elliot still had the power to throw her. The very thought of testing for a major motion picture made her dizzy with a desire she usually managed to keep tamped down.

Nathan burst into the kitchen crying, knocking her out of her reverie. Millie was behind him holding a broken Hopalong Cassidy holster. "I didn't do it," she protested.

Jill sighed and examined the broken holster. She had skipped her acting class last week when fevers and blisters required her attention. But tonight she was determined to go. Tomorrow was her birthday, and her fellow students wanted to take her out for a drink after class. Martin would be home by six o'clock. She could hold out until then.

2I

AFTER BEING COOPED UP WITH sick children, the long winding drive through Coldwater Canyon felt like a gift. The rain pounded steadily and made for slow going. Listening to the steady swoosh of the windshield wipers quieted her nerves. She thought of the scene she would be playing tonight with Tony Curtis.

Her character, Cleo, reminded her of herself as a young woman. When she lived in New York she'd seen Eleanor Lynn play Cleo in the original Group Theatre production of *Rocket to the Moon* at the Belasco Theatre. Morris Carnovsky had played opposite Eleanor, and now Morris was her teacher. Jill had been moved by Eleanor's performance, but Jill had her own ideas about Cleo. She knew the comparison was inevitable. And of course she was no longer Cleo's age. Still, the role was hers—for tonight anyway—and she intended to fully inhabit the tender waif who spoke with such determination. *"If there's roads, I'll take them. I'll go up all those roads till I find what I want...Don't you think life is to live all you can and experience everything?"*

She glanced at the clock on the dashboard. The rain was making her late. Morris expected punctuality from actors as much as he expected dedication. She hated to disappoint him.

The front door at the Lab was stuck because of the dampness. She pushed hard against it, and it finally swung free. The room was cold and dark. Morris sat on his stool facing the group like he usually did, but it became instantly clear to Jill that his talk was not about acting. She heard the bewilderment in his voice before she caught the grief.

"Senator Tenney from the California legislature seems to be the one behind it."

Then Phyllis spoke. Her voice had a desperate edge. "Are they saying that the Lab is a communist front organization because we've done Chekhov and Shaw?"

"In a word, yes. HUAC is on a rampage. As you all know, they've targeted Hollywood—the citadel of Bolsheviks." He noticed Jill and motioned for her to come in. She hadn't realized she was still standing; her mind was whirring to make sense of all this. Quickly, she found a seat.

Morris turned to Tony. "Tell everyone what you told me."

Tony Curtis, a handsome boy with a shock of curly black hair, was usually confident and playful. But tonight he seemed nervous as a schoolboy being confronted by a teacher about a test score. "I got a call and so did Janet, and I know others did, too."

"I did," said Charlotte.

Tony continued. "The studios don't want their contract players being associated with a place thought to be...well, you know...pink. They won't let us—"

"Won't let you?" Phyllis was on her feet, her voice rising in angry disbelief. "You have free will. They don't own you!"

Karen Morley, a starkly beautiful blond, stood and faced her. "You don't really know what it's like, Phyllis. Louis B. Mayer *does* think he owns me. He told me I shouldn't marry Alfred, that I should marry someone he approves of. He even told me that I'd better never have a kid."

Jill said to Morris, "But, legally, how can they shut us down?"

"They aren't shutting us down," Morris said, looking at her with tired, sad eyes. "They're just letting us bleed to death. Two years ago the IRS yanked our tax-exempt status. Last year we were forced to drop the Vets-training program. And now, with the studios pressuring students to drop out, our main source of revenue will dry up. We really don't have a choice."

JILL GOT IN THE CAR AND closed the door against what was now a light drizzle. She looked out the windshield at the wet blur of the street. Turning on the ignition, she sat there, the engine humming. Her head was pounding. She couldn't go home yet. Instead, she drove all the way down Wilshire Boulevard to where it dead-ended at a bluff overlooking the Pacific Ocean. By the time she got there, it had stopped raining. She got out and walked to the low wooden fence that hugged the edge of the cliff. Tall street lamps illuminated the nearby palms. On the other side of the wall, crumbled rock and mud became a steep drop-off to the highway a hundred feet below. She looked out past the highway into blackness where waves crashed onto the shore. The Actors Lab was a thing of the past. Her cherished sanctuary had been annihilated as completely as if it were a French cathedral demolished by a German bomb. Some form of fascism had crept into her very own life, and she was completely at a loss as to how to protect herself.

She wished she could see the horizon. She felt certain it would help her gain perspective, help her to see how small she was: a mere goose bump on the edge of the continent, on this fast moving ball hurtling through space. But thinking about these abstractions did nothing to snap her out of her gloom.

She walked along the narrow path, which zigzagged with the bends in the cliff. A slender moon struggled to break free of the cloud cover. It would be clear tomorrow. Tomorrow—her birthday. She thought of Cleo, and her heart constricted. Cleo was stillborn. She felt the curtain coming down on her dreams. What was she going to do? She was getting older. Was she going to be a housewife for the rest of her life?

She began to feel chilled and returned to the car. She decided to take Sunset back. It wasn't until she had passed UCLA that she realized she was not heading for Coldwater Canyon but for Elliot's house. It felt as if everything was coming apart and suddenly, tonight, she had to know if Elliot's flippant remark about M-G-M wanting an unknown actress was true, or if he had just been toying with her.

Elliot had been living in Beverly Hills for several months. She didn't have the street number, but she knew he lived on Altair and that his was the last house on a cul-de-sac. She followed the winding street as it climbed. The cul-de-sac was quiet and dark. There were three houses at the end of the street. She got out of the car and peered at the mailboxes and found COOPER. She stared through an iron gateway into the grounds beyond. It was a two-story Spanish-style stucco house that sat on a knoll, which rose steeply from the street. An iron railing framed the balconies of the tall, arched windows upstairs, and Jill could discern planters of geraniums hanging beneath them. She took a deep breath and unlatched the gate, following the brick path.

Lena opened the door. She was wearing a pale blue satin dressing gown that clung to her lithe body and gave off the light scent of expensive perfume. It didn't surprise Jill to find her at Elliot's front door, but it annoyed her. Lena was a sentry, someone to be reckoned with before being granted an audience with the king.

"Oh, Jill. Are you all right?"

Jill suddenly realized how late it was and how she must look, her hair matted from the rain, her mascara running.

"Yes, I'm fine, is Elliot…?"

"I'll get him," said Lena. She swung her long red hair as if it were an appendage and opened the door so Jill could enter. "You can wait in there," she said, pointing to the living room.

Lena disappeared down the terra cotta tiles. Jill stepped into the sunken living room with its plush wall-to-wall carpet the color of cantaloupe. A fire was blazing in a stone fireplace. She stood with her back to it, her coat still on.

Facing her above a white couch was an enormous abstract. A hodgepodge of bright oranges, yellows, and golds fanned out from a center partially covered by a flat green rectangle.

"Jill! What a nice surprise!" Elliot was barefoot, wearing a white terrycloth robe and dripping onto the carpet. "That's a Hans Hoffman," he said. "No matter how hard it tries, that rectangle just can't hide the chaos."

Lena was behind him carrying a bowl of fruit. Elliot said, "I've just gone for a dip, and I highly recommend it. Brisk!" Then, turning to Lena, "Find a swimsuit for Jill, sweetheart." Lena hurried out of the room.

Jill said, "No, Elliot, I don't want to go swimming."

"A drink then?"

"No, I—" Her face felt hot. She took off her coat and lay it on a white wing-backed chair. "A few weeks ago…you were probably only joking, but has that part been cast?"

Elliot didn't flinch. "No, I'm still testing for Phoebe. Seen about a hundred little tramps so far." He laughed one of his hearty, open-throated laughs. "I wasn't joking. I'd love you to read for the part." Then he looked at her with a wry smile. "Does Martin know you're here?"

"Of course. He's all for it," she said quickly. "He wants whatever will make me happy." Then added aggressively, "And what will make me happy is if I get a shot at this role."

He smiled. "Give my office a call. The sooner the better."

She felt a rush of affection for him.

On the drive home, she rolled down the window and inhaled the sweet, clean air. Streetlights shimmered in the black puddles. Like an incantation, she kept repeating, *"If there's roads, I'll take them. I'll go up all those roads till I find what I want."*

She opened the front door and inhaled the quiet of the sleeping house. When she climbed into bed, Martin didn't stir. The warmth of the electric blanket and the soft flannel nightgown against her skin began to lull her to sleep. It had been a very long day. Exhaustion was deep in her bones. She listened to Martin's rhythmic breathing. Tomorrow she would tell him everything.

She rolled onto her back and closed her eyes. Deep down, underneath the bravado and skirt chasing, Elliot was still a comrade.

22

SHE DREAMED ABOUT THE door at the Lab. It was stuck and she was leaning into it with her shoulder, pushing with all her weight, but still it wouldn't budge.

She awoke with the taste of bitter disappointment. Lying in bed with her eyes closed, listening to the muffled sounds of the children running up and down the hallway, she remembered it was her birthday. They had let her sleep in. She thought about how to spend the day, how to mark it in some way. She continued to lie there until she was sure they had all left. When had she ever been the last one to get up? She'd always made their breakfasts and lunches, helped them get dressed, and stood at the door waving good-bye as Martin drove off with them.

She went to the window and drew open the blinds. The sky was a dazzling blue; the honeysuckle sparkled. Everything had been washed clean. I'm thirty-seven, she thought, trying to register the change.

The kitchen was in total disarray. Millie had tried to wrestle a cake into being. It stood lopsided on a plate, chocolate smeared on thick. Jill set about scraping the remnants of batter from a bowl, then with a jolt, remembered Phoebe. She rushed to the phone and called Elliot's office; they could see her later that afternoon. She made hasty arrangements for the children to be picked up from school by a neighbor, then went to her dressing table. She brushed her hair in long sweeping strokes and carefully applied her makeup. She chose a flowery cotton dress that hugged her torso and flared out in an A-line from her hips. It was her birthday. She felt a frenzy of excitement.

Jill had never really considered dying her hair. Even when Jean Harlow was all the rage and now, Marilyn Monroe, she had remained happily planted in the Jane Russell camp. In the sun, her hair shone with chestnut hues; by moonlight, it looked as black as Higgins ink. She usually wore it down, letting it fall to her shoulders in natural waves. When she dressed up, she wore it swept back in a French twist with tortoiseshell combs.

She drove down Ventura Boulevard until she spotted a hair salon. She marched in and gave the order. Several hours later she emerged slightly stunned, running her fingers through her hair to reassure herself that it was still there. She shook her head, feeling the familiar sensation of hair tumbling into place around her face. She wandered down the street, glimpsing herself in the reflections of store windows. She looked like someone else—someone younger, sexier. She experimented with the way she walked, listening to the click of her patent leather heels against the pavement.

In one of the classes she'd taken at the Lab, the teacher began each session with movement exercises. "If you know how the character moves, you know who he is," he said. They had been sent to the zoo to study an animal that best represented their characters. Now, here on Ventura Boulevard, in the glow of this lovely spring day, the image of a panther presented itself. Phoebe might be a dumb blond on the outside, but inside lived a sable panther with its slow, deliberate, seductive loping.

She expected Elliot to be at the screen test, but it was only a casting director, who seemed unimpressed by her appearance or by the way she moved. Jill realized with a start that he'd no doubt seen blond actresses by the hundreds and that maybe she had acted too rashly. Maybe a brunette would be a more original way to depict Phoebe. She immediately banished that thought. Her Phoebe was blond. As long as Jill continued to let the panther guide her, she felt she could capture Phoebe's uniqueness.

She was asked to read two scenes, each showing a different side of the character. In one, she was hustling a drink in a bar, turning on her sexual charm, and for this scene the panther was in full force. The other scene was a monologue, words addressed to the grave of Phoebe's mother. Jill thought of her own mother, and there was a catch in her throat when she spoke the lines.

When she picked up the children, Millie didn't recognize her. Then, she was enchanted, touching her mother's hair ever so lightly. But Nathan shrank from her, disconcerted by the radical change in her appearance. "I'm still Mommy," Jill said, reaching across the seat to tickle him. But he shrank from her touch, staring at her through wide eyes.

When Martin came home, Nathan ran to him. "Mommy's different," he said, pulling on his father's coat, leading him to the kitchen where Jill was helping Millie put candles on the cake.

Martin stood in the doorway, hat still on, briefcase dangling, staring at his wife. In the evening light, her hair was a halo of white gold.

"Well?" Jill said with a nervous laugh.

He put down his briefcase and absently picked up Nathan.

Millie said, "I think she looks like a princess."

Martin crossed to her and ran his fingers through her hair.

"It's very different," he said. "Glamorous."

"I'm so relieved you like it!"

"I have to get used to it."

"We all do," she said. "Even me."

After the children ate their dinner, Jill blew out the candles and sliced up Millie's cake with promises that Mommy and Daddy would eat theirs after they got home. The babysitter arrived, and after many birthday kisses, Jill and Martin escaped into a grown-up evening.

They seldom went out to dinner, but on her birthday, Martin always took Jill to the Brown Derby. The big brown dome shaped like a hat stood on Wilshire Boulevard, its "hat brim" hovering just above the sidewalk. Inside, the room was dark and buzzed with conversation. Jack Lane's caricatures of movie stars adorned the walls. A recording of Frank Sinatra singing "Swing Easy" played in the background.

Martin and Jill sat next to each other in a corner booth drinking an expensive cabernet and eating prime rib. She leaned over and kissed his cheek. The flame that had once burned so strongly between them had gone out long ago. Jill accepted that as an inevitability of marriage. Martin had a bald spot now and his face, along with the rest of him, had grown fuller. But he still had an intensity in his eyes. He still had the ability to make her think, to challenge herself. He could still dazzle her with his creativity and the way his brilliant mind worked. They enjoyed each other's company. They enjoyed their children. They still enjoyed making love.

She had planned to bring up the screen test during dinner. But now she realized that actually there was nothing to tell. If she didn't get the part, why bring up the whole subject? It would only cause an argument and spoil her birthday. If she did get the part, well, she would deal with it then. Instead, she told him about the Lab, about what Tony had reported and what Morris had said. Martin sighed, "HUAC's tentacles are everywhere."

Then he reached into his pocket and pulled out something wrapped in tissue. Handing it to her he said, "But tonight we're celebrating, so let's forget about all that."

She unfolded the tissue and took out two Spanish combs. They were ivory. "To set off your black hair," Martin said with a wry smile.

They said in unison, "The Gift of the Magi!" and Jill added, "I hope you didn't sell your watch!"

He laughed and kissed her. "Happy Birthday, honey."

23

MARTIN WAS IN THE COMMISSARY eating a roast beef sandwich and making notes on the script for *Penny Lane*. It was about a girls' reformatory and starred Bette Davis as the head mistress. It was already in production, but Martin was being asked to rewrite scenes every day. Today, the studio wanted him to take out the word "community." It sounded too much like "communism."

He put his pencil down and took a bite of his sandwich. He thought about his "fellow travelers," as the press had pejoratively labeled his liberal friends. They were being called by the dozens to testify before HUAC. As his old writing partner Charlie Fisher quipped, "Cheer up. It gets worse."

Larry Parks was only the first of many who had, in his own words, "crawled through the mud," giving the Committee names of known or suspected communists. Martin figured it was Larry's union work that had made him a prime target of the witch-hunt. Dmytryk, one of the original Hollywood Ten who served time in prison, had gone running back to the Committee on his knees. Now they were trotting him out at American Legion meetings to speak on the evils of communism. For what? Martin wondered, then answered his own question: for thirty pieces of silver; now Dmytryk would be allowed to work.

Others had refused to cooperate with HUAC, citing the Fifth Amendment. Like a melon sliced down the middle, some fell to the right, others to the left. There was no middle road.

From the other end of the room, a stentorian voice rose above the din and Martin recognized it as belonging to Elliot. He stuck his pencil behind his ear and took his tray over to Elliot's table. "Don't generally see you around here," said Martin.

Elliot said, "I was just telling Kenny here that directors only scan the paragraphs of description."

Kenny, a slight man with nervous eyes, nodded hello. He turned back to hear the rest of Elliot's speech with a smile somewhere between gratitude and panic.

Elliot continued, "It's the dialogue that matters. I don't want to wade through a bunch of pretty prose. No audience will ever see it, so why should I?"

Kenny mumbled thanks and left. Martin sat down. "Still intimidating the junior writers, I see."

"He gave me a tome, the first draft of *War and Peace*. Then, with a wide grin added, "Well, pal, I never thought you'd let her out of the kitchen."

Martin took a bite of his sandwich. "Go on."

"I thought that's why you came over, to thank me."

"Thank you," said Martin. "Now tell me why I'm so grateful."

Elliot eyed him thoughtfully. "For letting Jill test for my movie."

Martin took his time swallowing. He reached for his bottle of cola. "Yeah, well, she's a grown-up. She does what she wants."

"I saw her test this morning and called her right away. I'm trying like hell to get Robert Montgomery to play opposite her."

Martin only half listened as Elliot rambled on about the shooting schedule, the script problems, location decisions.

Why hadn't Jill told him? How long had she secretly been going out on auditions? Or, had she tried to tell him and he hadn't been listening? Maybe he had cut her off without even realizing it. He thought they had agreed to wait until Nathan was older. But maybe they had discussed it again. He couldn't remember, and that bothered him.

Whenever he was doing re-writes he was distracted. Whenever he was in the beginning, middle or end of a script, he was distracted. He lived in two worlds—one of his own making, which required constant focus, and the other, which functioned fine without it. His wife and family were more important than his fictitious characters, but suddenly he realized how easily they could drift away if he didn't give them at least the same attention.

JILL STOOD AT THE KITCHEN sink in peddle-pushers patting meatloaf into a pan that was too small. The sounds of "Kookla, Fran and Ollie" drifted in from the den where Nathan and Millie were sitting cross-legged in front of the newly acquired television set, which had magically transformed them from wild monkeys into quiet little lambs. The pink hamburger bulged over the rim. She pushed in one place and it squeezed out another. She kept working it as she worried over her good fortune. Martin would be furious. Her mind bounced from how to manage his reaction to when to schedule costume fittings to how to find an agent. Elliot had referred her to Gerald Fisk and she already had an appointment for the next day. She wiped her hands on her apron and reached for the phone, placing a long-distance call to her father to share her good news. There was a catch in his voice as he said, "I wish your dear mother could've lived to see it happen."

She hung up and stared at the meatloaf. She was in a whirl-wind of excitement but still faced several hurdles. What to do with the children? What to do with her husband? It all kept coming back to Martin. She decided to forget the meatloaf and change her clothes, maybe something a bit dressy. She'd fix them martinis; make an occasion out of it.

But suddenly there he was, standing in the doorway.

She gave a little gasp.

"I saw Elliot today. He told me about the movie," he said without preamble.

She wiped her hands on her apron. "Oh, honey, I'm sorry...I mean I'm not sorry to have the part...but sorry that I didn't...look, it all happened so fast and before I knew it, Elliot—"

"I think it's great," he said.

She looked into his eyes to catch the sarcasm but there was none. "You do?"

"Sure I do," he said, taking off his hat and loosening his tie. "This could be a big break for you. You shouldn't pass it up."

"I won't be gone all the time. I thought I could get a babysitter who could come every day and—"

"That wouldn't be enough. I'll call my folks. Chances are the timing will work out since you'll be shooting during school vacation. Mama will be thrilled to have a whole summer with the kids. In any case, we should celebrate! After dinner we'll all go to Wil Wright's for ice-cream sodas."

She went to him and kissed his cheek. "Thank you, honey." There were tears in her eyes. "Thank you for wanting me to have this."

24

THEY HAD FLOWN BACK TO VISIT Martin's parents each summer, so the children knew their grandparents and adored them. They were excited about flying on the airplane, looking out at the miniature houses, getting little "wings" pins and box lunches. Jill knew that Martin's mother would teach them Yiddish songs and stuff them with kosher cooking. Martin's father would take them to the Bronx Zoo and let them feed the ducks in Central Park. Millie and Nathan would be safe and doted upon.

Yet, as Jill hurried toward the boarding area in the Burbank airport, a small hand clasped tightly in each of hers, she struggled to hold back tears. When Martin had announced this solution to the baby-sitting problem, she had pounced on it. But she didn't dream that this moment would be so excruciating. She had never been separated from them and now she was deliberately putting three thousand miles and a whole summer between herself and her babies.

They arrived at the gate. A line was already beginning to form. Martin went to make arrangements with one of the stewardesses.

Jill glanced at Nathan. He was clutching Mr. Rabbit with his free hand, staring wide-eyed out the large window at the snouts of the big airplanes.

Millie was struggling with her own tears. "What if Zadie isn't there when we get there?"

"He'll be there."

"But what if he isn't?"

Jill knelt and straightened Millie's new jacket, re-buttoning it correctly. "The stewardess won't leave you until Zadie gets there. That's a promise." Then she held Millie by the shoulders and looked into her eyes. "And Zadie will take you home and Bubbie will cover you with wet kisses and pinch your cheeks and give you peppermint candy and—"

"Take us to the zoo."

"That's right, and the symphony and the library and—"

"And the umpire state building," added Nathan helpfully.

Jill forced a smile. "Yes, even the Empire State Building. Why, the summer will fly by and you'll be back before you know it."

The last call for their flight rang out over the loud speaker. Jill pulled them both close and inhaled their lemony smell. She choked out the words, "I'll call tonight and we'll talk long distance."

ROBERT MONTGOMERY DECLINED the part. Jill was secretly relieved because, though she thought him a good actor, as the former president of Screen Actors Guild, he was a vociferous opponent of left-wing politics. Doing a love scene with him would've required a high degree of suspended disbelief.

At the last minute the studio agreed to let Elliot use an unknown for the male lead as well. Tom Blackwell was from the Midwest and what gossip columnists called "a natural." He had no formal training, but had all the ease of a Leslie Howard. He was tall and fair with a strong jaw and a head of sandy-colored hair. Jill liked him at once. Elliot watched the two of them together and uttered the magic word, "Chemistry!"

"*Stranger At the Gate*" was a war story set in France. Phoebe's husband has been killed by the Nazis, leaving her alone with two young girls who are being hidden on a farm. To make ends meet, Phoebe is forced into prostitution. One of her "johns" is an American soldier who sees the fragile soul beneath her hard exterior.

For Jill, working in front of a camera was a challenge. In theater, the story moved along in a logical sequence; in film, all the scenes that used the same set were shot at the same time regardless of where they came in the story. In theater, she had free range of movement; in front of a camera, particularly a close-up, she had to limit her movement. In theater, her efforts were directed to the balcony; on camera, she could speak naturally—there was no such thing as a stage whisper. In theater, her makeup was heavy, deep rouges and thick eye shadows; on film it was done with a light touch and done by someone else. In theater, the bigger the better. On film, "less is more," Elliot kept saying. She was getting on-the-job training, and she ate it up. She loved being on the set—nobody's mother, nobody's wife.

For the role of Phoebe, Jill was being dressed in low cut sweaters and filmy dressing gowns. Elliot had asked the makeup artist to give her fuller, redder lips. They had even changed her hair to make it less honey-colored, more platinum. Jill began to sit differently, arching her back slightly, thrusting out her chest. She smiled at crew members with a "come hither" look. When Martin visited the set he didn't seem to notice the change. He had been on movie sets before. His only comment was, "Different from radio, huh?"

Sometimes, if Elliot didn't need to work on set-ups for the

following day, he and Jill would run across the street and grab a drink at Mario's. Since movie people worked around the clock, especially if a movie was in production, Mario's was always noisy, dark, and smoky.

She would listen to Elliot talk about the movie: what kind of music he had in mind, what scenes needed re-writing, his concerns about the lighting.

"I'm trying to get the light like an Edward Hopper painting, a dramatic mix of lights and darks. I finally found a cameraman who understands that the play of shadow is just as important as the light."

"How did you get all your ideas about film anyway?" she asked, sipping a Manhattan.

He lit a cigarette and pondered her question. "I guess I began to see the camera in a new way watching newsreels during the war. Those cameramen on the battlefront had only one option—a hand-held camera, and natural light. Those films gave me ideas. Writers would be happy if I just nailed down the camera and let the actors say their lines. Ask Martin. I'm sure he'd say that the scene in *The Maltese Falcon* that runs thirteen minutes with no camera movement is brilliant. I say it's boring. If that's what you want, why not just mount the thing as a stage play? To me, the camera is a player every bit as important as the actor. Once you have the camera moving, the next obvious thing to consider is the movement of the light."

His face was flushed with enthusiasm, his excitement infectious. She felt a comfortable ease with him, as she had in the old days when they used to sit in the White Horse Tavern while Martin was in Spain.

She floated home each night, breathless with the novelty of her venture. How different her role was now compared to the one she'd been playing since the children were born.

Martin and Jill didn't see much of each other. Martin was on a deadline, and if he wasn't still at the studio when Jill got home, he was with Charlie Fisher, who had been subpoenaed by HUAC. Charlie's lawyer had advised him that taking the Fifth, if not done properly, could be serious. If Charlie was tricked into answering a question pertaining to a proscribed group on the Attorney General's long list of subversive organizations, he was required under law to name all the other members he might know—or find himself in contempt of Congress and go to jail. Furthermore, if they asked him, do you know so-and-so, he could say yes, we play golf together. But if they asked him whether he knew that so-and-so was a member of this or that organization, he'd have to plead the Fifth to avoid naming him. He couldn't simply tell about his own past political activities. Talking about himself meant waiving the right to refuse to talk about others. It was complicated, and meetings with the lawyers went late into the night. Martin was also helping to organize a fund-raising event for Charlie's legal expenses. Between his writing deadline and Charlie, it was as if he had two jobs. By the time he got home, Jill was usually asleep. She couldn't remember the last time they'd had a real conversation or turned toward each other in bed.

One night, she was the one who got home late. On the kitchen table she found a note from Martin: "Jill, look at this! Someone handed it to me at the market. I was afraid to throw it away. What if someone had seen me?" Jill skimmed over the American Legion tract:

REDS have acquired absolute control of Hollywood. Films made by Hollywood REDS are being used by Moscow throughout the world to create hatred of America. Hit the Hollywood Moguls in their pocketbook! Don't allow our theater screens to show films that sanctify MARXISM and ONE-WORLDISM! Put an end to RED control in Hollywood! Shun the theaters that show the REDS. Refuse to buy the products of sponsors who bring REDS into your Living Room via the TV set.

What followed was a list of the offending sponsors and the *"best known REDS and FELLOW TRAVELERS."*

She threw it in the trash can and went upstairs. She had an important scene to do the next afternoon and wanted to be well rested. When she slipped into bed, Martin stirred in his sleep. She looked at him. They were passing like ships in the night. She was traveling first class on an ocean liner; he was in a rowboat that had a small but steady leak.

25

It was still dark when Jill found herself suddenly wide awake, listening to the steady hum of the refrigerator, the distant rumble of trucks on Magnolia Boulevard, Martin's quiet breathing.

At first she thought she was still dreaming, but it was thoughts she was having, not dreams. She was thinking about a kiss she had shared with Elliot many years ago. She had totally forgotten that moment. Now that she and Elliot were in each other's lives again, that forbidden kiss had found its way into her consciousness, into the bed she shared with her husband.

She crept through the darkened house to the kitchen, got a glass of water and stood at the sink, staring into the back yard. It had been weeks since she and Martin had made love. He'd been distracted and so had she. There had been interludes like this before—after he returned from Spain, after each of the children was born. She missed his touch.

She tried to shake the disturbing dream, but it had a hold of her. She needed a distraction. Maybe she'd read Stanislavski's *Method*. It would give her insight into how to deepen the role of Phoebe. But she just stood there holding the glass, staring into the lavender sky. Then with firm resolve, she suddenly decided to clean the bathroom.

She went into the bathroom and opened the cupboard. When she reached for the sponge, her eye came to rest on her diaphragm box. She held it in her hand a moment before realizing she was thinking of Elliot, not Martin. She dropped it as if it were a hot ember.

When she and Martin had moved to Los Angeles, nothing brought her together with Elliot except social occasions. In fact, he was on a fast track with his career and moved in circles that seldom included her and Martin. She and Elliot had only superficial conversations. He continued to flirt with her the way he did with all women. But now, since rehearsals had begun, they were thrown together every day, sometimes hours at a time working intimately. Today they had worked on a love scene.

The setting was a foggy night, late and dark. Phoebe is walking on a bridge and sees a soldier about to jump. She goes over to him, but instead of trying to talk him out of his intention, she says, *"I'd jump, too, but I hate cold water."* He is startled by her nonchalance. She offers him a cigarette and ends up taking him to her place, a dingy room above a cafe. She lights a candle. She's wearing a scoop-necked peasant blouse, the kind that has elastic. He pulls the blouse off her shoulder and kisses her neck.

Tom played the moment with eagerness and lust. But Elliot wanted something different. He told Tom, "Your character is fragile. Remember, just moments ago he was willing to end it all." Then Elliot demonstrated the way he wanted Tom to touch her. "Tentatively, as if she might not be real," he said, as he slowly pulled the blouse down and lightly touched Jill's shoulder. She shuddered involuntarily and he caught the moment. Looking directly at her, he said, "Yes, that's right, Jill. That's exactly the reaction I want."

He was haunting her again. She put the diaphragm box back and closed the cupboard. Instead of cleaning, she turned on the bathtub faucets, slipped out of her nightgown, and melted into the hot water. The sound of the water helped drive away the thought of him.

She didn't go back to bed. Instead, she dressed in a sundress that hugged her bodice and showed off her legs. She made coffee and sat at the kitchen table writing a letter to the children. When Martin came in, she looked up, longing to have him touch her, to notice her pretty dress. But he poured a cup of coffee, saying, "You'll never guess what I dreamed. *'Share and share alike, that's democracy.'* Remember? Ginger Rogers' mother made Dalton Trumbo cut that line out of *Tender Comrade*." He shook his head and reached for the newspaper.

He used to be her tender comrade, but now he barely noticed her.

Later that day, they shot the scene where Phoebe prepares to meet the soldier played by Tom. Elliot showed Jill how he wanted her to slowly undress, down to her slip. "Then," Elliot explained in a soft voice, "Phoebe sits on the edge of her bed and washes her legs and feet. It is a slow, sensual moment of anticipation."

It was completely quiet on the big sound stage as the crew watched Jill go to the mark Elliot had set for her in Phoebe's room. She slowly unbuttoned her blouse and slipped out of her skirt. She sat on the edge of the bed and peeled off her stockings. As she picked up the pitcher and poured water into the enamel bowl, she could feel Elliot's eyes on her and it made her heart pound.

Afterwards, in her dressing room, she found herself trembling. There was a knock, and she heard Elliot say, "It's me." She took a deep breath, pulled her robe tighter and opened the door.

He came in, sat down, and said simply, "God, you're sexy."

"So, it's working, then, what I'm doing with Phoebe?"

"She's inside you. I like what you're doing very much." He lit a cigarette and offered her one. She shook her head. He took a long drag and stared at her intently. "Let's stop playing games, Jill."

"What do you mean?"

"You know what I mean."

The room was small and suddenly terribly hot. He was sitting on the narrow cot. She was standing with her back to the door, facing him. There was only a short, highly charged distance between them. He put his hands on her hips and pulled her to him.

"Don't, Elliot," she said weakly.

"Am I right? Since the day we met." He pressed his face against her mound and she could feel his hot breath through her robe.

She pushed away. "I'm married," she said, her voice quivering. He shrugged his shoulders. "I know."

"You'd better go, Elliot."

"You can't deny what's going on, Jill."

She gathered all her strength and in a firm voice said, "For God's sake, don't!" She felt she might cry, and turned away. "Please, Elliot, you're getting me all confused."

He caught her panic and stood up. "Okay, okay. I'm sorry."

She dared to look at him. He looked back without lust. "I guess sometimes I get carried away." He opened the door. "Keep up the great work. Phoebe is perfect." And then he was gone.

She clutched the dressing table and looked into the mirror. What's happening to me? she thought.

26

Phyllis lived in a cottage in the small beach community of Venice. Her house was built at the turn of the century when Venice had been a popular resort, with thousands of visitors arriving daily by red car, the electric trolley that ran all the way from downtown to the beach. In its heyday, Venice boasted the finest amusement park on the Pacific coast: three roller coasters, fun houses, and dozens of places for a game of chance. There had been a bathhouse, band concerts, and a dance pavilion. It even had canals where the tides flowed through narrow outlets out to the sea and gondola excursions that cost a nickel. Charlie Chaplin, Fatty Arbuckle, and Mary Pickford kept summer homes there.

Then, a series of disasters cost Venice its grandeur: a terrible fire, a fatal influenza epidemic, the Great Depression, the plugging up of most of the canals to make room for roadways. Finally, the discovery of oil brought the eyesore of hundreds of oil wells. All that remained of its previous glory was a weather beaten pier and a promenade where vendors peddled salt-water taffy and candied apples, and shops sold coral beads and picture postcards. The population was an eclectic mix of Russian Jews, Mexican-Americans, Negroes, bohemians, and artists. With its clapboard houses, stucco apartments, oil derricks, and sandy beaches,

Venice was an anomaly in the midst of the greater urban sprawl that was Los Angeles.

Jill got out of her car and inhaled the salty sea air. Phyllis' house was one in a row of neat white cottages interspersed with tall, gangly palms, their pom-pom tops waving in a bright blue sky. On her knees in a vegetable patch, Phyllis waved a muddy hand when she saw Jill coming up the walk, clicking along in red mules and a wide red skirt that billowed out when a breeze caught it.

"It's already one o'clock?" Phyllis said, jumping up. "I got involved with my tomatoes. I'm trying to outsmart an enemy who's too much of a coward to show his face in daylight."

Jill took off a glove and examined a leaf. "You might plant marigolds. That'll keep away pests."

"Come in and tell me the rest of your secrets!" cried Phyllis, clearly delighted.

They sat on the sun porch in white wicker chairs and ate salad that had come straight from the garden: carrots, radishes, scallions, cucumbers, and three different kinds of lettuce. They sipped ice-tea and talked about the downhill turn the country had taken, the loss of their beloved Lab, Jill's work on the movie.

After lunch, Jill borrowed a pair of sandals and a wide straw hat and they walked down to the ocean. They passed arched colonnades, remnants of Venice's grander days. On the promenade, old women sat in babushkas speaking Yiddish and feeding breadcrumbs to the sea gulls.

They bought salt-water taffy and slipped off their sandals, walking barefoot across the expanse of sand. It was a warm day and sunbathers lay on blankets under umbrellas. Children ran in and out of the surf. The water sparkled green and blue.

Jill looked across the ocean to Catalina Island. She thought of Elliot's face, his sharp features, his blue eyes. The touch of his hands on her body.

"Phyllis," Jill began, searching for the right words.

Noting the change in her voice, Phyllis cocked an eyebrow. Jill dug her heels into the wet sand, watching the water pool around her ankles. "What do you think about married women having affairs?"

Phyllis' mouth dropped open. "How could you possibly?"

"Not me," Jill said quickly, starting to walk along the water's edge. "A friend of mine. She met this man."

"Well, I guess if her husband is a bastard, then—"

"No, no, it has nothing to do with her husband. She loves her husband."

Phyllis said, "If she loves her husband then why on earth would she want to do it? Look, honey, I'm not married so what do I know? But I wouldn't trust a man who goes after a married woman any further than I could throw a bull by his prick."

Jill gave a little laugh.

Then Phyllis looked right at her and said, "Tell your friend: if you play with fire, you get burned."

On the way home Jill realized why she'd driven all the way out to the beach: she needed someone to knock some sense into her. She was Jill Fullbright, married to Martin Levy, with two beautiful children and the beginning of a career as a screen actress. Phoebe was only a character created by a writer, brought to life by Jill, thanks to years of professional experience.

She returned to work the next day with confidence that she could keep the difference clear.

27

ELLIOT ASKED HER AND TOM up to his house to rehearse, hoping that maybe in a different setting, away from lights and cameras, they would discover a level of relaxation. He was frustrated with the way a crucial scene was playing. It was the love scene, and Jill and Tom were too self-conscious.

Jill was wearing a tight sleeveless sweater and a narrow red skirt. Even when she wasn't wearing what Wardrobe had chosen for Phoebe, Jill had begun to dress like her. She had even started putting in her diaphragm before she left for work thinking it would help her sink into Phoebe's "ever ready" mental attitude.

Elliot showed them the dailies on his home screen and they saw how rigid they were. They rehearsed the scene in his living room, on the white couch, Elliot showing Jill how he wanted her to recline, on her back, propping herself on her elbows. She felt her nipples harden beneath her sweater and it became difficult to concentrate on Elliot's words.

"That's it! Right there. Whatever you're feeling, use it now, as you look at Tom. Make him come to you with just a look."

When the rehearsal was over she was breathless and stirred up. Elliot offered them a drink and she was about to accept when Tom said, "I'd love to, Elliot, but I promised Kate I'd take her to dinner as soon as we were finished."

"Jill?" Elliot asked. She hesitated. "Lena moved out, you know. I could use a friend."

"All right, one drink."

He made strong Bloody Marys. She drank the first one quickly and by the second, began to relax. She fell easily into a conversation with him about the old days in New York, their time in the Party.

Elliot leaned against the door frame, swirling the ice in his glass. "We were so young and naive, trying to fight the good proletarian fight when we ourselves were middle class."

Jill was on the couch, her shoes off, her legs curled beneath her. "Yes, but who better than we?"

A smile crept over his face. "Us? That's rather presumptuous, don't you think? Look at the plays Martin wrote. Here he was, a Jewish intellectual writing plays that preached the overthrow of capitalism led by the downtrodden working class. You have to admit, that was a bit of a contradiction."

She was feeling the liquor. "I guess life comes with contradictions."

"Example?"

Then she just looked at him. It was part Bloody Mary and part hunger, pure and simple.

"Well?" he said in a low voice.

She said nothing, but did not look away.

He slowly crossed the wide expanse of cantaloupe carpet and sat beside her. The house hummed with emptiness.

Her heart was pounding. He held her gaze with his eyes as he slid his hand under her skirt.

NORMALLY SHE WOULD'VE undressed in their bedroom. But she was afraid of standing naked, afraid that if Martin saw her, he would know. So she undressed in the bathroom, dropping her undergarments into the hamper, vaguely worrying about the "evidence." She looked at herself in the mirror, searching for signs, markings on her flesh, which, thankfully, she did not find.

In the shower, she let the hot water pound on her head. She got out, powdered her entire body, and wrapped herself in a fluffy white robe. In the bedroom, Martin leaned in to kiss her, but she pulled away. "Martin, what are you—?"

"You're—I don't know. You look so beautiful. Is that a new perfume?"

Despite her shower, he had smelled it on her. She brushed past him and went to her bureau, opening a drawer and pulling out a pair of nylons.

"It's been so long since we made love," he said, loosening his tie.

Her stomach clenched. Why tonight of all nights? After all these weeks of lying next to each other. She plunged her hand into a stocking to check for runs. "Doesn't the premiere start at eight?"

"We have an hour."

She could barely keep the tremor out of her voice. "Oh, Martin, I don't think—"

"I'll drive fast," he laughed, turning down the bed covers.

She couldn't possibly get into bed with Martin. She'd feel like a whore.

"Honey?"

"Really, Martin, I'm not feeling well."

"I'll make you feel better." His voice was husky, full of yearning.

She couldn't plead cramps. She had finished her period last week, which Martin knew because she had sent him out for Kotex.

He went into the bathroom and came out holding her plastic diaphragm box. "Catch," he said, tossing it to her.

She gave a little gasp as she caught it. She imagined the goo of her diaphragm slowly oozing out of her at this very minute. Would it still work now against Martin's sperm? The image of Elliot's sperm and Martin's sperm swimming together inside her body made her sick.

Suddenly, there was a loud rapping at the front door.

"I'll get it," she said quickly, putting the diaphragm box on her bureau and tightening the sash on her robe.

Two men in gray suits stood on the porch. One wore sunglasses and carried a brief case. "Is Mr. Martin Levy at home?"

Jill nodded, a new cloud of worry scattering her other thoughts.

Martin stepped forward. "I am Martin Levy."

"Mr. Levy," the man said as he thrust a large brown envelope at Martin, "you are being served a subpoena to appear before the House Committee on Un-American Activities." Then the men turned and went down the path to their car.

Martin closed the door. Jill said, "My God, it's happened."

He sighed. "Come on. Let's get dressed."

She followed him into the bedroom. "I can't believe it. I just can't believe it's really happened to us."

"It was just a matter of time. I'll have to call Charlie's lawyer and—Jesus, now this damned premiere..."

"But Charlie's lawyer will advise against testifying. Maybe you need to get a different lawyer, one who can understand the nuances of this whole thing."

He turned to her. "You know perfectly well that I would never be a friendly witness."

"But you hate the Party!" Jill insisted, sitting on the bed as Martin paced. "Why can't you just tell the truth? Tell them you were once a communist but you haven't been for years and that you left on principle. That you share their feelings about communism."

"I do? I think communism is a dangerous and alien conspiracy?" He reached for his pack of cigarettes.

"But you are one of the most adamant opponents of the Party. That's what they want to hear. Why is it so compromising to tell them that?"

"The fact that I quit the Party has nothing to do with this." He lit his cigarette and exhaled. "All that matters to them is that I give them names. That's the only way I can prove my patriotism. I can't just pick and choose which questions to answer. Once I start talking about my political past, I have to keep talking. That's the deal."

"If you give them names that they've already got, what harm is there in that?"

He looked at her and said deliberately, "I will not collaborate with a bunch of racists and anti-Semites."

"It's just plain dumb to hand over your job and blow your career all in the name of politics."

"It has nothing to do with politics. It has to do with morality."

They fell silent. She looked out the window. The summer sun was low in the sky, casting a rosy glow over the garden. "Martin, the best thing you can do for yourself," she paused and said pointedly, "and for Millie and Nathan and me—is to come out of this thing alive."

"During the Spanish Inquisition Jews were murdered if they didn't repudiate their religion."

Her voice was agitated. "How will being unemployed help

your children learn these noble truths, Martin? Do you really want to destroy yourself over this particular progressive ideology—not giving names of people whose names they already have?!" She banged the bureau for emphasis and sent the diaphragm box flying. When it hit the floor, it popped open. She bent quickly to retrieve it, but Martin had seen.

"Where's your diaphragm?" he asked, bewildered.

She didn't answer.

"You were already wearing it?"

The box made a little click when she shut it.

"But I thought you didn't want to…"

She turned away. The air in the room thickened.

"Who?" he asked.

She began to cry. "Oh, Martin, it really doesn't—"

"Who, damnit! I think I have a right to know who my wife is screwing!" There was a ringing silence in the room. Then, in the same demanding voice, "Tom?"

She shook her head no. Tears streamed down her face.

And then he knew. "Oh, Jesus, Elliot…" He sank onto the bed. "For God's sake, Jill. I can't believe you let Elliot draw you into his web."

She turned to him. "Only one time."

Martin jumped as if someone had thrown ice water on him. His skin was flushed, his eyes wide. She expected him to slap her, but he only enunciated each syllable as if she might be deaf. "One time, fifty times, what's the difference? You crossed a line!"

"I know," she said in a small voice. She watched as he opened the closet and grabbed his hat. Then he turned to her and through clenched teeth said, "I'm going to the premiere of my movie. When I return, I want you gone."

"Gone? You can't mean that!"

"You better damn well believe that I mean it!"

"Listen, Martin. It had nothing to do with you, with you and me. It's the film, the way Phoebe is, I got confused between—"

"I don't want to hear it!" He looked directly into her eyes with a flash of hatred that made him a stranger. "I want you gone by the time I get back."

Then he stormed out, slamming the door behind him.

My God, she thought, what have I done?

28

MARTIN DROVE DOWN Cahuenga in a daze. He had intended to change into his black suit and put on a fresh shirt. He touched his tie to make sure he had one on. He couldn't recall when he'd made the knot. Now it felt uncomfortably tight, like a noose. He pulled it apart and tried to concentrate on the road.

It occurred to him that he could turn right on Sunset instead of left. He could go directly to Elliot's, barge into his house, and tear him limb from limb. Physically, Martin was no match for Elliot. But he figured that what he lacked in muscle and girth he'd make up for in rage. He imagined Elliot standing by his pool, trying to explain away his treachery. But then he saw Jill by his side and suddenly the melodrama of it all produced a bitter laugh. This was the very stuff he spent day after day banging out on his typewriter. Waves of regret washed over him. He had spent too much time looking at his typewriter and not enough looking at his wife. When had she first begun to slip away?

He left his car with the attendant and started toward the theater, then realized that he couldn't possibly sit through the movie. He walked down a side street and wandered the neighborhood, going over and over the events of the past hour. When he figured the movie was over, he returned and stood in the back of the darkened theater watching Bette Davis, suitcase in hand, close the door behind her and walk away from the school forever. A mist fell on the narrow street. A small dog trotted by her side. Martin mouthed her last line with her: "Tomorrow is another day, Angie. And it looks like the rain has finally stopped." He wished he could feel an ounce of the optimism he had created for Davis' character.

The party at Chasen's served as a distraction, with its flow of champagne and high spirits. He made excuses for his wife's absence and as soon as he was certain that the requisite number of people had noted his presence, he left.

Alone in his car again, his fury took over. Elliot. His old friend, his old pal, his old comrade. He imagined pummeling him. But he knew he wouldn't. Martin was not cut out for such drama; he was only good at writing it.

There was one thing he could do. Something that would hurt Elliot far more than a good thrashing. Something that would kill his career and his appetite for other men's wives. A logical way to even the playing field. Martin could give Elliot's name to the Committee. The thought brought him pleasure. How to destroy a man—just utter his name. It was poetic, the perfect payback.

He got out of the car and let himself into the house, feeling lightheaded. He flipped on the hallway light and, as the quiet of the house settled on him, he could feel his spirits gradually sink. She was gone.

He wandered aimlessly from room to room in the semi-darkness. Suddenly, he was overcome with exhaustion. He collapsed onto the living room couch. He wanted a drink but doubted he had the strength to stand. Naming Elliot would not bring Jill back. Besides, he couldn't name only Elliot; if he gave them one name, he'd have to give them all the names.

He closed his eyes and a shard of memory pricked his consciousness. He couldn't have been more than five. His brother Daniel had just joined the navy and there was a party to give him a proper send-off before he took on Kaiser Wilhelm. Daniel looked very smart in his uniform—the wide pants, the red tie. He had let Martin wear his white cap. Martin was running on the street with his brother's cap playing war with another boy, Solly. They came upon a real soldier, sleeping on a bench. They stopped their play and studied him. His collar was crooked and a trickle of saliva ran down his chin. Solly plucked the cap from the sleeping man's head. Martin was shocked and insisted he put it back, but Solly was already skipping down the block.

Martin bolted upstairs and ran breathlessly into the apartment. His mother was playing the piano and the table and chairs had been pushed against the wall and everybody was dancing—Uncle Rudy and Aunt Ida and his brother Daniel and Daniel's sweetheart, Esther. His father came out of the kitchen holding a piece of strudel. "Ah, here's my dancing partner," he said when he noticed Martin.

"Pop! Pop!" cried Martin. "Solly pinched a soldier's cap right off his head because he was asleep and didn't—"

"Wait, boychek, tell me slowly."

After Martin had described Solly's naughty act in great detail, his father stared at him a long time. His mother stopped the piano and everyone got quiet. His father said in a somber voice, "What Solly did is between Solly and God."

"But, Solly is a thief and—"

"Are you God?"

Martin slowly shook his head no.

"Let there be no hope for those who turn one into the authorities. *La malshinin al tehi tikvah.*"

"Make it plain, Tateh," Daniel said.

His father turned to Daniel, his voice beginning to rise in anger. "It's in every prayer service, part of the eighteen benedictions. He should know it by heart."

"He's only a kid, Tateh." Then Daniel knelt in front of Martin. "Jews don't snitch on their pals, Martin. Do you understand?"

He had understood.

He opened his eyes and gazed at the shadows on the wall, which jumped every time a car passed on the street. He knew that the Jews didn't have a corner on this ethic. In what religion was being an informer considered honorable? Tongues had been cut out for nothing less. Nobody likes a rat.

So he would face the Committee and swallow their degradation. He would be dropped by the studio and no doubt dropped by some of his friends. He would have to figure out a way to feed his family. It would be hell, but he would get through it. Compared to his buddies who gave their lives in Spain, his would be a modest sacrifice.

Thinking of Spain brought back the warm memory of Jill's loyalty during that terrible year and a half. He absentmindedly rubbed his bum leg. He would never have made it without her. He choked back a sob. How could she do this to him now, when he needed her so much?

29

AFTER MARTIN LEFT THE HOUSE, Jill sprung into a flurry of activity, sobbing all the while. She pulled down a suitcase, stuffed in summer dresses, heels, hose, and slips. She thrust her makeup and earrings into her pocketbook and threw everything into the back of the station wagon.

It was a clear, warm night. The sun wasn't long gone and the sky glowed a violet-blue. She drove too fast. Patti Page was on the radio, singing in her country twang: *"Detour, there's a muddy road ahead. Detour, paid no mind to what it said..."*

It was true. Jill had paid no mind to the danger signs. She had played with fire and now she was feeling the burn. But she was feeling something else besides. Deep down, under the pain and confusion, was something raw and mysterious that compelled her. A deeply erotic, frightening curiosity. Something beyond her control was driving her toward Elliot.

She found him sitting on a chaise lounge lit by the blue green light from the pool. She went to him and just stood there holding her purse. He looked up. "Christ, what happened? You look like hell."

In a hoarse whisper she said, "Martin's been named."

"Oh," he said, sounding relieved. And then, "Not you?"

She realized with a jolt that if she had been named, *Stranger*

At the Gate would be in jeopardy. She sank down onto the bottom of his chaise lounge. "I wonder why I was spared."

"Whoever named Martin knows you're working. It was the friendly part of the 'friendly' testimony."

She let that sink in, wondering for the first time who had named Martin.

"I assume he'll take the Fifth?"

"We argued about that. It feels to me as if we're innocent bystanders getting splattered by the mud."

"It's rotten. The whole thing stinks."

"He's so stubborn."

"I see. So you stormed out of the house. I'm only a rest-stop in a domestic dispute."

She took a breath. "I told him about us."

He flashed her a look. "That was stupid, Jill."

He reached for a cigarette and lit it. He inhaled deeply and said wryly, "We're in trouble now, aren't we?" He drew her to him. She collapsed against his chest, feeling the warmth of his body. "Don't worry, we'll get through this."

They lay for a few moments and then he said, "C'mon, why don't you jump in the pool. It'll clear your head. I'll fix you a drink."

He went into the house and she began to undress. She considered leaving on her brassiere and girdle, but realized there was no longer a need for such modesty. She stood naked on the diving board a moment before plunging in, then swam the length of the pool and back, again and again until her muscles ached. She welcomed the fatigue. Then, breathless, she pulled a plastic raft toward her and climbed onto her back. There was no moon and the stars sparkled in a night sky the color of licorice. The warm air licked her nipples.

"You couldn't stay away, could you?" he said, with a hint of smug satisfaction.

She came off the float and watched him dive into the water. He swam over, brushing up against her. He pinned her against the side of the pool. "There's only one thing to do with a girl like you," and he pried open her legs with his thigh. The cool chlorine water rushed in and mixed with her own hot juices.

She slept a dreamless sleep and woke late staring out at the terrace and beyond to the pool. Pink bougainvillaea spilled over the iron grillwork and tangled with the climbing roses. A mocking bird was calling its mate. Or maybe it was calling someone else's mate.

Elliot had risen before dawn and would be on the set all day. She wasn't due until noon. She felt strange being here, in his bed. But lying in his arms through the night had brought her comfort. She had simply surrendered to what was happening.

She stretched out between the silky sheets and looked up at the pale wood ceiling that sloped at an angle. The room had a feeling of a Mondrian painting—angular and sparse. Glass ran the length of one wall catching the eastern light, opening to the terrace. Opposite was a walk-in closet. On the wall facing the bed was a lone picture, a nineteenth-century Japanese print in muted reds and ochres, surrounded by a thin gold frame. At first look, it appeared to be three children playing on swings, but as Jill studied it, the image became clearer. One girl was in fact on a swing, but her kimono was open and another girl was pushing her into the engorged penis of a man, his colorful robes in a tangle.

It shocked Jill, then amused her. It brought to mind another picture in another room from long ago. It was in her mother and father's bedroom. Jill was sick and to comfort her, her mother had permitted her to spend the sick days in her own large bed. Staying in her mother and father's bed had felt like a covert act and filled Jill with guilty pleasure.

Feverish and achy, Jill would roll off the place where it had grown damp from perspiration onto a fresh, cool place. She counted the squares on the quilt that her mother had stitched in what was called a wedding ring pattern. She buried her face in the pillows, hoping to catch her mother and father's distinctive smell, but the camphor her mother had rubbed onto her chest cancelled any other scent. She spent hours in a sleepy fog, staring at the picture on the wall facing her, a naked girl on a swing against a watery blue sky, leaning back against gravity's pull, her golden hair flying out behind her.

Jill ran her fingers through her hair. A couple of strands clung to her hand and for a moment she didn't recognize the platinum hair as belonging to her. There was much about herself that she did not recognize. She was in another man's bed, leaving her scent on his sheets. It was as if she had slipped into someone else's skin. Maybe Elliot was right. The panther-like Phoebe was growling inside her. Like the Hans Hoffman painting in Elliot's living room, Phoebe was the wild part of herself struggling to get out from under the determined rectangle that society and habit had imposed.

30

SHE AND ELLIOT NEVER discussed their arrangement. Jill was simply there and it suited them both. She expected that he might want to be with other women, but he said she was woman enough for him. On the set, they were strictly professional. Even the man who did her makeup didn't guess. But the knowledge of Elliot's lust for her fueled her work with Tom, and she turned in a strong performance.

She spoke with Martin periodically. Their conversations were civilized, polite; he held his rage in check. He reported that his parents were in favor of his decision to take the Fifth; they understood that even in America rights must be fought for. He dutifully forwarded letters from the children. Nathan and Millie were having a ball. It was their best summer vacation ever.

She felt as if she were on summer holiday, too. She didn't really think past the next day, the next scene in the movie. Then one afternoon she passed a toy store and noticed in the window a stuffed rabbit like Nathan's, and she felt a guilty tug at her heart. What would happen when they returned in a month? She pushed the thought from her mind.

As the completion of the movie drew near, however, the shadow of her children loomed larger over her life. She thought of them all the time. She couldn't get rid of the worry that gnawed at her. On the last day of shooting, she called New York. It was early in the morning and she was sitting on the edge of Elliot's bed putting on mascara, listening to Millie's excited report of her activities.

"Bubbie's teaching me to play piano and today I learned a song with both hands!"

"That's wonderful, sweetheart."

"Can I talk to Daddy now?"

The mascara was a sudden black smear on her cheek. She choked out the words. "Daddy's not here."

"Can we get a piano? Will you ask him?"

"Yes, I'll ask him, it's a good idea. I'll ask him."

"When he gets home?"

"Yes, that's right."

After she hung up she was shaking. It was a torment trying to hold the disparate parts of herself together.

THE WRAP PARTY FOR TALENT and crew took place on a cavernous sound stage where the theme was V-E DAY, and the buoyant atmosphere of a World War II victory party had been simulated. The art department had used props from the movie to decorate the place along with balloons, streamers, confetti, and ice buckets of champagne. V-Discs filled the room and couples danced to the sounds of Glen Miller's "Tail End Charlie." On a large screen a reel of outtakes ran in one continuous, hilarious loop.

The wardrobe mistress, a puffy woman with a helmet of tight gray curls, wandered over to Jill carrying a flute of champagne. "This movie will make you a star, honey!"

"I hope you're right, Mrs. Billington."

"I've been in the business since before talkies, and I can always spot the ones that'll make it."

"You made me look the part, Mrs. Billington. I'm indebted to you."

Jill went over to Harry, the cameraman, a big bear of a man who seldom smiled. "I hope we can work together again," she said.

"That's a nice compliment," he said. "I hope for your sake the offers start rolling in." He lowered his voice, "I read about your husband in the paper."

"It's a crazy world, Harry." She raised her glass. " That's why we have to celebrate when we can."

Her co-star came up behind her and seized her wrist as he whispered into her hair, "So, my little tart. And all along I thought you were just *acting* in our scenes. Now I know it was Elliot making you blush with desire."

She wriggled free and looked at him. The jaunty sounds of the Andrew Sisters boomed the "Victory Polka" and made it difficult to hear. "What are you talking about, Tom?"

His eyes twinkled. "Your secret is safe with me, darling," he murmured and drifted into the party, turning every few steps to wag a finger at her.

So, their affair was now public knowledge. In a way, it was a relief. It wasn't a secret from Martin, so who was she protecting? Now that the movie was over, let them say what they wished. It was all part of the way Hollywood worked.

Elliot glided by, his arm around the waist of the script girl. Jill smiled. All part of the Hollywood scenario.

Martin's hearing was in three days. Jill called early in the morning from Elliot's kitchen. "Do you want me there?" she asked.

"What for, Jill? So the press can document your wifely support?"

She took a breath. "Should I come or not?"

"It'll be televised. I'm sure Elliot has a television in his bedroom."

In spite of his sarcasm, she decided to go. She dressed in a navy linen suit and thought she'd wear her hair swept up for a more dignified look. Searching through her bag for something to hold it in place, among the bobby pins and lipsticks were the ivory combs. She touched their smooth surface and felt a stab of sorrow.

The Federal Building was an old building with a dirty stone facade. Reporters crowded the wide steps creating a gauntlet for anyone trying to gain entry. Rumor of Jill's forthcoming movie had already made her a minor celebrity; the press was waiting for her along with a swarm of curious onlookers.

Cameras flashed in her face and before she could find refuge in the hearing room itself, she was barraged with questions: Was her husband a commie? Was he going to cooperate? Would she stand by him no matter what?

She had almost made it to the heavy swinging doors, when a little man in a black hat thrust a microphone in her face and demanded, "What's your advice to young actresses about the casting couch?"

She was perplexed, completely missing the subtext of his question. When he saw her bewilderment, he put it more bluntly. "Isn't it true you're having an affair with your director?"

The question stung and she felt herself go red. This is what they want, she told herself, to watch me be humiliated. Her name and Elliot's were now linked; they had become the subject of whispered conversations. Her thoughts flew to Martin inside the building, and she had the sudden urge to run to him for protection.

She ducked the microphone and made her way to the marble-tiled corridor with its vaulted ceiling and WPA murals. Inside the hearing room newsreel and television camera crews were setting up equipment. The glare of their lights along with the overhead fluorescent lights made everything bright and hot. There was a stale odor that two ceiling fans did little to eradicate. A picture of President Truman hung on one wall and one of George Washington on the other. Spectators crowded onto long wooden benches fanning themselves against the oppressive heat. Others hovered along the walls between the tall square columns. The room buzzed with ghoulish expectation.

Jill squeezed onto one of the benches and removed her gloves, looking around for Martin. He was up front next to a man she didn't recognize, his lawyer perhaps. Martin was wearing a new blue serge suit. His hat sat on the table in front of him next to a pile of papers. She couldn't see his face, but from the way he was hunched over the table, she knew he was tense. He turned briefly, taking in the sea of faces. It startled her to see that he'd grown a beard. She tried to catch his eye with a little wave. He waved back, and she relaxed a little, but then realized that his wave was not for her. She turned and saw Alvah Bessie and Charlie Fisher. Alvah made eye contact with her, and then looked away. Charlie sent daggers.

On a raised platform in front of Martin was a long table where the Congressmen and their counsel were settling themselves. At eleven o'clock the gavel came down to bring the hearing to order. Chairman John S. Wood, Congressman from Georgia, was a lean man with a blotchy, pinched face. Rather than be unnerved by the photographers and the press, he seemed to bask in their attention. He smiled frequently, showing a row of gleaming teeth. He began by solicitously asking the photographers to please try not to disturb the proceedings and then turned his attention to Martin. He requested that his lawyer identify himself, then asked Martin to raise his right hand and swear to tell the truth.

Congressman Doyle, an older man with a paternal smile, verified the correct spelling of Martin's name, where and when he was born, and his current address. Doyle's shock of white hair gave him a grandfatherly look and his gentle smile made it seem as if they were all gathered for a family celebration. He interviewed Martin about his educational training, his employment history, which radio shows he wrote, which company published his book, what studios he worked for, what movies he'd written.

The questions and answers were proceeding so smoothly, so politely, that Jill began to imagine that Martin could escape the punishment of a blacklist. Then, out of the Doyle's mouth shot a question that made her dizzy.

Doyle didn't even look up from his notes when he said, "Mr. Levy, in the course of your time living and working in Hollywood, were you ever acquainted with a Mr. Elliot Cooper?"

Jill held her breath.

Martin leaned over and consulted with his attorney. Then he straightened up and mopped his brow with a handkerchief and said forcefully, "I decline to answer that question on the grounds of the First Amendment to the Constitution of the United States."

Jill sighed in relief. Then, she became troubled. Why had Martin invoked the First Amendment instead of the Fifth? Did he want to go to jail? She wished she had asked him about his legal strategy.

Donald Jackson, a pale Congressman from California with

sharp features and a menacing tone, asked the next question. "Mr. Kyle Livingston testified that you and Mr. Cooper were seen at a fund-raising function for the Joint Anti-Fascist Refugee Committee in December of 1943. Were you at this function?"

Martin said, "Again, I must refuse to answer on the same grounds."

Jackson said, "I have before me a photostatic copy of a letter of October 24, 1945, on the stationery of the Spanish Refugee Appeal of the Joint Anti-Fascist Refugee Committee, on which appears a list of sponsors." He passed the paper to Martin. "Will you examine the letterhead, please, and state whether or not you see your name as one of the sponsors?"

Martin didn't even look at the paper. "I decline to answer the question on the same Constitutional grounds."

Jackson continued, "Here is a photostatic copy of a 1939 issue of *The Daily Worker*. In a column entitled, '*Why This War?*' your name appears as the author. Isn't *The Daily Worker* the official organ of the Communist Party?"

The litany of questions seemed endless. Each time, in the same monotone, Martin refused to answer. Finally, not hiding his exasperation, the chairman scowled and said, "Mr. Levy, our country is in real danger from the enemy from within. You can prove your patriotism by helping us flush out that enemy."

Martin didn't blink. "Mr. Wood, if it is un-American activities you are interested in, I would like to direct your attention to the injustices being perpetrated every day in the South where Ku Klux Klansmen have defaced property and taken lives."

An agitated rumble in the crowd caused the chairman to pound his gavel. He gave Martin a withering look and said with mock patience, "Mr. Levy, this is a Congressional hearing into the conspiracy in the entertainment industry. You are here to give us information that will enable us to do the work that was assigned to us by the House of Representatives, to investigate subversive activities in the United States. All we're asking you to do is tell the truth."

Martin said plainly, "I am most willing to tell the truth about my life and my work. But I am not going to answer any questions as to my associations, or to my philosophical, my religious, or my political beliefs. These are improper questions for any American to be asked or made to answer."

"Mr. Levy," said Doyle, "let's get right to the sixty-four-dollar question. Are you now or have you ever been a member of the Communist Party of the United States?"

"I refuse to answer the question on the previous grounds."

Jill was agitated. Why wasn't he claiming the Fifth?

The chairman asked Doyle, "Has the witness declined to answer this specific question?"

Doyle nodded. "He said he's not going to answer any questions, give any names or anything."

Martin raised his voice. "If I may, sir, I would like to give my reasons for my answers."

Chairman Wood said, "Make it quick, Mr. Levy. Other witnesses are waiting."

Glancing at his notes Martin said, "I refuse to answer these questions because I feel they are an invasion of my rights and through me an invasion of the rights of all citizens in our country. My political beliefs are not secret. They are *private*. To answer these questions would be to admit that you had the right to ask them, and I do not concede to you this right. I will not be a party to the destruction of the basic American freedom—

freedom of thought. I believe democracy is strong enough to withstand all kinds of thought. Even dissident thought can throw light on the truth."

His voice rang out in the chambers with force and certitude. Jill saw not the man with a bald spot and a soft belly, but the man who once roused street corner crowds during the Great Depression, a man who put his life on the line to fight fascism in Spain. She heard that same unwavering conviction. In the pit of her stomach, she felt the same pull to him she'd felt so many years ago when he'd taken her to the Automat for lunch.

The crowd had broken into an uproar. Jackson spoke above the din. "Sir, it is apparent that you are assigning the First Amendment as legal grounds for refusing to answer the question. Now, do you have any other legal grounds upon which you claim a right to refuse?"

Yes, she whispered. Say yes.

"Yes, I have other grounds. I refuse to answer this question on my own highest sense of morality, which will not permit me—"

"Mr. Levy, that is not a legal reason."

"I believe this committee has entered into a conspiracy—"

"Mr. Levy, your opinion of this committee is not a reason for your standing on your rights to refuse to testify. Now please proceed," Jackson said, not hiding his irritation.

"I am trying to give my reasons."

"Well, Sir, you may not like my necktie, but that is not a legal reason. Now, I am asking you again if you have any Constitutional grounds upon which you desire to base your refusal to answer. I will object to anything except Constitutional grounds."

Martin conferred with his lawyer again and then said, "I further decline to answer this question on the grounds of the

Fifth Amendment to the Constitution, with specific reference to that portion which states that no one may be compelled to be a witness against himself."

Jill breathed easy again. At least he wouldn't go to jail.

Martin continued, "I believe this committee has colored the way people think about patriotism and—"

Jackson interrupted him, his tone harsh. "Patriotism comes in many colors, Mr. Levy, but red is not one of them." Then turning to the chairman, he said, "Mr. Chairman, having assigned the Fifth Amendment as a basis for his right to refuse to answer the question, I see no reason to pursue this inquiry."

Chairman Wood said brusquely, "You are excused, Mr. Levy."

With that, he pounded his gavel and waved his hand at Martin, shooing him away as if he were a smelly barnyard animal.

Martin put on his hat and walked stiffly toward the big swinging doors with deliberate steps, his chin thrust forward. Flashbulbs popped wildly.

He noticed Jill. With a slight incline of his head, he seemed only to say, "I see you."

31

ELLIOT WAS IN NEW YORK and wouldn't be back until the afternoon. Jill had spent a restless night and had just fallen into a deep sleep when the alarm went off. She dragged herself out of bed and tried to concentrate on today's meeting with her agent. She was a jumble of nerves, distracted by the hearing and the look on Martin's face when he had seen her.

She leaned against the elevator wall of the William Morris Agency, trying to clear her mind. Gerald Fisk's office was at the end of a long carpeted corridor flanked by movie posters. His secretary, a fair-haired girl with a bright smile, called her boss on the inter-com. "Miss Fullbright is here, Sir."

Jill remembered sitting at the kitchen table with Martin defending the use of Fullbright in Elliot's film. She argued that Fullbright wasn't only her maiden name; it was her stage name, her professional name. Martin saw her logic but felt that now that they had children, why not use her married name? It would save the children and their teachers any confusion. When she insisted, he accused her of a deeper resistance. "Levy is too Jewish, isn't it?" At the time, she was offended. But now, hearing "Fullbright," she realized Levy did sound too Jewish.

Why couldn't she admit that at the time? It didn't mean she was anti-Semitic; it meant that she wasn't willing to test how deep anti-Semitism ran in the movie industry. Neither was Danny Kaye. Or Melvin Douglas, or Edward G. Robinson. It was common knowledge that having a Jewish name was no asset for an actor or actress. She'd won the argument, but it had created tension between them.

The secretary's voice slashed through her thoughts. "Go right in, Miss Fullbright."

Gerald Fisk was a tall man with a goatee and a nervous habit of repeating himself. He greeted her with an ebullient clasp of her hands. "Good news, Jill, very good news! Drinks are in order!" He went to a cabinet and pulled out a decanter. His office had a modern look, decorated in shades of pale turquoise accented with orange. The windows looked out onto a quiet street off the main bustle of Beverly Hills. A single maple tree brushed against the glass.

Gerald poured her a drink and the first gulp landed in the pit of her stomach like a stone at the bottom of an empty well. It made her light-headed and calmed her jangled nerves.

"What are we celebrating?" she asked, taking a seat on the long aqua divan.

Gerald sat next to her, bubbling with excitement. "Dore Schary wants to extend your contract! Seven years. Seven years! D'ya know what that means, honey? He's trying to tie you up. You're gold, sweetheart, real gold."

Jill sipped her drink, nodding agreeably, trying to absorb the implication of his words, trying to keep thoughts of Martin from intruding.

"Arnold Keating is directing a mystery called *Mulberry House*. And, honey, they want you for the female lead! Opposite Alan Ladd!"

She snapped to attention. She was being paired with a real movie star.

"God, Gerald."

"They love you! This is big. Really big." He went to his desk and found the script. "Shooting begins in a month," he said. He handed her the script and, clapping her on the back, exclaimed, "Congratulations! I'm so happy for you. For us both!"

SHE WAS SURPRISED TO FIND Elliot in his study, stretched out shirtless on the leather couch, his arm flopped over his forehead as if he were shielding his eyes from bright lights. But the drapes were closed and the room was dark. Scripts lay in heaps everywhere. There was a mahogany writing table and behind it, tacked to the wall, were snapshots, sketches, pages ripped from magazines. Another wall held framed posters advertising *A Dance With Danger*, *Shadow Park*, and *Sailor's Delight*. There were black-and-white photographs: Elliot behind the camera, Elliot with his arm around Lana Turner, Elliot talking with Henry Fonda.

She wasn't sure if he was awake. "You got back early," she said.

"Umm," he mumbled, not moving.

"They've extended my contract."

"I expected they would," he said, not looking at her.

"I'll be working with Alan Ladd. Can you believe that?" He said nothing. "How was New York?"

"Hot."

She suddenly felt very hot herself and more than a little disappointed at his lack of interest in her good news. She went to the liquor cabinet and thought about pouring a glass of tonic, but reached for the bourbon instead. She sat at the writing table on the high-backed swivel chair. "Martin took the Fifth."

"Naturally."

She heaved a heavy sigh. "How am I going to explain all this to Millie and Nathan?"

Elliot didn't answer. She absently fingered the papers on his desk as she sipped her drink. Then something caught her eye. A large brown envelope. The light was dim and she couldn't make out the return address but its size and shape were familiar: it was like the envelope that had been handed to Martin on that day when all their lives had changed.

"Have you been subpoenaed, Elliot?"

"That's right."

"Oh, Elliot," she went to the couch and knelt down, touching his cheek. It was stubbled and his face looked gaunt and hollow.

"Save it," he said tersely, brushing her hand away. He got up and went to pour himself a drink.

"What will you do?" she asked.

"You can be sure I'm not going to chuck my career to defend a political point of view that revolts me." His voice was harsh and his eyes darted around the room as he spoke.

"So you'll cooperate?"

He knocked back the drink and poured another. "I met in closed session yesterday."

"Yesterday? But you were in...that's why you went to New York?"

He nodded, fixing his gaze on the photographs of himself.

"Why didn't you tell me?"

"I am telling you."

There was a long pause. Jill lowered herself to the couch and put her glass on the floor.

"I gave secret testimony. No reporters. No publicity."

"So you gave names?"

"The trouble is, nobody's looking at the big picture. In ten years, this will be a shabby footnote in history, but I will have made ten more films. I'm in a position of power. I won't give that up voluntarily. It's easy for Martin. A writer can always write. But what's a director supposed to do?"

He swallowed the rest of his drink. "Of course I gave names."

He was leaning against the bar top, making tiny circles with his finger on his forehead, a gesture Jill had never seen before. His shoulders drooped, his head was bowed and, for a moment, Jill glimpsed how he would look as an old man.

"Whose names?"

"What does it matter?"

"Carol and Ray?"

"Of course."

"Mine?"

"No. I didn't give them yours." He glanced at her. "I want to make another picture with you."

"How many names did you give?"

"There's no difference between giving one or giving one hundred and eighteen."

"One hundred and eighteen? God, Elliot." One hundred and eighteen lives, she thought. "Was Martin's one of them?"

"Yes, I gave them Martin's. They already had it. What difference does it make?"

It made no real difference. Martin's name was already going on the blacklist. But something caved in her chest.

He said, "I had to clear my name."

She drew herself up, suddenly very tired.

He continued, "I'm no saint like Martin. You've always known that. It's what attracts you to me."

She dragged herself into the bedroom. She was exhausted. She stared at the bed, but she couldn't get in. Her hunger for him was gone.

She went onto the terrace. The air was hot and dry. The sun beat down from a high, white sky. The pool glimmered azure. She stretched out on the flagstone and could feel the heat of the stones through her linen suit. She thought about taking off her jacket but her body had already begun to let go, as if she were lying on sand, not hard stone.

Did Elliot have a dark motive? Did he want to rub salt in a wound he had already inflicted on Martin? She knew Elliot was guiltless in that regard. Giving Martin's name to the Committee was done simply to help Elliot. Everything Elliot did, in fact, was to help Elliot, just as he had helped himself to Martin's wife. Not that she hadn't made it easy for him; she was fully aware of her part. So why was she surprised at Elliot's behavior? She had always known that he was incapable of caring about anything beyond his own interests. The only principle that governed his actions was: will this help me? But, what to her had once seemed bold and ambitious now seemed weak and selfish. When Martin had first told her he would be taking the Fifth, she couldn't believe he would do such a thing to his family. Now she realized he had done it not to them, but *for* them. She pictured Martin as she'd seen him yesterday—his new suit, his beard. The Committee had robbed him of his livelihood, but when he walked out of that hearing room, he still had his dignity.

She and Martin had traveled such a long distance together and had finally claimed a secure life. She had not wanted to face the disruption the blacklist would bring. But now, lying here with the sun pounding down, she realized that eventually she would have come to hate him if he had made any other choice.

She remembered a line from *Rocket to the Moon* that precisely described her in relation to Martin. She was tied to him, *"attached underground by a hundred different roots."* A deep longing for him took hold of her and she was overcome by the sudden urgency to leave Elliot's house.

32

SHE ROLLED DOWN THE CAR window, trying to catch a breeze. For two months, she had been under water, dependent on an oxygen tank powered by Elliot's breath. The world above—her husband and children—had been only distant echoes. Now she had surfaced and everything was altered. It seemed that the very look of things had the vividness of Technicolor.

As she began the gentle descent through the canyon that separated Beverly Hills from the sprawling San Fernando Valley, she imagined a bath. Even though it was a blistering hot day, she wanted desperately to fill her own bathtub with scalding water and soak in it for the rest of the afternoon. She wanted to put her things back in her drawers. She wanted to simply sit at her kitchen table and drink a cup of coffee. Mostly, she ached to put her arms around her husband and beg his forgiveness. The simple things she had taken for granted and cast off so easily presented themselves now as precious gifts. But she knew that she had lost her claim to them.

She turned onto Mountain View. The Chinese elms arched over the street creating a welcome bit of shade. When she first saw their front yard she thought it was a weird play of shadows, but then she gasped as she recognized the unmistakable shape of a swastika. It was so large it could have been seen from the sky.

She parked by the curb and stared in disbelief at what someone had dared to burn into their lawn.

She got out of the car and looked up and down the street. It was quiet. Had their neighbors seen this thing being done? Then, with horror, she realized it might have been one of them! She looked at Mrs. Murdoch's house. What did she really know about any of the people who lived on this block?

She ran inside calling, "Martin!"

She found him at his desk in the study, his shirttails outside his pants, his necktie hanging loose. He looked up, his eyes glazed and distant.

"Martin! Did you see?!"

"I know," he said, his voice flat.

"Do know who did it?"

He shook his head. "No idea."

"Did you phone the police?"

"They took a report, but what can they do?"

"So horrible..." she said, trailing off.

She dropped her purse onto the window-seat and stared out at the singed grass. A swastika. The symbol of the very thing Martin had staked his life against. She looked back at him. There didn't seem to be any more to say about it.

She sat down. "That was quite a circus yesterday."

He nodded, waiting for her to go on.

She looked at him levelly. "You came off well. Stuck to your guns."

He snorted. "They wouldn't let me finish my statement."

"Kyle Livingston gave you away? I don't even know who that is."

"Someone from my early days in the Party."

She couldn't get used to his beard. It made him look older, more distinguished. She glanced at the paperwork in front of him. "Are you writing?"

"Bills." His tone was cool and dispassionate. He turned his attention back to his desk.

"They extended my contract. The offer came from Dore Schary himself."

Martin gave her a sharp look.

"Can't you be a little happy for me?

"Dore Schary sanctioned the blacklist. How happy can I be?"

She noticed a stain on his shirt pocket. She wondered how he was getting his laundry done. He was probably sending it out and that thought brought a stab of pain. The idea that he'd have to pay someone to wash his shirts.

She took a deep breath and announced, "It's over with Elliot."

"Is it?" he said, not even glancing up.

She came over and stood by him. "It's been a crazy, kind of unreal time." She searched for the right words. "Playing the part of Phoebe...the way she...I was an idiot to run to Elliot, of all people. I'm ashamed of myself, Martin."

He stopped writing and turned to her. "Jill, what do you want?"

"I know I hurt you."

"And?"

"And...I feel awful. About the whole thing." She took a breath. "The children will be here in couple of weeks. Can't we put all of this behind us?"

He took off his glasses and wiped them thoughtfully with his shirttail. How many times she'd seen him do that. Watching him now, as he collected his thoughts, she was flooded with love.

"I don't think so, Jill. I don't think I can put this behind us.

I have no idea what 'us' is anymore."

"It'll take some time to find out. But, it's worth it, don't you think?"

He got up and crossed the room to where a pile of newspapers lay on a hassock. He picked up several and waved them in the air. "My name's all over the papers. My agent has dropped me. I'm out of a job. Nazis are burning my lawn. I have a few other things on my mind right now."

"Let me help."

He looked at her with hard eyes. Then he picked up her purse and handed it to her. "You'd better go."

He went back to his desk.

"I think if we just sat down and—"

He turned to her. "It's too late." He picked up his pen.

The conversation was over.

She walked to the station wagon trying to order her thoughts. She was shaking. In spite of the heat, she felt cold. She needed a plan. Where could she go? She thought of Phyllis, but a rush of shame made her eliminate that possibility. She suddenly saw herself from Phyllis' perspective. She had made a cuckold of her husband. She couldn't face anyone who knew them as a couple. She certainly couldn't go to Elliot's friends.

She got into the car, sapped of all energy. She gazed out at the lawn again and this time her eye skipped over the swastika and came to rest on her roses. They had grown leggy and brown, nothing but rose hips. Where were her precious roses? How had she allowed this to happen? A lump of regret grew in her throat. "My God," she whispered, "oh, my God." She collapsed onto the steering wheel, her body heaving with sobs.

She ran back to the house, tears streaming down her face.

She found him in the kitchen, ripping open a carton of Lucky Strikes. He glanced up but said nothing.

"Please, Martin," she begged.

"You think you can just waltz back in here—" he sputtered.

"I acted recklessly. I was wrong. You have to forgive me."

He gazed at her unmoved. "No, Jill. I don't."

"But what about everything we've worked for all these years? What about our plans? Our dreams?"

"You killed them."

It felt like an actor's nightmare; she was in the wrong play, she didn't know her lines. "But where am I supposed to go?" she asked, her voice trembling.

He lit a cigarette and inhaled deeply. "Get an apartment. You're the one with the salary."

"What about the children?"

"They can visit on weekends."

"But I'm their mother!" she shrieked. "You can't do this. I'll get a lawyer!"

His face was flushed. He spit out the words. "You want to fight this out in court? You want your philandering to be part of the public record? All right. And while we're at it, let's put Millie and Nathan on the stand and make them choose between us!"

"You would do that?" she asked, incredulous.

His lips curled in a sneer. "You would go to bed with Elliot?"

They fell silent, each breathing heavily. They had become worse than strangers; they had become enemies.

The tinkling of an ice cream truck drifted in from the street. She drew herself up and left the house.

The ice cream truck was stopped by the curb, "Twinkle Twinkle Little Star" repeating over and over again. A cluster of children gathered around, excitedly calling out their choices: "Pistachio!" "Chocolate chip!" "Eskimo pie!"

She felt a rising sense of panic. Where are Millie and Nathan? she thought. Where is my life?

33

WHEN JILL CALLED HER FATHER from Pasadena to say she was on her way, he wasn't surprised. He had been following the investigation into communist infiltration in the motion picture industry in the papers. He had read the list of people who had testified. He figured it was just a matter of time before his daughter came running home.

She spent the night in a motel in Barstow and began the journey across the desert the following morning. It was a torment, endlessly long and insufferably hot. She welcomed the punishment. She deserved a journey through hell, the fitting end to the venture she had so blithely entered into with the devil himself. Not that Elliot was the devil; he was merely one of the devil's servants, helping to bring pain into the world. And she had been his willing handmaiden.

A hundred miles outside of Las Vegas the car over-heated. She waited for hours by the side of the road with the mid-day sun beating down on her bare head. She had no water for the car or for herself and by the time a pickup truck pulled over, she was so parched she could barely speak. She got a ride to Mesquite. The owner of the Texaco station had a brother-in-law who was going to Vegas the next day and he could pick up a new alternator.

She spent a sleepless night in the Virgin River Inn, an airless dump with a sagging single bed and a view of the highway. The next day she searched for shade along the banks of the river, which was now only a sluggish stream. She sat on a boulder and watched the muddy trickle glinting in the sunlight. The script for *Mulberry House* sat in her lap, but she couldn't concentrate. A sparrow hopped in front of her, then lifted off. She followed it as it winged above the highway and became a small speck in the white glow of the morning.

She expected it would cool down as the day wore on, but the only noticeable change was the color of the desolate land-scape, which went from glaring white to grayish yellow. She sat in a broken canvas chair in front of the motel office with a pad of paper on her knees.

Martin,

You have every right to be angry. I'm trying to make sense out of everything. I'm very confused. But there is one thing I am not confused about. Millie and Nathan are innocent in all this. Please do not punish them because you are mad at me.

Jill

By the time the car was ready, she wasn't sure which way to point it. Denver seemed so far away. But the idea of going back was worse. So she climbed in, draped a wet bandanna around her neck and headed east. Her mind skipped from one troubling thought to another. She stopped to buy gas and, as the attendant was scraping dead bugs off the windshield, she remembered something her mother had often said to her: "You only get one reputation. Don't lose it." When she became a communist she knew her personal reputation was at stake, but she believed that there were things more important than her reputation; there were all the principles that Martin had taught her—fighting for the working man, fighting for war relief, fighting for progressive candidates. Now, it seemed she had thrown her reputation away, but for what principle?

As she passed through small towns, the car radio picked up the local stations. In Cedar City, Jane Wyman and Bing Crosby crooned, *"In the cool, cool, cool of the evening."* But the irony went by her. She was preoccupied with the tangle her life had become. She tried concentrating on the white line of the highway, but even that brought her back to herself. It reminded her how fragile agreements were between people. Like the centerline that separated her from oncoming traffic. It all operated on trust, on faith. As Martin had said, she had crossed the line.

Somewhere outside of Richfield, Johnnie Ray wailed, *"When waking from a bad dream, don't you sometimes think it's real?"* But in her life, the bad dream persisted. She wondered if she'd ever wake up. Over and over she asked herself why she had acted so rashly? Could she undo the damage to her marriage? Where would she live? How would she explain everything to the children? Her mind generated more questions than answers. Mile after mile of questions, of broken lines, broken promises, broken hearts.

When she began to climb into the cool, sweet rarefied mountain air, it seemed even the car was grateful. She found a rustic inn in Glenwood Springs. The next day, she stood by the railing on Lookout Mountain gazing out at the dense forest of mountain ash and juniper that stretched in all directions. A breeze came up making the leaves on the aspen jostle each other like wind chimes. She took the crisp, pine-scented air deep into her lungs and tried to soak up the dazzling view. But it made no mark on her gloom.

Though her father had visited Los Angeles often, Jill hadn't been home since she'd left for New York. In the twilight, Madison Street looked the same: row after row of red brick houses set slightly above street level so that each house was approached by cement steps cut right into the grassy hill. No fences, hedges or walls separated the properties. From one end of the block to the other, one green lawn rolled into another. Jill got out of the car. There was a stabbing pain in her right hip and her back was stiff. She stretched and rubbed her neck. Her hands were sweaty, her hair hung in limp clumps, and her skirt was wrinkled. She had hoped to be more presentable.

When her father opened the door the strong smell of coffee rushed at her. He was dressed up, his pants well-creased, his bow tie hugging his Adam's apple.

"Well," he said, studying her face, which was pale with dark pockets under the eyes.

"I made it," she said, giving a small shrug.

"You've changed your hair," he said, taking her suitcase.

The oriental carpet was threadbare and a Zenith television sat where the radio console once stood. But nothing else had changed— the same sofa under the window, the same filmy curtains, gray with age. Her mother's Singer sewing machine stood next to the radiator. He said, "You'll stay in your old room, I guess?"

They passed through the dining room with its Maplewood dining set. Two silver candlesticks sat in the middle of the table and Jill thought the white candles were probably the same ones her mother had placed there.

She went into her old room. Seeing the chintz bedspread with its matching curtains brought a bittersweet comfort.

"Is this okay?" he asked.

She nodded and sank onto the bed.

"Would you like a cup of coffee?"

She wanted to tell him everything. But even after so many days of being alone with her thoughts, she had no clue how to begin.

"It's a shameful thing," he said.

At first she thought he meant her affair with Elliot. But then she realized he was speaking of the hearings. "I'm not ashamed of Martin. I'm ashamed of my country."

She saw a flicker of indignation in his eyes. He said, "I know you never meant to help the commies, to sell America down the river. You were both dupes—"

The word, "Daddy!" flew out.

There was a long silence.

"I guess you're tired," he said.

She didn't look at him. "You have no idea."

He made a little cough, then mumbled something about going to water the lawn as he closed the door behind him.

She collapsed onto the bed. She had hoped for refuge, but she'd been a fool to think she'd find it here. She was beyond exhausted. Her clothes stuck to her body. She felt like taking a shower, but was too tired. She closed her eyes. The last time she'd slept in this room she'd been an innocent girl full of dreams.

THE BARKING OF A DOG WOKE HER. She wondered what time it was. The chintz curtains flapped lightly in the cool breeze of the open window. She reached for the lamp on the nightstand. Her hand found the switch, drawing on its own memory. Her wristwatch said four o'clock. She lay there a moment, trying to get her bearings. The gay daffodil wallpaper was faded and drab. Two ornate oval frames held photographic wedding portraits of her parents. Her mother was dressed in a white gown with small pleats buttoned to the throat. She held a bouquet of violets in her lap. Her back was rigid, her mouth a thin, wan smile. Her eyes showed a spark of eagerness. What had been her expectations of married life? Had she ever looked at another man?

34

JILL HAD TROUBLE FINDING HER way to Hillside Memorial Park, but locating her mother's grave was easy. She knew it was near a row of blue spruce. She had a memory of their heavy, dark branches sheltering the spot where her mother had been lowered into the earth. The early morning sky was gray as she walked among the trees, climbing a small hill, reading the headstones, trying to remember what had been carved on her mother's.

It was smaller than she remembered, flat on the earth, not standing.

MILLICENT ANNE FULLBRIGHT

1895 — 1935

CHERISHED WIFE & MOTHER

She wasn't much older than I am, Jill thought with a shock. She shuddered at the idea of having only three more years with Millie and Nathan.

The air was heavy with morning mist, and the bench, which faced her mother's grave, was damp. She spread her sweater on it and sat down. Gazing out over the endless rows of tombstones that dotted the hillside, she tried to conjure up a picture of her mother. But she could only imagine her as she had looked in the hospital, white and drawn, her eyes shut against the possibility of life. Jill couldn't hold onto a lively image—her mother bent over her sewing machine, her nimble fingers pushing the fabric under the needle. Or her mother arranging lilacs in a vase, or at the dining room table polishing the candelabra. These images would flash but quickly disappear, as if the slide projector were misfiring.

Her mother had indulged her. Made sure she had piano lessons, ballet, and tap. By the time Jill was fourteen and showing an interest in theater, Millicent hired a tutor to coach her in acting technique. "Everyone has a gift," her mother had told her. "Mine is stitching a dress. Yours is dramatics."

Jill had always felt a deep gratitude for her mother's devotion to her talent. Millicent attended every recital, sat in the front row of each performance. When Jill was around Millie's age, she had played the lead in the school Christmas play. The teacher had written a long monologue especially for her. Afterwards, people gushed over her splendid performance. As she walked home with her parents in the cool dusk, Jill chattered non-stop about the show. "I got the biggest part because I'm the best in the whole school!"

Later, as she lay in her bed, she overheard her parents arguing in the kitchen. Her father was saying that Millie had spoiled Jill, that an only child would always be spoiled. Her mother said she had wanted another child and then: "You can't blame me for the way it went." Her father said they could try again. Her mother answered, "I couldn't stand to lose another."

The incident came thudding into Jill's consciousness. At the time, she had no understanding of what they meant. Now she realized that her mother had suffered a failed pregnancy. Maybe more than one. She recalled the pain of her own miscarriage, something she hadn't thought about for years. She was overcome with a sense of loss. She had lost a brother or sister, she had lost her first pregnancy, she had lost her mother. She had lost her husband, and depending on how vindictive Martin was, her own children might be lost to her as well. Tears came in a steady stream. Then her grief collapsed into shame for what she had stupidly risked for a fling with Elliot. Facing her mother with her transgressions was as bad as facing Martin.

Jill sat a moment hoping for some absolution. The mountains stood in silent silhouette, dark and jagged against an ashen sky. She stood up, peeling her sweater from the bench. She wondered if the ache in her heart would ever leave. A strand of memory as fine as gossamer floated toward her. It was a line from Balzac she'd memorized for a class in Oral Interpretation. *"The heart of a mother is a deep abyss at the bottom of which you will always discover forgiveness."*

Suddenly a clear image of her mother sprang to mind and held there. Jill had been inside the school auditorium trying out for the part of Juliet. When she burst through the big doors, there was her mother-rouged cheeks, polished shoes, erect posture. Jill stumbled past her, whimpering, "Ina Jones got it…" and began walking so fast her mother had difficulty keeping up. Then Jill felt her mother's grip on her arm. The expression on her face was fierce. "Don't whine and don't complain! So you lost. Now, what's the next play you can try out for?"

Jill looked at the headstone. "Thank you," she said softly.

35

AMONG THE MANY CHANGES Martin had trouble getting used to was the emptiness of the house. The uninterrupted quiet. Even on those days when he had worked in his home office, times when he needed quiet, he had enjoyed the noisy buzz of family life humming along in the background. Without it, he felt disoriented. He yearned for the company of his children, for their ongoing chatter, the way they moved through the house thumping, skipping, bouncing, bursting with life and energy.

He missed Jill, too, but the Jill he used to be married to, not the mate who had jumped ship, not the wife who had thrown fidelity into the toilet. When he thought of Jill now, it was with fury, not longing. Knowing that she no longer shared Elliot's bed did not alter that.

Charlie had told him, "It's just a roll in the hay. She'll be back." Charlie was right. It had been just a roll in the hay, and she had come back. But in the meantime, everything had changed. They could not pick up where they'd left off. She had destroyed the most important thing that bound them together: trust.

The day after he had turned Jill away, he telephoned Al and offered to take him out to lunch. Al had been on the west coast for only six months. He'd grown from a tall, earnest boy into a lanky, loose-jointed man with narrow, hunched shoulders. His wife was also a journalist, their lives happily intersecting through their mutual passion. Then, two years ago, she succumbed to cancer.

Al was devastated. He hit the bottle and bottomed out—lost his job, lost his savings. At Martin's urging, he moved to California. Martin lent him money. They had him to dinner a few times. But he remained reclusive, communicating only occasionally by telephone.

It was the first time Martin had been to Al's run-down bachelor apartment in West Hollywood. Its dirty exterior was partially masked by overgrown shrubs and a pink bougainvillaea that lay heavily across its roof. The place had obviously not received much attention since it was first slapped together sometime in the twenties. Martin knocked, but there was no answer. He pounded louder.

Finally, the door opened and Al stood staring out of red-rimmed eyes in a puffy face. His orange hair was in a tangle, he was badly in need of a shave and his undershirt was stained. The room was dark and stank of cigars and whiskey. Martin thought of the dingy basement they had shared in New York and wondered if Al had ever lived with sunlight.

Martin edged past him into the room and sat on the unmade bed. He offered Al a cigarette. Al took it, but his hands shook too much to light it. Martin lit it for him and one for himself. Al collapsed onto a chair and inhaled. Then he began to cry. Not loud convulsive sobs, just tears running down his cheeks. Next door, someone was practicing violin. The notes were repetitive and sharp, grating on Martin's nerves. He noticed Al's old portable typewriter. Leaning against it was a snapshot of a woman, her eyes bright and full of laughter. There were stacks of books everywhere. They brought to mind the endless conversations he and Al used to have about the workers' struggle. It seemed so long ago.

Al blew his nose and managed a look of chagrin. "Sorry," he mumbled.

Martin put out his cigarette and said, "I need your help, pal."

Al looked at him blankly. Martin pulled him to his feet, peeled off his stinky undershirt, and helped him into the shower. Then he returned to the main room pulling up shades and opening windows. He tucked in the old, gray sheets and smoothed the bedspread over it. He threw away a stack of yellowing newspapers, emptied ashtrays, and poured what remained of the whiskey down the drain.

He took Al to Pig 'N Whistle and told the waitress to keep the coffee coming. Al's drab brown suit hung from his frame. Who knew when his last meal had been? It was clear he hadn't had breakfast, so even though it was well past one, Martin ordered for both of them: eggs, pancakes, sausage, hashed browns, biscuits. But Al only picked at his food. After the third cup of coffee, Martin thought he was sober enough to listen.

"No one will admit there's a blacklist, otherwise they'd be subject to lawsuits. I owed Paramount another four weeks and they told me they thought I'd written myself out. What could I say?"

Al studied him through heavy-lidded eyes. "Why don't you write under a pseudonym?"

"Pseudonyms don't work. The producers want to meet the writer, talk with him about the story." He looked at Al. "I need a person."

Al reached over and helped himself to a cigarette from Martin's pack.

"I'm a bit pink myself, Martin."

"But no one out here knows that. You're a fresh face."

Al exhaled a plume of smoke and snickered. "Fresh. That describes my face, eh?"

They shared a laugh, and then Martin continued. "I have a mortgage and two kids."

"Jill's working, isn't she?"

Martin didn't blink. "Jill's gone. Moved out weeks ago."

"She what?"

Then Martin lit a cigarette and exhaled slowly. "Elliot."

"Jesus," Al winced. "Sonofabitch."

They sat in silence, smoking, wondering at how their lives had gone. Martin finally spoke. "So, I need your help. Millie and Nathan need your help."

Al suddenly welled up with emotion. He blew his nose into his napkin and cleared his throat. "All right, partner, I'll try."

They arrived at a financial arrangement that seemed fair. Al would hand over ninety percent of what he was paid. His ten-percent would be the same as an agent would get. The only thing that Martin would lose besides credit would be the Social Security. Martin had a script ready to peddle. He would give it to Al and instruct him on how to go about setting up meetings with producers. It was a high-wire act, but for each of them, the only act in town.

By the time they said good-bye, it was late afternoon and cooling off. Al got out of the car and leaned into the window. "Thanks, Martin. You may have just saved a friend's life."

"Likewise," said Martin.

He drove along Magnolia Boulevard feeling lighter than he had in months. When he passed a brick building with a large sign posted above the entrance, Burbank Animal Shelter, without thinking, he swerved into the parking lot.

It was fifteen minutes before closing time, so he went with his first hunch, a black Gordon setter, a mutt from the sheep-herding family. The dog was huddled in a ball amidst the cacophony of barking, yelping, and growling. Martin felt an immediate kinship. They gave him to Martin in a cardboard box along with a bag of puppy kibble. He named him Daniel, after his brother.

At night, he put the puppy in the cardboard box at the foot of the bed, but the poor thing didn't stop whimpering. If he allowed Daniel into his bed, he'd never get him out. Martin considered that for a moment. Why was that such a bad idea? He realized it was Jill's voice he heard, full of dismay at the very idea of letting an animal sleep with them. But this was no longer Jill's bed.

He reached over and picked up the furry bundle. Daniel looked at him with grateful brown eyes. He was shaking all over and Martin brought him close to his body. The two of them drifted into sleep, the first restful sleep either had enjoyed in a long time.

36

JILL'S PARTING FROM HER father was cordial. She realized that she would never change his opinion of Martin or herself when it came to their political beliefs. There were limitations to what she could expect from Russell. But then there were limitations in any relationship.

When she returned to Los Angeles, she drove directly to Phyllis' house. If Phyllis was horrified by the recent events in Jill's life, she didn't say. She had an expansive, generous nature and the words "I told you so" were not in her vocabulary. She offered Jill her couch for as long as she needed it.

Martin had cooled off. He agreed that going to court would not help anyone. He met Jill at a restaurant and discussed the logistics of sharing the care of the children. They were careful with each other, considerate with their words. It seemed as if they had arrived at some kind of truce.

Two weeks later, Phyllis helped Jill move into a two-bedroom bungalow on one of the Venice canals. It was tiny with all the charm of a doll's house. The outside was covered with wisteria, which even at the tail end of summer had one or two lavender blossoms. In front was a tiny patch of earth. It got the morning light and Jill imagined herself and Millie planting a garden while Nathan fed the ducks that swam in the canals. There was a ladder propped against the side of the house and after Phyllis left, she climbed onto the roof, propped herself with her feet, and gazed at a thin sliver of sheet metal gray ocean. Seeing that small piece of shimmering water brought a sense of peace, something elusive these days.

Between costume fittings for the new movie, Phyllis took her to the Merchant of Venice, a great mix of old and new furniture where she picked up a burgundy rug and a loveseat. She also bought a cedar toy chest. She would make a project of filling it when the children visited. She painted it to match the walls, egg-yolk yellow. She had brought her mother's sewing machine back from Denver and sat stooped over it, struggling to thread the bobbin. She finally figured out how to run the machine but couldn't get the fabric to cooperate. After ripping out the hem twice, she gave up and just looped the polished cotton over a curtain rod and held it in place with safety pins.

Martin grumbled about how long the drive would be from the Valley. She wouldn't like the drive either, but it was well worth it to be able to inhale ocean air, to gaze out onto palm trees, and to be able to walk along the promenade. Furthermore, M-G-M was right around the corner in Culver City. She looked forward to sharing her little nest with Millie and Nathan.

THEIR PLANE ARRIVED THREE days before the first day of school. Jill met them alone; Martin had granted her that. As she waited for them to disembark, she felt anxious. She knew their summer had been a success, but she worried that her own summer would make her a stranger to them. Or worse, that they might somehow sniff out her treachery.

When they stepped off the plane, it took her a moment to realize they were hers. Nathan had a haircut that made his ears stick out. Millie was a head taller. They rushed into her arms, and she pressed them close. She had forgotten the silky feel of their skin. Words tumbled out of them, they had so much to tell and it had to come all at once or else they'd forget.

Daniel met them at the door barking with delight. Jill jumped back and shot Martin a surprised look.

"Is he ours?" asked Millie, beside herself with joy. Nathan was a bit shy, but watching his sister's ease gave him the courage to pet the creature. Millie hugged her mother, "I've always wanted a dog!" Nathan showed them the Yankee cap that Zadie had bought him. Millie brought out a potholder she had made herself. Bubbie had taught her how to knit! She presented it ceremoniously to her mother. Jill made a fuss over it. But she wasn't really feeling enthusiasm. Like a bad actor, she was merely "indicating" interest, showing for the sake of her audience. She was preoccupied with the conversation about the separation, which she and Martin had agreed to have with the children after dinner. The two of them sat at the kitchen table in pained silence as their children raced through the house filling it with their cries and laughter, the dog yipping as he followed them from room to room. Jill studied the blue wallpaper as if she'd never seen it before. Martin lit one cigarette with another.

Millie set the table, but she was puzzled when it was Martin, not her mother, who served the meal: Swanson T.V. dinners with applesauce and chocolate milk.

Nathan told a story about going with Zadie to his restaurant and being allowed to serve knishes to the customers but spilling one and breaking a plate and then a waitress helped him. His storytelling was one long breathless sentence. Millie was trying to be a polite listener but was bursting with her own tales, about meeting a girl named Francine and going on the subway all by themselves. "Francine's mother gave her a permanent wave. Will you give me one, Mommy?"

"Sure I will, honey. Maybe this weekend."

Martin and Jill exchanged looks. Choosing her words with care, Jill said, "Daddy and I are trying something new. We're going to live in two houses instead of one."

Nathan thought it meant everybody taking turns with different houses and said, "Goodie!"

But Millie caught the other meaning and in a small voice, asked, "Why?"

Martin said, "Mommy and I need some time away from each other."

Millie's face fell. Nathan asked, "Are you getting a divorce?"

The word stunned Jill. She had no idea Nathan even knew the word. She rushed in with too much good cheer. "No, no, a separation, not a divorce."

"What's a separation?" asked Nathan, picking up on the sudden tension in the room.

Trying to steady her voice, Jill said, "It means I'll have a house where you can visit, and Daddy and you will have this house."

"Where you can visit?" asked Nathan, confused, hopeful.

Millie looked tiny and frail. "Where will we sleep?"

"Oh," said Jill, all smiles, "I've got that all figured out. A bunk-bed!"

"I hate bunk-beds," Millie exclaimed.

Nathan said quickly, "You can sleep on top, Millie."

Martin got up to get his cigarettes. "Now, Millie," he

began, but she interrupted, her voice rising in panic. "What about my birthday?"

Her birthday was the following week. Martin and Jill had decided that Jill would have the birthday celebration on the weekend. But when Jill patiently explained the plan, Millie exclaimed, "I want my party here. With Tina and Pamela and Allison." She burst into tears. "I wish we'd never gone to New York! Then nothing would be different when we came home!"

Jill reached over to take her daughter onto her lap, but Millie jerked away. Jill looked helplessly at Martin. Martin was pale, his mouth taut.

Nathan looked from his mother to his father to his sister, trying to decipher the hidden meanings. He began to cry too. "I want Zadie," he wailed.

Jill struggled to keep her own tears in check. Stay strong, stay strong, she thought. She had known it was going to be difficult, but she had no idea it would be so brutal. Out loud, she said, trying to inject brightness into her voice, "I'll see you Saturday. We'll buy sno-cones. It's only four days away."

Millie's nose was running. Jill went to wipe it with a napkin, but Millie turned away.

Daniel let out a high whine. Martin was by the refrigerator. "They need time with this."

She stood up. Nathan ran to her and threw his arms around her skirt, hysterical. "No, Mommy, no!"

Jill peeled his hands off. It broke her heart. "Millie?" she said. But Millie wouldn't even look at her.

37

WALKING OUT WHEN HER children were so distraught catapulted Jill into another downward spiral of self-incrimination. What had felt quaint about the canals and cozy about her little home now made her feel lonely and frightened.

The plan was that Martin would bring them over Saturday, and then Jill would drive them home Sunday in time for the birthday party with Tina and Pamela and Allison, which Martin would organize. Saturday morning Jill found herself biting her nails while she waited for the coffee to percolate. It's only Millie and Nathan, she kept telling herself, but she couldn't quiet her nerves. Finally, at ten o'clock, she heard the familiar sound of the Packard. She ran out to greet them, but Millie wasn't in the car. "She refused to come," Martin said with a shrug. "What could I do?"

Jill pasted on a smile for Nathan and took his Mickey Mouse overnight bag saying, "We'll have our own special time, won't we, Nathan?"

Clutching Mr. Rabbit, Nathan ran ahead to investigate the new house, and Jill leaned into the car. "What exactly did she say?"

"Pamela's mother won't let her play with Millie anymore. I tried to explain everything to Millie about the Committee and the fear, but she blames you for everything." Martin saw her wince and his tone softened. "It's a lot to get used to."

Jill helped Nathan climb onto the roof, knowing he'd be thrilled at the height and sense of danger. They sat there a while, looking out at the ocean and the seagulls and the palm trees swaying in the light breeze. He was unusually subdued, and Jill found herself babbling to fill the silence. "After lunch, we'll go to a big amusement park. There's a fun house with wobbly stairs and a mirror that makes you look like a giant and another one that makes you look like a midget. They have a merry-go-round with shiny horses and a roller coaster that flies out over the ocean. And we get to eat delicious cotton candy. Have you ever had cotton candy?"

He shook his head. She dove in again, her voice high and eager. "Oh, you'll like that a lot. It's like sweet pink clouds. And hot dogs. We'll get hot dogs, too."

"Are we atheists?" he asked suddenly.

She looked at him, dumfounded. "Atheists? Where did you learn such a big word?"

"We had a bomb drill and we were hiding under our desks and I was next to Alex and he said that his dad said we're atheists."

Jill took a deep breath as she searched for the right words. "Atheists don't believe in God, but we do believe in God, so we're not atheists."

"Anthony called Millie a pinko and then so did all the kids at recess and it's because you moved away."

"What? Pinko? Who's Anthony?" She felt as if she were on a runaway train.

"Millie was crying and crying and Daddy tried to give her a permanent but it looks like a million wires sticking out and she didn't want to go to school but Daddy made her so she had to wear a scarf all day."

A wave of failure came over her. The name-calling. The permanent.

Then: "I want to go home."

"Oh, honey, you just got here." She looked at him. He was staring at a duck gliding soundlessly through the water. "Would you like to feed the ducks?"

"I want to go home."

"Tomorrow, Nathan. You can go home tomorrow."

He stared at her through large eyes the color of Martin's and said, "But Millie needs Mr. Rabbit today."

She could have put her foot down, but she was too unsure of herself. She sighed, and helped him down off the roof.

38

SHE THREW HERSELF INTO HER WORK, concentrating on Lucinda, her character in *Mulberry House*. The screenplay had been written by Isobel Rugio, one of the few women scriptwriters around. Isobel had a flare for the way women spoke, and it made learning the lines easy. Mulberry House was a publishing firm, and Lucinda was Alan Ladd's secretary. Lucinda stumbles across a shady business deal and is caught between her loyalty to her boss, whom she's in love with, and the pressure to tell the truth. The irony of playing a character who contemplates betraying the man she loves was not lost on Jill.

Today was the first table read. En route to the studio she was thinking about her character, only half-listening to the radio, which was broadcasting a live report from the Federal Building. She turned up the volume when she heard that Libby Roth had been called to the witness stand—Libby, her old comrade from the New York days. Jill listened anxiously as she heard Libby answer the questions. She gave them name after name. Libby was cooperating! The last name in the long list was Jill Fullbright.

She felt the wind go out of her and she veered to the side of the road. She sat there trembling, gripping the wheel. Libby. She couldn't believe it.

She found a pay phone and called Martin, but there was no answer. She called her agent, but he was in a meeting. She got back in the car and sat for a moment, trying to think what to do. She looked at her watch. She was late.

When she entered the large conference room the other actors were already seated in chairs around a table covered with scripts and coffee and donuts. It was clear from the somber tone in the room, from the way people averted their eyes, that it was already common knowledge. Alan stood and gallantly pulled out her chair. She smiled at him gratefully. His eyes gave nothing away.

When it came time to say her lines, they came out stiff and awkward, as if she were speaking a foreign language, each word new and peculiar in her mouth. She heard herself talking as if she were an observer watching someone else perform. She couldn't lose herself. She sensed others shifting uncomfortably in their seats and this heightened her self-consciousness.

When the reading was over, Arnold Keating, the director, called her over. Before he could say anything, she jumped in with, "I'm sorry. I know I was off today."

He smiled and said, "Don't worry about it," then handed her a memo. "Dore Schary wants to see you."

Her stomach clenched. Word had already reached the ears of the head of the studio.

She had met Dore Schary once or twice at Elliot's when Schary was still production chief at M-G-M. He had only recently assumed full command of the studio; Louis B. Mayer had angrily resigned after three years of butting heads with him.

Jill entered the Irving Thalberg projection room. Schary was seated in front with three other men. She stood in the back, trying to adjust to the dim light, wondering if she should announce herself. Then he saw her and said, "Come in, Jill," not bothering to introduce her to the others. He called to some unseen person, "We're done here, Johnny." The others left the room as she came down the aisle.

She sat down, leaving a seat between them. Schary was a trim man with horn-rimmed glasses and an easy smile. His tie was blood red, like a blunt sign in the middle of his chest proclaiming his power.

"Well, Jill," he said, opening a small pouch and sprinkling tobacco into the bowl of a cherry wood pipe. "I've seen footage from *Stranger At the Gate*, and I'm confident *Mulberry House* will be equally terrific. You're a fine actress."

She breathed a sigh of relief. They loved her here. She had a seven-year contract.

He tapped down the tobacco with his thumb. "However," he continued, putting a match to the bowl, "that's not the reason I called you in. I understand you were named in this morning's hearings."

Her heart quickened.

He drew on the pipe stem, making a sucking sound. A woody smell filled the room. He noticed her blanched face. "It's nothing to be alarmed about. It's simply a matter of clearing your name. The Congressmen are fully aware that we have a picture to make."

Her heart slowed to its natural rhythm. The ax hadn't fallen after all. Dore Schary was one of the most powerful men in Hollywood. He knew how to finesse such matters.

"Here's what you need to do. Set up a meeting with Eugene Sloane. He's a brilliant lawyer, used to work with the ACLU. He'll put you in touch with the right people. And then we can get back to the business of making movies."

"You make it sound so easy."

"It won't be. You'll have to write a statement. Swear you're not a communist, that you detest communism, renounce all past left-wing activities."

"Will I have to testify?"

"Possibly. Sloane will know about that. The idea is to avoid a subpoena and get this handled quickly."

"My God..."

He puffed on his pipe, choosing his words carefully. "It's lousy, I know. Personally, I deplore the whole thing. Look, I'm a liberal, too. When I was at RKO I did quality films. I voted against the producers' Waldorf-Astoria decision. But I still have to abide by it. Dalton Trumbo, Hugo Butler, Waldo Salt—they were my friends. Now they won't even talk to me. Any way you cut it, everyone loses. The fact is, the Committee is calling the shots and in order to keep making movies, we're forced to follow their rules."

She said, more to herself than to him. "I'm reeling from all this...an hour ago I was playing Lucinda...there's suddenly so much to think about."

He laid his pipe on the edge of a marble ashtray and cocked his head. "The thing is, we have to take care of this immediately. Once filming starts, it's harder to re-cast."

Re-cast? She was dumfounded. "But we've already begun rehearsals. I've had costume fittings."

He shrugged. "We have to be realistic, Jill. Look at the trouble Irving Allen had when Howard Da Silva became an unfriendly witness. Allen had to splice him out of *Slaughter Trail* to a tune of a hundred thousand bucks! We don't want to cancel your contract, but right now, you're tainted. Once the studio begins to get complaints—"

"But who? Who would complain about me playing Lucinda?" Indignation colored her face.

"One call from Ward Bond at the Motion Picture Alliance, and we've got trouble."

She dropped her eyes to her hands, which were clutching her pocketbook. He picked up his pipe and re-lit it, studying her as he sucked on the stem. The smell of his pipe suddenly made her sick. "You're part of the M-G-M family, Jill. The family can protect you, but only if you help."

The word family brought a lump to her throat. She stood up. He extended his hand. She offered her own, limp and trembling.

Schary held it in a tight grasp. "I know how rough this is."

"Thank you," she said dumbly, her voice barely under control.

She drove directly to the William Morris Agency. Gerald Fisk was in a meeting and she had to wait for an hour in the reception area with nothing to do but read the papers that littered the low table in front of her. She scanned them quickly. But she knew the report of today's hearings wouldn't be in the papers until tomorrow. Then Hedda Hopper's column caught her eye:

> "I'd like to run every one of those rats out of this country starting with Charlie Chaplin. I urge all loyal Americans to boycott pictures with actors who have had Communist connections or any film made at Metro Goldwyn 'Moscow'."

By the time she was admitted to Gerald's turquoise office, Jill was near panic. His reaction did nothing to calm her.

"What's wrong with you people?" he said, his voice unnaturally high as he paced in front of her. "This is the greatest country on earth!"

"I never said it wasn't! That's not the issue."

"Do you realize what will happen if your name gets on the blacklist? You won't be able—"

"You're my agent, you should defend me! Why don't you stand up to the studios and tell them that if they blacklist one of your clients, then they won't get any of your other clients!"

Gerald sighed and said, "That's all very nice to imagine but the fact is, there is a blacklist, and there's not a damned thing I can do about it. Not one damned thing."

He sat down next to her on the divan. "And if you get on the blacklist, not only will you never work again as an actress, but honestly, I don't know where you could get work, period. After *Stranger* comes out, your face will be as familiar as Rita Hayworth's. You won't even be able to sell clothes at Penney's."

This shocked her. The blacklist cast a wide net.

"Look, honey, I understand your marriage is in trouble. Do you want to lose your career, too?"

She felt herself redden at the mention of her marriage and looked quickly out the window.

He ignored her embarrassment. "Just write the damned statement. Say whatever they want you to say."

"It's not that simple."

"It is simple: become a friendlie—or get black-balled."

"What if I have to name names?"

He put a hand on her shoulder. "Just name a few little people."

"Little people?"

"Jill. Listen to me. This is a time for expediency, not morality."

SHE RACED TO THE OFFICES OF the Screen Actors Guild. She ran a red light and laughed out loud. Red light, red scare, red menace, red hunt, red baiting. It was about seeing reds everywhere! Well, right now, she was the one seeing red.

She parked haphazardly and rushed into the building. The union was strong and could protect her. She was shown into the office of the administrative head, a buxom Mrs. Gibson with bifocals and several chins. Mrs. Gibson listened with forbearance as Jill related her predicament, then asked, "Were you in fact a member of the Communist Party?"

That question, that so-called sixty-four-dollar question, hung in the air like a bad smell.

"Mrs. Gibson, you have no right to ask me that. Don't you realize that's what this whole damned thing is about? I came here today because I'm a dues-paying member of this guild, and I deserve its protection. I demand its protection! My job is at stake. I have a seven-year contract at M-G-M, and I want my union to fight for it!"

Mrs. Gibson stood up. Her chins shook as she spoke. "You don't seem to understand, Miss Fullbright. This is deadly serious business. The Guild Board believes that the international communist conspiracy is a clear and present danger to our nation, and that all participants should be exposed. All of the unions stand together on this point. Are you familiar with the statement made by the Motion Picture Industry Council last March?"

Before Jill could answer, Mrs. Gibson continued, her voice rising in agitation, "It offers commendation to those former members of the Communist Party who have repudiated Party ties and who join their fellow Americans in the fight for freedom. All the guilds signed the statement. AFTRA members can be fined, suspended, or even expelled for failure to cooperate with HUAC. The SWG has even amended its rules about screen credit so the studios can omit the names of writers who have not cooperated with the Committee. And the Motion Picture Academy has decreed that no unfriendly witness can be nominated for an Oscar."

Jill's voice was shrill. "But the blacklist is illegal. My name is about to go on it, and I'm about to lose my job!"

Mrs. Gibson leaned forward, supporting her enormous weight on flabby arms and spoke in sharp, jabbing thrusts. "As a labor union we will fight any secret blacklist created by any group of employers. On the other hand, if an actor has so offended American public opinion that he has made himself unsaleable at the box office, the Guild cannot force an employer to hire him!"

Jill slung the strap of her pocketbook across her shoulder. "What a lot of bull, Mrs. Gibson. Pure bull. Whatever happened to 'all for one and one for all'?"

"Ronald Reagan is president of your union. Talk to him if you think it's bull."

39

MARTIN PUSHED THE LAWN mower methodically back and forth. The sweet scent of the newly cut grass comforted him. It had been a hard day. Nathan had lost his first tooth and put it under his pillow, but Martin forgot to leave a dime. Nathan was crestfallen, and even Millie couldn't convince him that the tooth fairy would come for sure tonight. It was the kind of thing Jill took care of.

Then, this afternoon, he had a meeting with Millie's teacher. Mrs. Harvel was a stately woman with long silver hair, which she wound in a tight braid on top of her head. She had shown Martin Millie's spelling tests and book reports. They were very poor. "Millie's report cards from past years show that she's always been a cooperative and enthusiastic student." Then, in hushed tones, she added, "They carted away Bill Robinson yesterday. Two policemen, just as he was explaining the Gold Rush to his fifth graders. He was certainly not teaching communism."

Martin was surprised at her bluntness. She continued with a sympathetic tilt of her head. "Millie has had to make some big adjustments this year. If there's any way I can be of help..."

"Thank you," he said, moved by her warmth and sincerity.

He was concerned. Millie had become withdrawn and overly sensitive. He wasn't sure how to handle her. He missed

Jill. He wanted to share his worries. He yearned for her companionship. He ached for her touch.

He dumped the grass into the garbage can and went into the house, Daniel trotting by his side. He sat at his desk and looked at the notes he'd made for the new script. So far, working on the black market with Al as his front had worked. Not to say that there weren't frustrations. Martin was being paid a fraction of his old price since he couldn't use past credits as a negotiating lever. He got no credit; he had no contact with the producer or director. Still, he—that is, Al—had sold *Fast Track* to Paramount.

But yesterday during a meeting with the producers, Al had been asked for other story ideas. Al kept his cool and stalled for another meeting. This morning, he told Martin, "The fact is, I do have some ideas." They were at their usual meeting place, Pig 'N Whistle. Between mouthfuls of buckwheat pancakes, Al said, "I'm on the studio payroll already. I'm ready to go back to work. Besides, I don't like getting credit for work that's not mine."

Martin saw that Al was taking an interest in life again. He looked better, too, had gained weight, and he was on the wagon. But it put Martin in a quandary. Who else he could trust with his material? Another writer might not be as forthcoming as Al. Another writer might sell Martin's ideas as his own and take the full pay. Martin certainly wouldn't be able go to court if that happened. He wondered if he dared write under a pseudonym and risk being discovered. The bills were piling up. He was still in debt for legal expenses from the hearing. Each time his name was uttered in those chambers at the Federal Building, and then published the next day in the newspapers, it was like getting hit again. Furthermore, each time he got named, the slim hope that an old producer friend might look the other way and take a chance on him was further diminished. The Committee was gaining stature. Each time a witness became an informer, it made it that much more difficult for the next witness to resist.

Neighbors avoided him; the woman at the dry-cleaners wouldn't meet his eyes. When his guard was down, he became self-pitying. His fortunes had turned around because of activities in a political party, which had turned out to be terribly flawed and which he no longer would defend on any grounds. He had lost twice.

His thoughts were interrupted by a sound at the door. He thought it might be Daniel scratching to get out, but Daniel was sprawled on the floor, asleep by his feet.

He opened the door and found an ashen-faced Jill.

"What is it? What's happened?" he exclaimed.

"Did you listen to the news today?"

He'd been caught up in his own worries. He hadn't been tracking the hearings. "You've been named?"

She looked frail and afraid, her eyes hollow. "Come in," he said. "I'll make some coffee."

"I'd rather have a drink."

She sat at the kitchen table watching him pour scotch into a glass.

"Who was it?" he asked.

"Libby."

"Christ...Libby..."

They sat in mute silence united by their disbelief.

"Dore Schary wants a letter. Tell them that I love America, that sort of thing."

"Name names, that sort of thing?" he said, pointedly.

"It might not come to that."

"Oh, yes, it will. No one gets cleared without cooperating."

"I have a seven-year contract. I can't throw that away."

He said nothing.

She looked at him imploringly. "Isn't that what's most important now, with all these changes—to keep working?"

"You want Millie to be singled out as a daughter of a stoolie?"

"She's already singled out as a daughter of a pinko. What difference does it make? She'll suffer either way."

"You know my position, Jill. You'll have to find someone else if you want permission to squeal."

She stood up. She hadn't touched her drink.

IN BAD NEED OF A FRIEND, she drove to Phyllis' house. The sun was low in the sky and the orange glow above the ocean hinted at the beginning of a beautiful sunset. She wanted to sit on Phyllis' sun porch, gulp down a drink, and spill out her troubles. But when Jill knocked on her door, Phyllis didn't open it. Jill could hear Beethoven coming from inside. She knocked louder and yelled, "Hey, it's me!"

Then she heard Phyllis' voice through the closed door.

"They're watching my house, you can't come in."

"What are you talking about?" Jill said, looking around at the sleepy little street. But then she saw it: a dark sedan with two men sitting in it. "Who are they?"

"F.B.I. Now that you're in trouble, you've got to stay away."

"But Phyllis, they can't hurt you."

"My name showed up in *Red Channels*."

"It did? But why? You were never in the Party."

"My name was in an ad in the *Hollywood Reporter*

opposing the re-election of Jack Tenney to the State Senate. I studied at the Lab. Who knows what else? I'm under some kind of cloud. I think they've put a tap on my phone. You'd better not call."

"Oh, Phyllis," said Jill, leaning against the door. She was bone tired.

"Please, Jill, I mean it. You've got to go."

Wearily, she turned and let herself out the latched gate.

She remembered a line from *The Children's Hour*, the play she'd performed on Broadway all those years ago. Her character and the character she was believed to be having a homosexual relationship with confronted their accuser "with their lives spread on the table for you to cut to pieces." How innocent Jill had been when she did that play. Now it was not a fiction, now she herself was about to be blackballed by the community for an imagined sin.

40

MILLIE HAD BEEN BOYCOTTING the weekend visits, even though Nathan had come. Finally, one Saturday, she was in the car, too. She wore a blue and white gingham dress and a scowl. Jill didn't mind the scowl. Millie had made the choice to come, and that was enough.

Nathan was glad to be back now that Millie was there. He pulled Millie into the house, pausing to show her how the Dutch door worked, then showed her their bedroom. The bunk bed stood against the wall, a silent reminder of the day they had been told of the separation. Nathan scrambled onto the top bunk and almost hit his head on the ceiling. Jill stood in the doorway watching. Still holding her overnight case, Millie sat on the bottom bunk and pointed to the toy chest. "What's that?"

Nathan answered enthusiastically, "Mommy's going to let us fill it with toys!"

Millie shrugged indifferently as if she were too grown-up for such things. Jill bit her tongue. She believed Millie *had* grown up too fast these past weeks, though she looked very much like the ten-year old she now was. The permanent gave her a scarecrow look. Parts were singed and it sprang out in an unruly frizz around her head.

"I like all those curls," said Jill softly. "Very grown-up."

Millie's hand floated up to her hair. "Where's the restroom?" she asked formally; Jill half-expected her to raise her hand and ask permission to go.

"I'll show you!" Nathan boomed and jumped off the bed, skipping into the bathroom. Millie rose listlessly and passed her mother without a word.

After lunch, they walked the three short blocks to the beach, weighed down with a blanket, thermos of cold lemonade, a big red and yellow beach ball, towels, pails, and shovels. Nathan rolled around on the blanket, clutching Mr. Rabbit, sucking his thumb. He hadn't sucked his thumb since he was a toddler and it worried Jill to see him doing it now. Millie took off her shoes and socks and walked down to the water. Jill hoped a wave might crash loudly sending her back with frightened eyes, arms open for comfort. Good God, thought Jill, I want it so badly I'm hoping for her to be terrified. But Millie merely stood there, letting the water lap at her toes, and then she returned to the blanket, lay face down, and fell fast asleep.

Sea gulls circled lazily. Beachcombers and sunbathers came and went. As Jill watched Nathan build a sandcastle, she struggled with the decision facing her. What if she had to testify? If she took the Fifth, then she'd have to live with the word "incriminating" since the Fifth Amendment was about not incriminating oneself. But she didn't do anything incriminating.

Besides she didn't want to spend the rest of her life being branded a communist. Taking the Fifth would force her to be tainted forever.

Nathan ran toward her, all sandy and glowing with the delight of watching the water gradually cave in his castle. He was thirsty and she poured him some lemonade. They played catch, until a breeze carried the ball down the beach and Nathan had to run like crazy to keep it from rolling away. Jill held onto the ball while Nathan splashed in the water. She glanced over at Millie. Still asleep.

Jill had no great love for the Communist Party. Wasn't defending the Soviet Union worse than naming names? Furthermore, she was poised on the brink of success. How could she deliberately turn her back on that? Was it so wrong to want her life to count?

When Millie woke up, Jill gave her a quarter for Popsicles and watched as she and Nathan crossed the stretch of sand to the promenade. She looked out at the water. The tide was edging closer. She thought about what her agent had said. Maybe he was right. This was a time for expediency. Becoming an informer was a hoop she had to jump through in order to receive the Committee's blessing and keep working.

When the kids came back, the three of them drew their names in the wet sand. Still, Millie would not look at her mother and would not address her unless necessary. They stayed until the tide was licking the edge of the blanket and the sun lay squat on the horizon, just about to melt into nothingness.

By the time they got back to the house the sky was a smear of gold and pink. They were all cold and hungry. Millie sat on the bottom bunk feigning interest in a cookbook she'd found in the kitchen. Nathan was whining that they'd forgotten to go onto the roof. Jill promised they'd do that first thing tomorrow. She was grilling cheese sandwiches when Nathan said suddenly, "Where's Mr. Rabbit?"

"You had him at the beach," Jill said and her heart sank at the very real possibility that Mr. Rabbit was still there. "Go look in your room." He came out a moment later, panic on his face. By now the tide would have covered the spot where they'd sat. Nathan without Mr. Rabbit was like Nathan without an ear or a toe.

"Let's go get him. Millie, get your sweater!"

The air was cooler and the wind had come up. The beach was dark and empty, and Jill cursed herself for not having brought a flashlight. They each had a different idea of where they had been sitting and so they looked in each place as best they could by the slim light of a crescent moon. Millie said, "You shouldn't have let him bring Mr. Rabbit here." Nathan gripped his mother's hand and sniffled. Millie's voice rose above the ocean. "If Mr. Rabbit is gone, Nathan will die!"

"We'll find him," said Jill, but her heart trembled.

Millie continued. "What if a dog got him? Or some kid took him? It's your fault!"

Though Jill couldn't see her, she could hear tears in her daughter's voice. "Your fault! Your fault!" she shouted. Jill was on her knees stupidly digging in the sand. Nathan stood beside her, now bawling loudly. Jill's own tears came and she whispered, "My fault," as Millie was yelling, "Your fault!" and their words blended with the crash of the waves.

Finally the three of them were in a collapsed heap on the damp sand weeping together. Nathan had dropped his mother's hand and was holding Millie's, and Jill was hugging her knees to her chest, rocking.

Their tears finally spent, they sat in silence staring at the black water. Their eyes had grown used to the darkness. The shape of the waves and the dull white of the foam had become familiar. Jill reached out to Nathan. "I'm sorry, sweetheart." He let himself be drawn onto her lap, where he curled into a small ball and stuck his thumb in his mouth. Millie was within arm's reach. Jill hesitated, then touched her daughter's hair. Barely above a whisper, she said, "I know you're hurting inside. It's okay to be mad at me." She stroked her daughter's frizzy hair. Millie did not say anything. But she did not move her head away.

41

JILL SENT WORD TO DORE SCHARY that she was working on the statement, that she had an appointment with Eugene Sloane, that she was willing to do whatever was necessary. During rehearsal breaks, she sat in a corner bent over a legal pad, weighing each word, trying to walk the fine line between her own truth and the kind of statement that would clear her name.

I am a proud American. I believe in democracy. The reason I signed a petition for the Hollywood Ten was not because I agreed with what they had to say but because I believed they had the right to say it.

She tore it up and tried again.

I am proud to be an American. I fervently believe in democracy. I believe in the freedom of speech and freedom of thought which is why I signed a petition for the Hollywood Ten. I believed they had the right to their beliefs.

She had no concentration for her work. Normally, she

prided herself on memorizing lines effortlessly. Now, they eluded her. Her characterization of Lucinda was still clumsy. It would be a pathetic irony if she were fired for a lackluster performance instead of for her political affiliations!

By nature an optimist, Jill usually saw the glass half-full. But now, even when she squinted, the glass didn't hold a drop.

THERE WAS AN EXPANSIVE feeling to Eugene Sloane's law office: overstuffed chairs and black lacquer cabinets. The table lamps were ornate and looked Chinese. Eugene sat behind a wide desk talking on the phone. He waved Jill in. She sat opposite him, studying his face, trying to decide if she could trust him. In fact, he had a trustworthy face—boyish good looks, smiling eyes, and a strong chin. He was dressed in a camelhair suit; he wore diamond cufflinks.

Finally, he hung up and reached across the desk to shake her hand. "I understand you're about to have a big hit!"

His comment relaxed her at once, and she smiled. "My only hit if I don't get the Committee's blessing."

He laughed easily, waving his hand as if the Committee were nothing more than an annoying mosquito. "Oh, what an ugly business. Would you like some coffee?" He spoke brusquely and with a certitude that calmed her.

"Yes, please."

He buzzed his receptionist and ordered two coffees, then turned back to Jill. "All right. Let's get down to business."

"Mr. Schary told me I'd need to write a statement." She took a folded paper from her purse and smoothed it out. "I've started, but I'm afraid I need some help."

He took it from her and glanced at it. "You'll want to say

that the Committee's undertaking is strengthening our government at home and abroad. How you admire their work, that sort of thing." He scribbled in the margin as he talked. "We'll finish this together then get it mimeographed and circulated to the studios and, of course, to the Committee." He looked at her. "Now, give me a little background so I know if you're headed for the graylist or the blacklist."

Jill's eyes widened in surprise. "I didn't realize there were two lists."

"For signing petitions, marching in May Day parades, union activity, that sort of thing, a letter should do," he said, adding with a laugh, "the 'smear and clear' process. But if you were actually in the Party, then you'll need to do more than write a letter."

Jill scrambled through her mind for reasons not to tell this man the truth about her Party affiliation. Could it hurt her? In fact, he was the only one who could keep her from being hurt. In a low voice she said, "I was in the Party."

He tapped the tip of his pen against his teeth with a look not of judgment, but of consternation. She added quickly, "But I was only a kid. It was so long ago."

"Doesn't matter when. The important thing is to renounce past affiliation."

"I can do that."

Then he said directly, "Staying off the blacklist for former Party members means giving names."

She winced. "I don't know if I have the stomach for it."

"Yes, it is distasteful. It takes guts to be an informer. But there's no other way. Otherwise, your past will cost you your future."

"What if I don't mention any names that haven't already been mentioned? I don't want anybody ruined because of me."

"That's fine. You'll just corroborate names that have already been corroborated. We'll make that clear in the meeting."

"What meeting?"

"It's best if you agree to a voluntary interview with the Federal Bureau of Investigation."

She was aghast. "The F.B.I.?"

The door opened and a pretty brunette with shiny red nails set down a tray with cups, sugar, cream.

"Thanks, Lois," Eugene said as he absently handed her several envelopes. "These need to be notarized."

Lois took the envelopes and left.

Eugene handed Jill a cup and poured cream into his own. "Now, where were we?" Noticing her pallor, he laughed lightly. "Oh, yes. The F.B.I. Nothing to worry about. They're just a bunch of men doing their job."

"It's all so upsetting." She heard the pitch of her voice. She didn't want to break down. He was trying to save her career. She looked into her cup and tried to steady her nerves.

"Did you know, Jill, that...do you mind if I call you Jill?" She shook her head. "Did you know that I worked with the Committee for the First Amendment?"

She looked up in astonishment.

"I think the whole idea of HUAC stinks. But," he said, his voice softening, "it's easier to work with them than against them. I'm a lawyer. I take the long-range view. I don't see sacrificing one's self to a useless end. My job is to serve my clients. How can they be served by being on the blacklist?"

He was so logical, so clear. Of course he was right.

"Just think of it as an elaborate ritual, or maybe a better word is maze. You have to walk through this maze in order to keep your job. First we set up a meeting with the F.B.I. We send out your letter and include in it an offer to the Committee to cooperate as a witness. That avoids the subpoena. Then we have a preliminary meeting with William Wheeler. He's the Committee's chief investigator, a real gentleman; you'll like him. Then the hearings."

"Can't I testify in secret session? I was hoping—"

"Well, no. You see, you've been named publicly so you have to appear publicly. You're in the spotlight now with the movies and so on. Besides, since your husband took the Fifth…"

He noticed her surprise.

"It's public record, of course." He let this sink in. Then added, a lightness to his voice, "After the hearings, bingo! You're done! Once it's over, I'll follow up with the studios. Make sure you remain hirable."

"And I won't have to name anyone who hasn't already been named?"

He nodded and dug into a drawer, pulling out a square blue pamphlet with red and white stripes across the middle. He pushed it across the desk toward her. "This should help clarify things."

"Thank you, Mr. Sloane," she said sincerely.

"Please," he said, "Call me Eugene."

42

SHE WISHED SHE COULD discuss everything with Martin, but he had made it clear that there was nothing to discuss. She needed a man to talk to. She certainly didn't want to speak to Elliot. Her father was out of the question. Who could she turn to? What she really needed was someone who was objective.

Dr. Milton Shapiro was a Hollywood analyst who had worked with many actors and writers. Jill had heard about him from Isobel Rugio, the screenwriter of *Mulberry House*. Apparently others who had been called by HUAC had found him helpful.

Jill knew that Martin would disapprove of her decision to seek psychological counseling. In his opinion, Freud and Marx were antithetical. Even after Martin had shed the Marxist line, he clung to the belief that psychoanalysis was misguided because it justified the inequities of society by attributing them to personality flaws, rather than to the system.

Jill disregarded Martin's opinion and also pushed aside the outrage she felt when Dr. Shapiro's receptionist told her that the fee was twenty-five dollars an hour. Twenty-five dollars to talk to a stranger! Nonetheless, the next day she found herself in Dr. Shapiro's semi-darkened room gazing at his paneled, book-lined walls, the framed certificates attesting to various licenses and degrees, the photograph on an otherwise empty desk featuring him on the deck of a boat holding a large fish. Light filtered through filmy curtains. Jill eyed the couch but instead sat gingerly on the edge of one of the leather chairs facing him.

He was a portly man with a large nose and a ruddy complexion. "So," he said with sincere interest, "what brings you here?"

Self-conscious, not knowing where to begin, she spoke about her contract, about the blacklist.

His voice was deep and soothing. "Ah, yes, I'm familiar with that particular quagmire."

She quickly forgot the expense and basked in the comfort of pouring out her story to a sympathetic ear. "I'm so confused, Doctor. What should I do? The only way to clear my name is to implicate people, and that rubs me the wrong way. My husband—he also appeared before the Committee—"

"As a hostile witness or—?"

"He took the Fifth. There are supposedly detention camps just waiting for subversives. Obviously, those who took the Fifth would be the first to go. I moved out. Not because of that, but because...you see...I had an affair..." She studied his face for a reaction, but he gave nothing away. "The children are with him..." She felt herself well up and, despite her awkwardness, allowed the tears to flow. "It's all too much..."

He handed her a box of tissues, then said gently, "You seem to have a lot of inner conflict."

"If I don't cooperate, I'll lose my contract."

"Do you need to support yourself?"

"Well, yes. My husband can't get hired. And because we're separated, there are more expenses. Besides, if they actually do start to put people into the camps…" Then she added with some embarrassment. "I really do enjoy working."

"Umm. That's connected to your sense of personal worth. Which we shouldn't dismiss lightly."

"So you think I should cooperate?"

"I can't direct your actions. But I do encourage you to look at all sides of the question. Is career suicide what would serve you best in your life right now?"

43

JILL GOT TO THE TAIL O' THE Cock before the others and waited nervously in a booth at the farthest end of the restaurant. She ordered coffee and opened the pamphlet Eugene Sloane had given her.

THE ROAD BACK
(Self-Clearance):
A Provisional Statement Of View On The Problem Of
The Communist And Communist-Helper
In Entertainment Communications
Who Seeks To Clear Himself.

In the middle of the first page was a biblical quote. "That they should have a change of heart and mind, performing deeds fitting this change. Acts 26, Chapter 20." She flipped to the middle of the pamphlet. "...hatred of communism does not mean hatred of individual communists. It means informing in the noble sense of warning, educating, counseling..."

Wearily, she closed it and watched the waitress set down a mug of coffee. She took a sip and scalded her lips. The restaurant was filling up with the breakfast crowd—studio people, other actors. She hoped Eugene would get there soon. She didn't want to be left alone with William Wheeler the way she had been left alone with the F.B.I. agents. Eugene had been held up in a meeting, which left her and the two men staring at each other for an hour. She had agreed to meet them in her house, but once they showed up, she regretted it. She didn't like feeling so uncomfortable in her own home. The men sat stiffly on the loveseat and waited for her attorney to appear. She made small talk to fill the silence but worried she might let something slip which later could be used against her. Once Eugene arrived, everyone breathed easier. It shocked her to learn that the F.B.I. knew everything there was to know about her. All her political activities, including her Party work in New York. They knew about meetings and rallies that she'd forgotten she had even attended. And they knew everyone else who had attended them, too.

"I like punctuality!" It was the warm voice of Eugene Sloane, sporting a new haircut and a bright blue tie. "Of course, you might not guess that given my own record. I would've been here fifteen minutes ago if my son hadn't needed a lift to school at the last minute. Usually rides his bike. You have kids, don't you? Oh, good timing, here's Bill."

William Wheeler had appeared behind them. He was a solidly built man who looked as if he should have been coaching football. In fact, he and Eugene spent the first ten minutes talking about the Rams. She smiled politely, pretending interest. That's when she saw Elliot sashay into the room, surrounded by an entourage. Her stomach did a flip. He took a seat at the far end of the room, in her line of vision. She watched him hold court—his expansive gestures, his booming voice. So confident, as if he owned the place and everyone in it. He obviously had no fear of running into people whose lives he had wrecked. She was filled with disgust. How is it possible that she'd fallen so completely under his spell? She recognized several of the people with him, all of them stoolies. It struck her that by cooperating with the Committee, she was placing herself in his camp.

"Well, Miss Fullbright," said Wheeler, finally turning his attention to the matter at hand. "I'm delighted that you've agreed to assist the Committee, and I speak on behalf of not only the Congressmen, but the entire government. Democracy depends on citizens like you who are willing to demonstrate their patriotism."

Her eyes wandered over to Elliot's table as Wheeler droned on. "We are deeply indebted to our citizens who have chosen to expose the men and women who would rather defend Soviet Russia than our own great nation."

When it was her turn to speak, Wheeler listened attentively as she emphatically stated her refusal to give any new names.

"Eugene has made that clear to me." He took out an envelope and removed a paper. "That's why I've brought this list, to facilitate things."

She held the paper gingerly, as if it were fecal matter. She ran her eyes down the list. Names of her friends, people she had swapped stories with, people she had done scenes with in acting class. "And these people have already been named by other witnesses?"

"That is correct, Miss Fullbright."

She handed the paper back to him, "Yes, all right." Then she added quickly, "I'd like to explain to the Committee on the day of my hearing, so that it becomes a matter of public record, the reasons why I originally joined the Communist Party because, Mr. Wheeler, I am not ashamed of those reasons."

He considered this request and exchanged looks with Eugene. Then said, "I have no objections to that, as long as you make it perfectly clear that presently you oppose what the Party stands for."

Eugene's reassuring smile told her that she would not be compromising herself to agree to this stipulation. "All right," she said.

Eugene picked up the tab. While he was fishing through his wallet, Jill said pointedly to Wheeler, "May I ask a rather obvious question, Mr. Wheeler?"

"Of course."

"Since you already have the names, what's the point of going through this whole charade?"

"I can understand your question. Congressman Jackson explains it this way. The Committee just doesn't place any credence in the testimony of a witness who isn't prepared to fully cooperate with it. Naming of names is the ultimate test of a witness's cooperation. You see, if you don't name names, you're protecting your old comrades. We see the naming of names as the final proof that a witness has broken with the past."

THAT AFTERNOON SHE WENT to another appointment with Dr. Shapiro. This time she stretched out on the couch, grateful for a place to lie down, a place to sort things out.

"It's normal to have ambivalent feelings, Jill. They don't go away completely. But the scale begins to tip in one direction, and that helps you take action."

"Instead of stewing, like I am."

"It sounds as though you have excellent legal counsel."

"When I was in his office I felt completely committed to this course. But then, after those meetings, I don't know..."

She tried to find the words to describe her dilemma. The dull ticking of the wall clock made her jittery. "See, it's not new information they're after. They have all the information. They don't need me to teach them about the Communist Party. They want to make sure citizens know the Committee can get them to do whatever it wants them to do. They want to put on a show. Those two meetings, the one with the F.B.I. and the one with Wheeler, were dress rehearsals. I'm the dancing monkey."

"Because you're a star?"

"That's part of it. The studio's done a lot of publicity for my movie. And the fact that I had an affair with the director has given people a lot to talk about. So, yes, I'm already in the spotlight. My cooperating with the Committee makes them look good, as if I think they're doing a great job. Which I don't. By cooperating I dignify the proceedings. I was against the Committee years ago, when it was first formed. What will people think when I endorse it now?"

She felt him shift slightly behind her. "Instead of worrying about how you look to the rest of the world, how do you look to Jill?"

"I don't know. What are my principles here? I keep feeling them slip and then I can't remember what they are. What can I do and still hold my head up? I don't trust my impulses."

He didn't answer. The silence began to weigh on her. She wished he'd solve her problem. She was paying him enough. Finally he cleared his throat. "Since you've already met with the F.B.I. and with Mr. Wheeler, you have actually already cooperated, isn't that true?"

"Well, yes...I suppose so."

"Then I suggest you stop torturing yourself."

She swung her legs over the side of the couch and looked at him in the dim light. He had kind eyes. He wanted the best for her. She felt touched by his compassion. But there was nothing he could say that would really make a difference. Nothing anyone could say.

44

HER CHEST ACHED. Something heavy was pressing down. Her rib cage would surely crack. Her breastbone would be crushed onto her dying heart. Her heart was beating like an injured bird, frantically flapping its wings against the rib cage—a canary struggling to get out.

She awoke, her body in a cold sweat, her heart thumping loudly. She tried to calm herself by taking slow, shallow sips of air. She remembered Rudy Vallee, the canary in New York. How she had hated his song. Somehow, she had become that bird, ready to sing, ready to squeal.

She sat up in bed and pushed aside the curtain. The sky was gun metal gray. It wasn't even 5 o'clock yet. She had to go back to sleep. She couldn't afford to be groggy. She had to be sharp. She had to look sharp. She tried to focus on something besides the hearings. She thought of Lucinda, the character she was playing, and tried but failed to remember the lines from the opening scene. M-G-M had extended her contract. Dore Schary loved her. She pictured him pressing tobacco into his pipe. "We're family," he had said. She tried to hold onto that fact.

But it was Martin's face she kept seeing. Martin was her real family. *"Attached underground by a hundred different roots."*

She wondered if he would be there today and thought for one terrible moment that he might bring the kids. But children weren't permitted into the proceedings. They would be at school, ignorant of the path their mother had chosen. Larry Parks had described what it felt like to give names: "crawling through the mud."

She staggered out of bed and squinted into the mirror above her bureau. In the half-light, she saw only her own eyes peering back. She let out an involuntary gasp. When she flicked on the light her features lined up in their regular pattern. She took a long breath. Well, she was awake now. No sense in trying to go back to sleep. The day that she so dreaded had begun.

IN FRONT OF THE FEDERAL Building, a small crowd waved placards: "AMERICA! LOVE IT OR LEAVE IT!" "IF YOU DON'T LIKE IT HERE, GO BACK TO RUSSIA!" She knew that the placards were aimed at the enemy, at people like Martin. Once she had testified, she would not be vulnerable to such taunts.

The press was waiting for her with microphones and cameras. She held her breath and wished there were another way into the building. Just then, Eugene came running up.

"You look terrific!" he said, noting her new charcoal gabardine suit. He took her hand and ran interference for her past the crush of reporters.

They rode up to the fourth floor and sat on a bench outside the hearing room under a portrait of President Roosevelt.

"Nervous?" he asked.

She nodded her head.

"Come on now, you're an actress. You should know that butterflies make for a good performance. At least you didn't have to memorize a bunch of lines."

She looked down at her shoes and realized with horror that she had a run in one of her stockings. "Oh, no," she said, swallowing back tears.

Eugene covered her hands with one of his own and said, "It'll be over soon."

The room seemed smaller than she remembered it. Television camera crews and newspaper photographers were in the front. The place was packed, but she was careful not to look at faces. She did not want to see anyone she knew. By not looking, she could pretend she was playing a part in a strange pageant before a crowd of anonymous spectators. As she walked down the center aisle, she heard coughs and murmurs, felt people shift in their seats.

Eugene led her to the front. They sat in the first row behind the table where she and Eugene would soon be sitting. Now another attorney sat there, conferring with his client. Jill recognized the witness as a contract player from Paramount. Andrea Stouffer had been in one of Martin's movies. She was young with a pug nose and slightly bucked teeth. She spoke softly but with conviction to the four Congressmen who sat facing her behind their long table. Jill recognized Chairman Wood and Congressman Doyle and, of course, William Wheeler. Counsel for the Committee, Frank Tavenner, was the one whom Andrea was addressing. "I made a great mistake in entering the Communist Party, and I feel that I am doing the right thing to come here today because if there's any way I can help stomp out this evil menace then I owe it to my country to do so. I'm only sorry that I did not come forward sooner."

Tavenner had a slight lisp and spoke in a solicitous manner, as if he were speaking to a child. "It's only because of the willingness of people like you to come here and give us a full statement of the facts that we are able to show the American people the great danger of this international conspiracy. We are deeply appreciative of your efforts to assist us. My son died in the war for Americans like yourself, Miss Stouffer."

"Thank you, Sir."

He turned to the chairman and said, "I have no further questions."

Wood nodded and pounded his gavel before saying the magic words that would send Miss Stouffer scurrying back, untainted, into the workplace. "Thank you for your cooperation."

What a travesty, Jill thought. An American flag caught her eye. It hung limp, as if it had given up trying to stand proud. That's dangerous and useless thinking, she told herself. As Dr. Shapiro had reminded her, she had already as much as testified. There was no turning back.

The chamber was filled with chatter as Andrea Stouffer came up the aisle, a look of triumph shining on her face. That will be me soon, Jill told herself, grasping onto the promise of relief. She followed Andrea with her eyes and, despite her earlier determination not to note who was in the room, now that she was facing them, it was impossible not to see Martin's green eyes fixed upon her. Next to him sat Charlie, and on his other side, Al, a face she hadn't seen in months. Surprisingly, Phyllis was there too. Jill's eyes flickered past them quickly before any contact could be made. On the other side of the gallery sat a different group of old friends, among them Libby, wearing a nervous, anxious look.

The gavel pounded again. "Let us come to order, please."

Mr. Tavenner said, "I now call Jill Fullbright."

She and Eugene moved to the chairs recently vacated by Andrea and her attorney. Eugene arranged his papers on the small table then gave her hand a little squeeze. Suddenly she was blinded by the hot light of flashbulbs. She said, her voice breathless, "May I request, please, that the photographers..."

Wheeler saw how thrown she was and said brusquely to the photographers, "Please hurry."

Mr. Tavenner, held out a Bible to her and asked, "Do you solemnly swear to tell the truth, the whole truth, and nothing but the truth, so help you God?"

The only other time she had taken an oath before God was that rainy day so long ago when she had promised to love, honor, and cherish her husband. Jill took a deep breath and said, "I do."

The chairman showed his toothy smile and said, "It is our hope, Miss Fullbright, that you, like many witnesses who have made the mistake of associating themselves with the Communist Party, will have the courage and loyalty to make an honest disclosure of all you know about its activities."

She did not answer, but her face was open and her eyes said she was willing.

"Are you represented by counsel, Miss Fullbright?"

"Yes, Sir. Mr. Eugene Sloane."

Eugene was asked to identify himself for the record, and Jill was asked to do the same. Finally, Mr. Tavenner began the questioning.

"Miss Fullbright, what is your occupation?"

When Jill said, "Actress," she suddenly felt her higher sense of purpose. She was a professional actress. It defined her. And now she had an opportunity to fight for the right to pursue her art, her soul's nourishment.

The questions came in a predictable monotonous order. She was asked about her education, her professional career in radio, when she had first come to Los Angeles, when she began to work as a screen actress.

She could get through this. One foot in front of the other.

Tavenner asked, "Please state the names of the organizations with which you have been affiliated in Hollywood. To jog your memory, I have a list."

She took the sheet from him and glanced over it. "I was a member of the Hollywood Independent Citizens Committee of the Arts, Sciences and Professions."

"Was that organization an outgrowth of the Hollywood Democratic Committee?"

"I think so, yes."

"What other organizations were you affiliated with?"

"What do you mean 'affiliated with'?"

"Either by membership or by way of aid and support."

"I supported all of these."

Tavenner paused and scanned his notes. "Were you a member of the Actors' Laboratory Theater?"

Her stomach clenched. Her Lab, her precious Lab.

"I was."

"Did you hold any official position in that organization?"

"I was a treasurer for a while. It was more of an honorary position than an official one."

"When was that?"

"In 1949 or 1950. I can't remember exactly."

"What were your duties as treasurer?"

"I signed checks."

"To whom were those checks written?"

"To the office help, the janitor, the teachers, the utility bills, paint for scenery. That sort of thing."

"What office help? For what organization?"

"For the Actors' Lab."

"Please tell the Committee whether or not there were, to your knowledge, communists in the Actors' Laboratory Theater?"

She took a deep breath. This is the beginning, she thought. The roller coaster had completed its long slow ascent and was about to drop into a wild ride.

"I believe there were some. Though," she added quickly, "the Lab was not a communist organization in any sense. It was an acting school, a place where actors could learn their craft and put on plays. It had nothing whatsoever to do with politics or political parties. We weren't stealing atomic secrets."

Tavenner ignored this comment and asked pointedly, "Do you know a woman named Phyllis Gladstone?"

Her heart shuddered. "Yes," she said, barely above a whisper.

"Please speak up, Miss Fullbright."

"I know Phyllis Gladstone." It suddenly felt terribly hot in the room. Jill noticed that the overhead fans were not turning. "I wonder if I might have a glass of water. I'm feeling..."

"Yes, yes, of course." He whispered something to an aide who scurried over to a side table where a pitcher and several glasses stood. Eugene met the aide halfway and hurried the glass to Jill, whispering, "You're doing fine." He looked confident, almost happy.

She took a swallow and put the glass down.

"Now, Miss Fullbright. What was your opportunity to know and to observe the fact that there were communists in the acting school?"

"I just knew. We discussed political ideas at Schwab's drug-store, after class. But they were only swimming pool communists."

Laughter erupted in the room, but it died down when Tavenner asked the next question. "Miss Fullbright, were you ever a dues-paying member of the Communist Party?"

At last: the big question. She reminded herself that she had nothing to hide. That being a member of the Party was not a crime. She glanced at Eugene. He wore the same look of calm confidence.

"Yes. I was a member."

"Will you please tell this committee the circumstances under which you joined the Communist Party? "

She took a breath. "Yes, Mr. Tavenner, I would like to do this because I think it will help you to understand the evolution which I, and many of my friends, went through."

"Please, proceed."

Jill felt herself on more solid ground. She just might be able to take charge of this situation. Like a good audition, she'd show them her interpretation of a scene, not necessarily the one they expected to see.

"I joined the Communist Party in 1936. It was during the Depression and as you might remember, it was a sorry time for our nation. I wanted to help make things better. The Communist Party made sense to me. They wanted to help unionize, to struggle against racial prejudice, that sort of thing. Our aim was not to overthrow the government, it was to make our government serve people better." Though she was not comfortable with theater improvisation, she felt herself warming to her subject. "Many of us who joined at that time later dropped out because we felt the Communist Party was no longer the best organization for realizing those dreams."

"Do you believe that the Communist Party takes orders from Moscow?"

"I no longer attend meetings so I cannot answer that question."

Tavenner whispered something to Wheeler and Wheeler spoke next. "Will you state to the Committee where you first became a member of the Party?"

"In New York City."

"Who recruited you into the Party?"

She had been going along so well, in control and suddenly, she felt trapped. "I — I don't remember. It was many years ago."

"Where did this person live?"

"In New York, I presume. I can't recall."

"What was this person's occupation?"

"I can't remember. He was in the arts somehow. We all were."

"So, this person you can't recall was a he?"

Jill swallowed hard. "Yes, a man. But I can't remember his name."

"What were the circumstances under which you met?

"I can't recall."

"Was it at a meeting or where?"

"I really don't remember."

"Did others counsel you about joining the Communist Party before you were recruited by this man?"

"I don't think I discussed my decision with anyone."

"Were you assigned to a Communist Party cell?"

"I guess you could say I was assigned. I was part of a group which met regularly."

"What was the name of that cell?"

"It had no name. We were actors and writers and directors who worked in radio or theater."

"Is it true that your group helped organize a fund-raising event for refugees of the Spanish Civil War in the aftermath of Franco's victory?"

"Yes. More than one."

"So you were a member of that particular cell from 1936 until when?"

"There was no official date I dropped out. I just sort of drifted away. 1939 or 1940."

"Will you tell us what you know about the Communist Party since your time in Hollywood?"

"I wasn't a member of the Party in Hollywood."

"Did you attend a meeting at the home of Mr. Lionel Stander that dealt with a conflict in the Screen Actors Guild?"

"No. I was not a member of the Guild until recently."

"Do you know writers or actors in Hollywood who were members of any particular branch or group of the Communist Party?"

"I would say that certain writers and actors met as communists, but I can't say for sure, as I didn't meet with them."

She felt relieved. She had walked the tightrope of her New York days evading the question, hedging the truth. But then Chairman Wood asked, "In New York, who were the leaders of your cell?"

"There were no official leaders."

"Who directed the meetings that you attended in New York?"

"Well, no one really. They were more like discussions. We discussed unemployment. We talked about problems that we were having at work. It was a social occasion, too. We drank wine and listened to records."

There was a ripple of laughter in the room and Jill dropped

her eyes to her lap where her hands were twisting one of her gloves. "Sir, I am not ashamed of my activities as a communist. We were working for the general good and—"

"Miss Fullbright, who directed the activities that this group was engaged in?"

"I must repeat, Sir, that to my knowledge no one directed our activities."

"Who called the group together?"

"Well, I can't say for certain."

"Did you have a set, scheduled meeting time, or was it called by some individual?"

"We usually met once a week. Various individuals would call."

"So, it wasn't run by mental telepathy."

Again, the chamber filled with laughter. She took a breath, trying to hold onto her slipping sense of dignity.

"Someone issued the call, isn't that right?"

"That's right."

Tavenner and Wheeler consulted between themselves. Tavenner looked directly at Jill and leveled the next question. "Miss Fullbright, do you either through blood or marital relationships, have any relatives who are or have been members of the Communist Party?"

The question came fast, like a blast of hot air. She had dodged their bullets, but now she felt her back against the wall. She turned to Eugene. "What should I say?"

"Just tell the truth, Jill. It's almost over."

"Miss Fullbright?"

She felt Martin's eyes on her. He had already been named. This wouldn't hurt him. She thought about *Stranger At the Gate* and *Mulberry House*. She thought about her seven-year contract.

About her rising star.

Impatiently, Tavenner declared, "Miss Fullbright. We are waiting."

She began to speak, "Mr. Chairman..." Then a series of images flashed before her in rapid succession—herself on Elliot's satiny sheets, her children crumpled in tears on the beach, the look on Martin's face the night he saw the empty diaphragm box.

She picked up the glass of water and drained it. Then she set the glass down firmly. Enough betrayal, she thought. "I can't," she announced.

Mr. Tavenner eyed her. "Miss Fullbright?"

She cleared her throat. "Mr. Chairman, Mr. Tavenner and members of the Committee, I cannot answer that question. I will answer questions about myself and my own activities, but I will not discuss anyone else's."

Wheeler's face reddened. Eugene rose. The room erupted in a confused mix of protestations and applause. Chairman Wood narrowed his eyes. "Order!"

Wheeler said, "In our private meetings, Miss Fullbright, you corroborated a list of names and agreed to do that for the record today."

She didn't flinch. "I know I did. But now, now that I'm actually here, in front of my family and friends, I can't. I just can't hand over names of people who weren't disloyal or subversive in order to clear my own name."

"If you knew a man who'd committed murder, wouldn't you feel obligated to give his name to the authorities?"

"But murder is against the law. Being a member of a political party is not." Suddenly, it was all so easy.

Eugene, still standing, addressed the chairman. "Chairman

Wood, I request a recess so that I may speak with my client and explain the—"

Jill interrupted him. "There's nothing to explain, Eugene. I thought I could do this, but I can't."

Congressman Doyle spoke up. His white hair, his elderly demeanor reminded her of her father. He said in a soft voice. "Now, Miss Fullbright, you must realize that we do not accept the answers you are giving."

Jill said, in an equally soft voice, "That is your prerogative, Congressman."

"Understand, you will be held in contempt if you do not cooperate with this committee. It's too late to plead protection under the Fifth Amendment. You waived that right when you disclosed that you were once a member of the Communist Party."

Her heart was pounding. She would go to jail like the Hollywood Ten.

His voice grew sterner. "I strongly advise you to take a moment and consult with your attorney and accept the counsel he offers."

"I have no reason to do that, Mr. Doyle."

The Congressmen whispered amongst themselves. Mr. Tavenner said to the chairman, "I move we adjourn, Mr. Chairman. There is no point in continuing with this witness."

Chairman Wood sighed. "Very well, Mr. Tavenner." And to Jill he said, "It saddens me that you have made a choice, which is not only dangerous to yourself, but puts our country in danger as well. You are excused."

SHE WALKED DOWN THE WIDE steps of the Federal Building, making her way through a hostile crowd. She hurried her step, pushing away the thoughts that came flying at her. Her career was over. She was unemployed. She would go to prison. Despite these gloomy prospects, she felt strangely elated.

She thought of her children. Now she could look them in the eye. She kept repeating to herself: for Millie and Nathan, for Millie and Nathan.

People jostled her and taunted her. Reporters and photographers shouted questions. She concentrated on the crisp outline of the San Gabriel Mountains in the distance. Then she felt someone grab her elbow. She turned quickly. It was Martin. His eyes were full of tenderness.

Without a word, he held her arm and guided her through the crowd.

ACKNOWLEDGEMENTS

Writing a period piece cannot be done without the deep research of other writers. As I began this project, it was my good fortune that editors Cary Nelson and Jefferson Hendricks had just published their extraordinary volume, *Madrid 1937: Letters of the Abraham Lincoln Brigade from the Spanish Civil War* and that Patrick McGilligan and Paul Buhle had recently published *Tender Comrades, A Backstory of the Hollywood Blacklist.* I was also helped enormously by *Naming Names* (Victor S. Navasky) and *Additional Dialogue: Letters of Dalton Trumbo, 1942-1962* (edited by Helen Manfull). I am indebted to The Southern California Library, whose mission is to "document, preserve, and provide access to the histories of communities in struggle for justice." I am reassured just knowing it exists.

For lending their critical eye to early drafts, I am indebted to Maryedith Burrell, Candace DuPuy, Jeanne Field, Dennis Hicks, Randi Johnson, Phoebe Larmore, Tessa Hicks Peterson, Deborah Robison, Jo Sadalla, and Jessica Williams. I am grateful to Marxist theoretician Jonathan Arthur, who clarified the historical framework, and to Brian Cooke, who kept me on track with the music of both eras. Thanks also to agents Mary Alice Kier and Anna Cottle of Cinelit who gave it their all.

I thank my agent and longtime friend, Jeanne Field, for her ongoing encouragement and especially for supporting my decision to put aside Hollywood pursuits and write a novel.

I am grateful for the editorial expertise of Annalisa Zox-Weaver. My deep appreciation goes to Beth Escott Newcomer for her artistic sensibility.

In the 1950's the term "fellow traveler" was pejorative. I'd like to reclaim that term with pride as I acknowledge my fellow travelers Deborah Robison, Jo Sadalla and Eve Poling, whose ongoing deep affection and long shared history gives this project special meaning.

Naomi and David Robison, Nate and Buddie Zahm, and Hope and Jeff Corey provided safe havens in my childhood. They are my chosen family, along with their children and their children's children. I am also grateful to those other families who stood by ours during the blacklist years, in particular Nate and Faye Abkin, Dora and Al Caraco, and Berte Taube.

When I was a girl, David Ellis, a longtime family friend and gifted writer, gave me confidence by taking my artistic aspirations seriously.

My parents, Stanley and Rena Waxman, were a blessing in my life in more ways than I can count. In this instance, it was my father who suggested I write a novel instead of a screenplay, a thought that hadn't occurred to me. My mother generously offered tales of her life as a struggling actress in New York, which opened up possibilities for Jill's story. Both offered invaluable suggestions along the way. Above all, they provided the example of how to live as artists without compromising their principles.

I thank my daughters Jessica and Tessa, their husbands

Robe and John, my brother Mark, and my sister-in-law Paula for their ongoing support of my work. A deep well of gratitude to my dearest comrade, Dennis, for his understanding of the demands of made up characters and for believing in the importance of telling this story.

STEPHANIE WAXMAN is the author of *Sex and Death*, a collection of short stories. Her nonfiction work includes *A Helping Handbook —When A Loved One Is Critically Ill, Growing Up Feeling Good*, and *What Is A Girl? What Is A Boy?* She has contributed to *The Missouri Review, The Bitter Oleander, North Dakota Quarterly*, and *West*. Stephanie has conducted workshops in Japan, the Netherlands, Nicaragua, Alaska and Hawaii, and currently teaches writing in Los Angeles, where she lives with her husband Dennis Hicks.

www.stephaniewaxman.com

www.ingramcontent.com/pod-product-compliance
Lightning Source LLC
Chambersburg PA
CBHW022029240626
47154CB00007B/2336